RUTHLESS

An abandoned chapel burns. In this part of Manchester, destruction is not unusual. But this time, the body of a man lies inside. And it's down to Scott and Bailey to save them all... Detective Constable Rachel Bailey is struggling to come to terms with huge change, just as her partner, D.C. Janet Scott grapples with a horrifying tragedy. But they must put aside their own troubles if they are to solve this murder investigation. Especially when a second building goes up in flames...

RUTHLESS

RUTHLESS

by

Cath Staincliffe

Magna Large Print Books
Long Preston, North Yorkshire,
BD23 4ND, England.

British Library Cataloguing in Publication Data.

Staincliffe, Cath
 Ruthless.

 A catalogue record of this book is
 available from the British Library

 ISBN 978-0-7505-4256-2

First published in Great Britain in 2014 by Corgi Books
an imprint of Transworld Publishers

Concept and text copyright © Transworld Publishers 2014

Cover illustration © Roy Bishop by arrangement with
Arcangel Images

Cath Staincliffe has asserted her right under the Copyright,
Designs and Patents Act, 1988 to be identified as the author of
this work.

Published in Large Print 2016 by arrangement with
Transworld Publishers

Magna Large Print is an imprint of Library Magna Books Ltd.

Printed and bound in Great Britain by
T.J. (International) Ltd., Cornwall, PL28 8RW

For Ellie, who lights up my life

Wednesday 9 May

1

Rachel stopped at the brow of the hill to catch her breath, a stitch in her side and sweat trickling down her back. Panting, she bent double, touched her toes then straightened up.

It was almost dark and she watched the streetlights come on in the valley below, delineating the ring road and the motorway and the web of residential streets that sprawled up the sides of the hills. Mills and churches and tower blocks were dotted here and there, rising among the terraced housing.

She hadn't brought a torch and the track back to the car would be treacherous in the gloom, rutted and riven by tree roots and the gnarled heather that clung to the slope.

Rachel felt something nip her neck and waved a hand to swat it away. Gnats.

As the darkness deepened it seemed to bring a silence with it, an interruption of the distant traffic sounds so she could hear the tick of the ground cooling and something rustle in the foliage behind her.

A flash of black disturbed the air by her face and she cried out then felt like a right tit. A bat, that was all. Fetching its supper.

The glow caught her eyes, down in the west of town. A rich orange that reminded her of bonfire night. Looked too big to be a bonfire, wrong time of year – May. Perhaps a car had been torched, the petrol tank going up in flames. Joyriders, some lowlife toe-rags, getting rid of a vehicle used in a robbery. *Looks bigger than that, too,* she thought, flinching slightly as the bat swooped past again.

A shriek carried on the still air, high and hoarse. Fox, owl? Some predator. She felt her muscles stiffen in her calves and kicked each foot in turn. Time to head back. The thought brought a sullen burn in her guts. Daft. She was just being daft.

As if on cue, her mobile trilled. She yanked it from her pocket. *Sean* on the display. Her husband. How the fuck had that happened? She knew of course. He asked her and she said no, joked with him, shagged him, kept saying no and he kept on asking until one day, everything else gone to shit and he was still there, kind, shaggable, cheering her on and she had buckled, said yes, defences down.

She read the text: *spag carbonara half an hour x.*

He was more of a pie and chips, kebab and onion rings bloke. Born on the same estate in Langley as she was. Dragged up like Rachel and her lot had been. And like Rachel he escaped into the police. But since the wedding

14

he'd gone all Jamie Oliver on her. Trying out this and that. Rachel hadn't a clue why. She'd be just as happy with egg and chips or burger and beans but she went along with it. A phase, she reckoned. Least Sean never had any expectations that she'd be cooking or ironing his boxers or any of that malarkey. That was one thing they had going: he knew the score. He was a PC, the fire-fighting side of crime, out on patrol, while she was a detective on MIT, investigating murder and serious assault.

She texted him back: *OK x*. Considered putting a smiley face instead. Kisses on texts seemed adolescent – well, on texts to Sean anyway. And they weren't kids, were they, not now? But they'd had a thing back then, from time to time, when there was nothing better on offer.

She ran as hard as she could on the path back down, savouring the feeling of speed and power, feet thudding and her heart beating fast in her chest. If she could just keep running, how great would that be? To just go, leave it all behind, Sean and her mother and her brother Dominic. Except for the job, she didn't want to leave the job. Or Janet, who she worked alongside.

Halfway down she pitched forward, her left foot catching on a stone, she yelled out, slammed into the ground with a jarring thud. She staggered to her feet. Her knees stung.

She took a couple of deep breaths then carried on.

At the car, she saw the dark slashes of blood on her knees. Nothing to worry about. She ran a towel over her face and neck, her arms.

The route back to her flat, *their flat,* she reminded herself, took her through Manorclough, where the blaze she'd seen from the tops was still raging. One of the buildings was on fire. Curious, she parked in the car park at the small shopping precinct and walked past the shops and on to the road where the fire was.

She knew the area. They'd done a few jobs roundabout here in her time: a domestic where the bloke had paid a mate to knife his ex, to teach her a lesson for chucking him out; and the rape and murder of an elderly woman.

Closer to the blaze, the stench of the fire filled the air and she could see fire tenders at the scene, three of them, as she walked up the road. Uniformed officers were keeping the crowd away from the site. The Old Chapel, she realized, now belching clouds of acrid smoke into the air, the inferno roaring. Hoses were spraying water but bright flames were still visible through the holes in the roof and the windows where the shutters had burned away.

Fire always drew a crowd, a spectacle and

free at that. It hadn't been a chapel for ages. Probably closed back in the seventies and she remembered it was a carpet place for a while then that went bust. Rachel had no idea what it was used for now, if anything. The state of the grounds, neglected and overgrown behind the wire fencing, and the holes in the roof suggested it was derelict. Just begging for some fire-starter to come along and set light to it.

She looked at the crowd. Whole families, mum with a pram and a bunch of kids around. Teenagers, some of them filming with their phones. A few older people too; one man had made it with his Zimmer, determined to be at the party. A lad on a BMX bike, stunt pegs on the rear wheel. Dom had wanted one of them, their dad had played along but they all knew the only way it would happen was if it was robbed. So it never happened. Rachel had found an old racing bike at the tip and dragged it home and Sean had begged new tyres off a cousin and they'd done it up for Dominic. Never had working brakes but Dom was made up.

All we need is an ice cream van, she thought, *or toffee apples.* A loud cracking sound and the crowd responded, oohing and aahing, as part of the roof collapsed and fell inside the building sending fresh flames and sparks heavenwards. Rachel shivered, damp from her run and not near enough to the heat from the fire.

She should go. She hated the word *should*. She *would* go. Get some grub, glass of wine, swap news of the working day with Sean. She was already late.

As Rachel went back to the car she caught a different smell on the air, the stink of skunk, dark and pungent. Saw two figures walking away down the alley next to the old dole office, hoodies up, slogan emblazoned on the back in Gothic typeface, *CLASS OF 88* and an outline of an eagle. More interested in getting smashed than watching the fire. Or maybe they'd just gone to get refreshments at the shops for the next round. The dole office closed down some years back. People had to travel into town to sign on nowadays.

'I'll zap it,' Sean said, when she apologized for being late, 'you get a shower, no worries. What have you done to your knees?'

'It's nothing, I tripped, that's all.'

'You want to clean it.' He peered closer, touched the side of her leg.

'Don't fuss,' she snapped. Then felt awful for the edge in her voice. 'I'm fine. Big girl.'

'In all the right places,' he winked. Not put off his stride at all.

Why couldn't she just relax? She had it all, didn't she? Job, flat, fella? The run was supposed to get rid of it, the tension, the irritation, the sickening sense of disappointment. Only weeks since they wed, this was meant to be the honeymoon period. Instead she felt trapped, stuck and restless. She kept waiting for Sean to go but he was here, always bloody here.

Give it time, she thought, I need to get used to it. Too comfortable with her own company, too used to her own way of doing things, to her hard-won independence. So she sat and ate pasta and shared a bottle of wine and listened to Sean. She smiled and nodded and chewed and swallowed and kept on breathing. And they went to bed and shagged and then she lay in the dark, listening to him breathe. Wondering what the fuck was wrong with her.

Day 1

Thursday 10 May

2

Janet was making packed lunches, cheese and tomato butty for Elise, peanut butter for Taisie, crisps, apples, fruit juice, muesli bars. She snapped each lunchbox shut and set them on the counter by the door. She probably ought to get the girls to do their own, they were old enough, but she'd not got round to talking to them about it. Best to discuss it first with Ade, who made the lunches more often than Janet, as he didn't need to leave the house as early as she did. Better to present them with a united front. Not that there had been much unity since he'd moved back in. He seemed to disagree with her at every chance he got. Still punishing her.

She tried to be conciliatory, play the penitent, smooth the waters but it rankled. She heard the slam of the letter box, the thud as the paper hit the mat, Ade's footsteps coming downstairs. He was scanning the front page as he came into the kitchen, his hair wet from the shower, smelling of deodorant. In his teacher's garb, white shirt, navy tie, black trousers. He always wore a tie. School expected staff as well as students to conform to their dress code. Smart, respectable. Dull, a little voice whispered in her head.

'I've done their lunches,' Janet said.

'Right.' He put the paper down. Janet took her breakfast, a round of toast and a cup of coffee, to the table. Read the headlines upside down, *GROOMING GANG GUILTY*, while Ade filled the kettle and put bread in the toaster.

'Mum?' Elise, still in her pyjamas, stood at the door. 'This party. Can I go?'

'Yes,' Janet said.

'No,' said Ade.

'We've not had time to discuss it.' Janet took a bite of her toast.

'What do you need to discuss?' said Elise.

'Whether you can go,' Janet said.

Ade poured water into coffee. 'Whose party is it anyway?'

'A friend.'

'What friend?'

'John Planter – well, his brother,' Elise said.

'We don't know them,' Janet said.

'So? Please?'

'Look, we don't have time to talk about it now,' Janet said.

'Olivia is going. We can share a taxi back to hers.'

'Where is it?' Ade said.

'Middleton.'

'Middleton where?' he said.

'Don't know.'

'What's the party for?' Janet said.

'Why does it have to be for anything? It's just a party, God!'

'Look,' Ade said, 'if you want to go, here's what you do: you find out exactly who is having it, what they're called, where they live. Whether their parents will be there to supervise.'

Elise opened her mouth in protest. 'I can't believe this.'

'You're fifteen, Elise,' Ade said, 'we're not letting you swan off, God knows where, with a bunch of strangers without asking any questions.'

Elise rounded on Janet. 'You said yes, you said I could. If Dad hadn't said–'

'Enough!' said Ade.

'Find out,' Janet said, 'and when it starts and finishes. When we know all that, your dad and I can have an informed discussion and let you know our decision.'

'This is outrageous,' Elise said.

Janet did think Ade was going a bit over the top but better safe than sorry. 'We're not doing this to be awkward,' she said, standing up.

'Yes, you are. It's like living in a prison camp.' Elise kicked the back of the door with her foot and stormed off upstairs.

Ade sighed, Janet choked back a laugh. 'She might want to turn the poor-oppressed-victim act down a bit if she wants to go,' Janet said. 'Not like Elise to be so moody.' Elise

25

was the sensible one, the elder daughter, hard-working, responsible. Usually it was Taisie who tested their patience. 'I'm off, so we'll talk about it when she's done her research, shall we?'

'Yeah,' Ade said, face in the paper. Janet had a sudden urge to share a memory with him, a party they'd gone to as teenagers. One room full of couples smooching, the kitchen crammed. Janet had felt jittery, sensed people watching her, and Ade had tried to help her relax by pouring her a large glass of Southern Comfort which she drank far too quickly. They indulged in some heavy petting out in the alley behind the house then Janet had been sick as a dog all down her front: Ade had walked her the four miles home as they didn't expect to be allowed on the bus.

She'd not been out of hospital long then and social situations were still awkward. She'd feel people's curiosity, sticky and keen, could hear their unspoken comments and questions as they swapped glances, *she's a psycho, a nutter, been in the loony bin. Did they strap her down, shock her? Do we need to hide the sharp objects?* And their fear, as if having a breakdown might be catching and distress was an airborne virus. Keep your distance.

Not Ade though. God knows where he got that compassion, that understanding, mature beyond his years – but it wasn't much in evidence nowadays. Maybe it had all been used up, burned out. Maybe Ade was spent. He'd said at Rachel's wedding perhaps they should get divorced. That it wasn't really working, them sharing the house, putting it up for sale and not expecting to sell, stuck there. Had they just run out of steam, of passion, of love? Didn't the years of backing each other up, of pulling together, of routine and quiet affection, didn't they count?

Twenty-six years. She owed it to him to hang on. It was Janet who had risked it all for a few snatched nights with another man. Janet who had brought mistrust and jealousy and disruption into the marriage. The least she could do now was bide her time, see if it really was possible to salvage anything.

She looked at the back of his head, the hair thinning, and the folds of skin where his neck had thickened over the years. The warm flush of nostalgia evaporated.

Janet picked up her keys and bag and left for work.

The Old Chapel reeked. DCI Gill Murray could smell it as soon as she parked, even before she opened her car door. And once she'd been logged in and admitted into the scene, the acrid smell filled her nostrils and clawed at her throat.

Not the worst smell at a crime scene, the worst were the corpses left undiscovered until nature had its way. Decay blooming like green and black flowers on the skin, body fat and fluids breaking down, melting, leaking from the corpse, flesh rotting, home to blowfly and their maggots. That truly was the most god-awful reek. This was simply unpleasant.

The fire service had alerted the Major Incident Team earlier that morning, when officers doing a sweep of the Old Chapel had recovered human remains half buried among the charred debris of the fire.

On the threshold, where the main doors had once hung, Gill surveyed the building. Or what was left of it. Above her, open sky, blue and streaked with thin clouds, was framed by the jagged remnants of roof beams. The centre, the spine of the roof, had collapsed taking many ribs with it but others, broken, split, now ringed the gaping hole like so many blackened, jagged teeth.

The place was simply designed, a rectangular prayer hall with a rounded apse. Small anterooms off to either side of where the altar would have been. She could pick out several lumps of beams, charcoal now, among the ash and smashed roof tiles that covered the floor. The brick walls had withstood the ferocity of the fire though they were coated black with soot. Here and there were holes on the ground where the wooden floorboards had burned away.

'Theresa Barton, crime scene manager,' the plump woman introduced herself.

'Trevor Hyatt, fire investigation,' the man with her said. He was tall and bald with a red face and a nose that looked like it had been broken.

'Body's over here,' Barton said, pointing. Gill followed her, taking care to tread only on the stepping plates. The figure, burned black, was partially concealed by a timber. Face and shoulders exposed, lying on its side, fist and forearm close to its neck. Pugilist pose – a side effect of the fire, the intense heat causing the muscles to contract. The wreckage covered the torso and abdomen but poking out below were the legs and feet, the feet curled like claws. No clothing remained.

'No shoes?' Gill said. 'They'd burn?'

'Yes,' Hyatt said.

Here and there the scorched skin was split to reveal seams of meat. The lips had shrivelled back to expose long, discoloured teeth, an uneven skeletal grin. It was impossible for Gill to tell from the remains whether this was a man or a woman, to determine age or ethnicity. All questions for the pathologist.

'Could it be accidental?' she asked the fire officer.

He shook his head. 'Almost certainly deliberate. It looks like an accelerant, petrol or something, was used and we can tell by the spread that the seat of the fire was here,' he

29

gestured to the body, 'and around this area.'

So whoever had used the accelerant had been inside the building. It wasn't a case of petrol poured through the doorway, which was three or four yards away.

'Self-immolation?' Gill wondered aloud. 'They usually want an audience, don't they? Act in public.' And as for suicide, burning was an appalling way to die, our fear of fire as intense as the pain it delivered. She could not recall one sudden unexplained death she had been asked to investigate where the victim had set themselves on fire as a way to end it all.

'The body was set alight?' she said.

'It's a possibility.' Hyatt was cautious. They were all cautious until they had the evidence, theories were no more than that. The job was about facts, science and hard data. The body on the floor might be a fatality due to some awful accident but for now the very presence of accelerant meant it was suspicious. And that meant Gill needed to inform the coroner and ask permission to carry out a forensic post-mortem.

She coughed, hot inside her protective suit. The face mask did nothing to hide the smell.

'When were you called?' she asked the fire investigation officer.

'999 came in at eight o'clock last night,' he said, 'no reports of occupants. Place had been empty for several years. Last officially used as storage for a carpet wholesaler in 2009.'

'We will document as much as we can here,' Theresa Barton said, 'but there's little chance of recovering trace materials after an inferno like that.'

In the normal course of things they would hope to find evidence of any recent contact between the victim and other people. Fingerprints, DNA from hair or saliva, blood or sperm that might lead them to witnesses or, if foul play was suspected, to potential suspects. The fire compromised all that.

'The remains are at risk of further disintegration when we move them,' Barton said.

'Just do your best,' said Gill.

'Seeing as it's you,' Barton said.

'Let's just suppose it was an accident,' Gill said, 'our victim decided they were going to make a fire, to keep warm.'

'Not especially cold last night,' said Barton.

'Not outside,' Gill agreed, 'but in here it might be like a tomb. No heating for several years. Damp.'

'OK, go on,' the crime scene manager nodded.

'So they build a fire, they've got some petrol, slosh it on and don't realize they've splashed some on their sleeves or shoes. They light the fire and puff!' She splayed her fingers wide. 'Up in smoke.'

Hyatt was pulling a face, not convinced.

'But it is possible?' said Gill.

'Possible,' he said slowly.

'We found a container?' Gill asked.

'Not yet, still a lot of debris to sort through. It may have been destroyed with the heat,' he said. 'Third case of arson in the area in the past six months.'

'Really?'

'The mosque at the far end of Shuttling Way in December,' he said, 'and the school, the one over the road, in February.'

Gill nodded. St Agnes's, a little primary school, most of the kids on free school meals, a significant number on the at-risk register. Manorclough was dirt poor and beset by all the problems that came with poverty, including a high crime rate.

'We'll be comparing them,' Hyatt said.

'You think this might be the same person?'

'Often is, and there are clear similarities with the first two incidents.'

'So maybe this is them,' Gill pointed to the body, 'the fire-setter, and we're looking at a case of arson that went horribly wrong. We need an ID, whatever cause of death is, doesn't get us very far if we don't know who this is. Right, I'll let you get on.'

Gill made her first call, waited for the coroner to answer. 'Mr Tompkins, it's DCI Gill Murray. I'm at the site of an unexplained death at the Old Chapel, Manorclough. I have a body discovered in a suspicious fire, accelerants found. Identity unknown as yet. I'd like permission for a forensic post-mortem in order to determine cause of death.'

'Go ahead, DCI Murray.'

'Thank you, sir.' He liked to be called sir and it was no skin off Gill's nose to be respectful. Best to keep on the right side of the coroner. It was his dead body now: the body officially belonged to the coroner, not the police, not the family, and the coroner would determine whether and when the body could be released for burial or cremation, when an inquest was required, and whether to interrogate the police on their actions.

Next she rang Garvey, the home office pathologist. 'Got a victim, burned to a crisp but I still need a doctor's certificate of death.'

'Be there in five,' he said.

'Express service? I'm honoured.'

'I'm heading into the General, you're on my way,' Garvey said.

'That's it,' she joked, 'destroy the moment.'

It was a matter of minutes for them to complete the documentation Gill required, once Garvey had pronounced the death. She liked working with him, he was meticulous, pleasant company, had a sharp intelligence that she appreciated and was easy on the eye too, more than easy. Sadly for Gill he was also gay and happily ensconced in a civil partnership.

'Doesn't seem much point taking body temp,' he said. The measurement was routinely used to help estimate time of death of the victim, but given he or she had been consumed by fire the body had undergone catastrophic changes. 'And could be destructive to try.'

Theresa Barton agreed with him. 'Leave it. Suggest we bag the victim and recover all material beneath and around the body,' she traced an oval in the air, 'say two metres either side.'

'Pray it doesn't rain.' Gill nodded to the open roof.

'We'll erect shelters in any case,' said Hyatt. 'From our end we'll want to spend several days examining the scene.' In the same way that the work of the crime scene manager and CSIs was to find the evidence to try to build the narrative as to how someone died, so the fire investigating officer would be doing the same to establish the story of how the fire started and developed.

'Buzz me,' Gill said as Garvey peeled off his protective suit outside the building, the all-in-one smudged with soot and ash despite his efforts to disrupt the scene as little as possible.

She watched him leave, taking the chance to lower her mask, breathe some less tainted air and let her face cool a little before returning to the chapel. Most people who died in a fire died of smoke inhalation, not from the ravages of the flames. Losing consciousness and dying before the heat reached them. But if this victim had been doused in accelerant and then set alight it would have been a truly horrific death.

Garvey rang as soon as the post-mortem was ready to start and Gill attended along with Pete Readymough, who would be exhibits officer for the investigation. She had briefed her syndicate to stand by in case they were unable to rule out foul play. And she had met with the press officer to instruct her as to the facts that could be made public at such an early stage: *Unidentified body recovered from a fire at Old Chapel in Manorclough. A post-mortem will be carried out later today, after which police hope to release further details.* The fire itself would have made the front pages of the local paper. With news now of a body, interest would be even keener.

The smell filled the dissection room, the stink of burned bone and charred meat over-powering the background smells of bleach and disinfectant. Gill listened to Garvey dic-tating notes as the body lay on the mortuary table, in exactly the same pose as it had been in at the chapel. The effects of the heat had fused the body in position, carbonizing the flesh. Once the external exam was over it would be necessary to break the limbs to gain access to the internal organs, most of which were likely to be cinders, Gill thought.

Garvey measured the body in sections to ascertain the height. Crown of the head to top of the spine, the curved back, the zigzag of the cramped-up legs. Added together it translated as six foot two inches. 'Victim presents in the foetal position, left side uppermost. Cranial base evaluation and angle of the pelvic bone tells us victim is male.' Garvey analysed the shape of the skull and concluded that the man was Caucasian. 'Substantial charring, absence of clothing, body hair. Visible fractures to the lower ribs on the presenting left thorax. Dislocation to the hip.' From the beam that had fallen, crushing the man where he lay. Fragments of rib poked through the frazzled skin, reminding Gill of the gaping roof at the chapel.

A wedding ring on the victim's left ring finger, thick with sooty grease, was photographed in situ then Garvey removed it, small crumbs of flesh dropping from the finger as he did so. He peered at the band under one of the powerful lights above the table, took a sample swab from inside and out, then cleaned it up. 'Inscribed,' he said, 'R.K. and J.S. 23.4.72.' He glanced at Gill and sketched a bow. Gill smiled: this could be a useful lead, to identity if nothing else. Pete got an evidence bag ready and placed the ring inside.

As well as photographs of the victim, a number of X-rays were taken of different sections of the body, Garvey, Pete and Gill withdrawing from the room each time while the scanner did its job. The resultant images came up on the computer screen. Garvey clicked on the first, the skull.

'Forensic odontology?' Gill said, suggesting another route to identification. The teeth were uneven, some missing, some broken. 'Doesn't look like he had a check-up every six months.' *Must cancel my check-up,* she thought, the day after tomorrow but she'd be up to her neck with this. Garvey clicked on the second picture. The hand and neck.

'Some evidence of wear in the vertebrae,' he pointed out.

'Middle-aged?' said Gill.

'Most likely.'

Then the third image. The mesh of broken ribs, the main part of the chest. Gill noticed the dark smudges at the same moment as Garvey said, 'What have we got here, then?'

He clicked closer. The smudges were clearer now, two of them, small cylindrical forms with a conical nose, the size of cigarette butts.

Gill's heart missed a beat. 'I think we can safely rule out accidental death, or suicide,' she said. 'The poor bugger's been shot.'

3

They were ready and waiting in the incident meeting room when the boss arrived, having sent word that she was launching a murder inquiry. Rachel had been part of DCI Gill Murray's syndicate for three years now. Could've been sergeant if things hadn't conspired to make her miss her exam. But there'd be chance again if she stuck at it. And she was determined to do so. Things had been rocky and Godzilla had been on her back on more than one occasion, making Rachel feel like shit, but she'd not yet been chucked out. Janet reckoned that the boss rated Rachel as a keeper, someone who'd fly up the career ladder if she put her mind to it, but Rachel wasn't so sure. She'd been on the receiving end of Godzilla's tongue-lashing so many times that she sometimes thought the boss had it in for her. Though to be fair there had always been good reasons for the bollockings. Not as if they were trumped up, bullying or whatever.

'This morning I attended the scene at Old Chapel, Lower Manorclough.'

'There was a fire,' Rachel said, interrupting without thinking, 'last night.'

'There was indeed,' the boss went on after a short pause, 'reported on the local news.'

'No,' Rachel said, wanting to set the record straight, 'I saw it, I was there...'

Janet, on the other side of the conference table, raised her eyebrows at Rachel, either querying why she'd been there or warning her about butting in when the DCI was speaking.

'...that's how I know,' Rachel tailed off.

'Glad we've cleared that up,' the boss said smartly. 'What you won't know is that our victim, male, Caucasian, identity unknown, was inside the building and initial evidence suggests he was shot, twice, then doused with accelerant and set alight. I must warn you the photographs are not particularly pleasant and are not required viewing. Avoid looking at them if you wish. Garvey found no soot inside what remained of lung tissue, which suggests the victim was already dead when the fire started.'

The photographs were projected on to the large screen. Kevin Lumb, on Rachel's right, reared back. 'Whoa!' he said. 'Barbecued or what?'

What a knob.

Kevin, dim though he was, realized he'd spoken out of turn when stony silence greeted his adolescent comment. 'Shock, innit?' he said weakly.

It wasn't enough.

'DC Lumb,' the boss said, no iron in her voice as yet but Rachel could tell it was coming, 'our role as members of a major incident team is to represent the interests of victims of serious crime and attempt, to the best of our ability, to determine who perpetrated said crime. To make every effort to see a suspect apprehended, charged and, God-and-the-jury willing, convicted of that crime. And we carry out that role with professionalism, affording every victim the respect and dignity that any one of us might expect if it was one of our own in the mortuary. So just close your gob and put your brain in gear. Got it?'

Pete Readymough, to Rachel's left, put down his breakfast butty and wiped his fingers on a tissue. Put off by the photos, she imagined. Pete could do with skipping a few meals, Rachel thought. He could probably survive several weeks on his reserves of body fat.

'Sorry, ma'am,' Kevin said. He gave Rachel a sideways, shamefaced look, as though he expected her to feel sorry for him. Ever since Sean had chosen Kevin as best man (fuck knows why, he barely knew the guy) Kevin had acted like he was one of the family. Chumming up to Rachel, oblivious to her put-downs, thinking she was joking when she told him to do one. Like his mind couldn't really compute a universe where he wasn't at its centre, loved by one and all. She might, feel sorry for him if he had the nous to learn from his mistakes but he just repeated them.

The boss resumed, 'Our priority is to establish identity: who is this man? Once that's clear we may be able to establish who had reason to want to kill him.'

'Could he have been killed elsewhere and dumped there?' Mitch asked.

'It's possible,' the boss answered.

'Any sign of how they got in?' Rachel said. 'The place was boarded up, wasn't it?'

'No answers yet,' the boss said. 'Find out who the current owner is, talk to them, any history of break-ins and so on. CSI and fire investigation still ongoing. Could be some time. What we do have is a gold wedding ring recovered from our victim, inscribed R.K. and J.S. 23.4.72.'

'Forty years,' said Pete.

'To that end, Kevin,' Her Maj's beady eyes bored into Kevin's head, 'start a trawl of the marriage records, beginning locally, that date and those initials.'

'Narrows it down,' Lee said dryly.

'I know,' the boss agreed, 'without an ID, motive is likewise obscure. But perhaps Kevin will be able to help us with the name and next of kin and we can trace the widow. Rachel, Janet, Lee and Mitch, house-to-house in the area. Janet, you're still acting sergeant, you co-ordinate it,' Godzilla instructed. 'Did anyone see any activity at the chapel on Wednesday? I'll be meeting with the area intelligence manager.'

'Use of a firearm,' said Mitch. Ex-army was Mitch, good on hardware. 'That size – we're talking a small handgun.' Mitch pointed to the magnified image of the two bullets that had been taken once they were recovered from the body. 'Do we know what weapon?'

'At the lab now,' Godzilla said.

'Could be a hit,' Mitch said. 'Though no bullet to the head, which is a little unusual.'

'An assassination?' the boss said. 'Why burn the body? With an organized hit half the intention is to send a message, "Look what big scary fuckers we are, anyone else tries it gets the same."'

'Setting the fire, that's quite different, that's twisted,' Rachel said. 'The desire to hurt, isn't it?'

Lee nodded in agreement. 'Yes, think of all the ex-partners who stuff burning rags into houses, kids upstairs in bed. Whole families.'

'Personal,' Her Maj mused, 'which doesn't sit easily alongside the organized hit scenario.'

'Drugs?' said Rachel. Drugs and guns, like fish and chips, rum and Coke.

'Mitch,' the boss said, 'have a chat with the drug squad, find out what little sleaze-ball's running the supply on Manorclough. We should know later today or tomorrow what weapon we're looking for and whether there's a tie-in to any other shootings. The first call to the fire service was from a Zainab Muhammad at the flats opposite. Several more calls came in after. So house-to-house, speak to Mrs Muhammad and her neighbours.'

'Any reports of gunfire?' Rachel said.

'Nothing logged,' said the boss, 'see what the locals tell you. The residential properties are across the road from the chapel, no homes on the chapel side. Our colleagues in the fire service are also looking into similarities between this arson and two prior incidents.'

Rachel thought of the crowd she'd seen gawking at the inferno. Wondered if any of those watching knew that a man was inside the building. Would any of those who'd rubber-necked feel differently once they heard? A harmless spectacle, a bit of a thrill in their dull, tedious little lives transformed into a tragic loss of life. Some would probably get a kick out of the notion, Rachel thought, that *X-factor* moment of coming close to murder, death, scandal.

'What were you doing loitering on Manor-clough?' Janet asked Rachel as they got in the car.

'Why?' Rachel said.

'I'm nosy, humour me.'

'I'd been for a run.' Rachel started the engine.

'A run. I'm not sure I could run for a bus,' Janet said.

There never seemed to be any time to take exercise.

'Running, twice a week. Boxing club every Tuesday. Well, that was the plan,' Rachel said.

'*Boxing!* What does Sean think about you boxing?'

'*I'm* not boxing,' Rachel laughed. 'I'm helping train 'em up. Self-defence. Though I can do a mean kickbox if pushed. It's the youth project. Keep 'em off the streets. Community-minded, right?'

'I suppose,' Janet said.

'There's fuck all else for kids to do, I used to help out back when I was on probation. Good for the CV. Tried to get Dom along–' She stopped abruptly. Janet knew Rachel was still devastated about her brother and also that she hated talking about it. Before Janet could say anything Rachel ran on, 'Anyway, what's Sean got to do with it? He's not the boss of me.'

'No, I am,' said Janet.

'Sarge!' Rachel laughed.

'Give over.'

'Someone should ring Andy, let him know.'

'Shut. Up,' Janet enunciated clearly. Sergeant Andy Roper had been abruptly transferred to another syndicate in the meltdown that had followed their brief affair, with Andy morphing from Janet's secret lover to stalker then saboteur. His removal had led to Janet's temporary promotion. She hoped it wouldn't last too long. She didn't need any new challenges, was eager to just let everything settle, subside. She craved some stability. She owed it to the girls, as well. No sooner had Ade moved out after a miserable, gut-wrenching row than their grandma, Janet's mum, Dorothy, had moved in needing support after her hysterectomy. Now Dorothy was back in her own home and Ade was back in the marital bed. It felt like musical chairs. Without the fun. And now Ade was talking divorce.

Janet looked at the map of the area surrounding the Old Chapel. A large roundabout marked the middle of the estate, perhaps designed as Oldham's answer to the village green. The main roads met at the roundabout. Off Manorclough Road was the shopping precinct. On the far side of the roundabout two tower blocks stood. Opposite the Old Chapel, slum housing had been cleared in the 1980s and replaced by new-built maisonettes. There were a few larger buildings marked on the map to the north between the canal and Shuttling Way, the dual carriageway they were driving along. Janet looked up and identified the mill, now converted into retail use: paint, furniture, mirrors, fabric and lighting. Further clues as to the area's past were in the names of the streets, Fullers Yard, Tanners Back Lane, Mill Lane and Spindle Road. Cotton had driven the expansion of the area, cotton too brought workers from Pakistan, India and Bangladesh. Ade, a geography teacher, would be proud of her.

Janet directed Rachel to take the next turning off Shuttling Way and to park at the precinct.

'I'll start with Mrs Muhammad,' Janet said, touching her finger on the map to the houses opposite the chapel. 'You do the neighbours.'

'There may be some CCTV at the shops,' Rachel said.

'Yes, we'll go there next. If anyone's got tapes, we'll take them,' Janet said.

'After that?'

'See where we're up to.'

Mrs Muhammad's small yellow and cream brick house had been embellished with fancy double-glazing, etched diamond patterns on the windows and elaborate wrought-iron gates with oval tips on top of the upright rods, reminiscent of a row of spears, Janet thought. Handy for security though, slip on those and you'd soon know about it.

There was no answer when Janet repeatedly rang the bell, so she tried the mobile number that Mrs Muhammad had left when she reported the fire.

'Soapy Joe's,' a woman answered.

'I'm looking for Mrs Muhammad,' Janet said.

'That's me.'

Janet explained the reason for her call and was directed to the launderette. 'Go up to the shops and we're the next to last unit on the parade,' Mrs. Muhammad said, 'before the tanning salon.'

There were eight units altogether, two-storey buildings. Two blocks of four with a gap in the middle that led to an alleyway behind. Chippy, newsagent cum off-licence, hairdresser, then an empty unit either side of the cut-through, a pound shop which covered half the pavement in brightly coloured plastic boxes, baskets and bins, Soapy Joe's and beyond that the tancab.

The launderette was noisy and humid, a bank of washing machines down one side, several in use, dryers at the far end, bench seating and areas to fold clothes. The smell of detergent and fabric conditioner and hot metal.

One customer sat on the benches, intent on her phone. Mrs Muhammad emerged from the door at the back. 'Police?' she asked Janet. Janet nodded.

'We'll go outside,' Mrs Muhammad said, 'can't hear yourself think in here.' She pulled up her headscarf and threw the length over her shoulder to hold it in place.

Janet checked Mrs Muhammad's details and asked her to describe what she'd seen on Wednesday night.

'I'd just got back from here and I was putting the youngest to bed, he's at the front in the boys' room. I went to draw the curtains and I could see smoke coming across the road, from the chapel.'

'You didn't see anything unusual before that?'

'No,' she said.

'And you didn't hear anything?' Janet was thinking of the gunshots.

'No. I looked to make sure, you know, then rang the fire brigade. By then there was even more smoke. Now they're saying this bloke died in there.' She looked at Janet, keen, curious.

'That's right. Did you ever see people going into the building or in the grounds?'

'Now and then. Not often, you know. I don't know how they'd get in. Wire fence all round,' she said, 'and the building is all boarded up.' Her eyes flicked over Janet's shoulder and narrowed She stepped to one side and yelled, 'Oy, Rabia. Get here, now!'

Janet turned to see a teenage version of Mrs Muhammad in black jeans, a white blouse and spike-heeled boots, carrying a large sequined bag

The girl hesitated – she was at the end of the row of shops – then walked up, her heels smacking on the pavement.

'Why aren't you in college?' her mother snapped as she drew close.

'Free period,' the girl said, contemptuously. 'I'm going back after.'

'Make sure you do,' Mrs Muhammad said.

'I will. I said.' The girl scowled. 'OK?' She spun around and stalked off.

'Girls,' Mrs Muhammad breathed, 'ten times more trouble. You got kids?'

'Two,' Janet said, 'girls.'

'Good luck with that,' she said and Janet smiled.

'People trespassing?' Janet prompted her.

'Oh right, so sometimes there's been kids in, not recently. Don't know why they'd bother, what's there to do in there, all weeds, i'nt it? It were a right blaze.' She shook her head, patted at the scarf on her shoulder. 'The house still stank even with all the windows shut.'

'There have been other fires started deliberately?' Janet said.

'Yeah, the mosque, the school. It's not good,' she said. 'Thought it was racists, the mosque, you know, but the school, we all use the school. What's all that about? And this,' she tipped her head in the direction of the Old Chapel, 'well, it's not good, is it? Who

49

could do that to a person? That is really horrible'

'Are you aware of anyone causing problems in the area, antisocial behaviour, that sort of thing?' Janet said.

'You always get a few.' She grimaced.

'Can you think of anyone we should be talking to?'

Her expression altered slightly, becoming guarded, suspicious. 'No,' she said.

Janet wasn't sure whether she resented the implication that she might know criminal elements in the area or whether she did know and was frightened to say so.

4

Rachel spoke to the residents at numbers six and eight Low Bank Road, all of whom had seen the blaze but nothing else. She recognized the woman at number six, she'd been there with the buggy and all her kids. The bloke at number ten, Mr Hicks, was housebound. He thought he had seen someone going down the side of the chapel. Running. 'I think there were two of them,' he said.

As soon as she asked for more details he faltered.

'Men?' she said.

He shrugged. 'Don't know.'

'Black, white?'

'More likely Pakis round here,' he said.

'Could you tell?' asked Rachel.

'No.'

'Height?' Thinking of the victim who was six foot tall. Might he have seen the victim and someone chasing him?

'Couldn't say,' Mr Hicks replied.

'What were they wearing?'

His rheumy gaze brightened, like some part of his brain had coughed into life. 'Them jackets.'

'Jackets?' Rachel said. 'What like?'

'Football,' he said.

'Football strip?' Hardly counted as jackets.

'No,' he sneered. 'American football.'

What the fuck did American footballers wear?

'Wi' hoods.'

Hoodies? Rachel's sense of progress evaporated. 'You mean hoodies?' That'd rule in most of the local youth and half their parents.

'Like…' he waved one crabby fist, thumb and fingers together as though holding the answer, '…baseball.'

Make your mind up.

'Wi' numbers on,' he said.

Rachel's heart skipped a beat. The couple she'd seen in the alley, puffing billies. Class of 88. 'Both of them had these jackets?' she asked.

'One did, the other was further away and

these glasses aren't so good, need a new prescription from the optician. But how am I supposed to get there? They expect me to fork out for a taxi?' Shit eyesight didn't exactly make him prime witness material but still.

'You make out the numbers?' Rachel said.

'Two fat ladies.'

'Eighty-eight,' Rachel supplied.

'Right,' he said.

'What time was this?'

'About half past seven. Half an hour later it's all on fire.'

Rachel left him and headed for the shops, the buzz that comes with a promising lead simmering beneath her skin.

She found Janet at the parade. 'Witness sighting of intruders in the chapel grounds,' Rachel said. 'The description matches two lads I saw down here last night. Wore hoodies with matching numbers on the back.'

'A gang thing?' Janet said.

'No idea.'

'Worth asking about,' Janet said, 'see if we can get names. I've spoken to the launderette, that's where Mrs Muhammad works, and I've done the tancab. I'll do the hairdresser's if you take the off-licence and the chip shop.'

The off-licence cum newsagent was staffed by a young white guy with elaborate tattoos on both forearms and around his neckline. Rachel had noticed the CCTV camera outside the shop overlooking the entrance, and another behind the counter. 'The cameras working?' she asked him once she'd flashed her warrant card and noted his name. Liam Kelly.

'Yes.'

'We'll take any recordings from last night.'

'Sure,' he said.

She asked him about the fire but he couldn't tell her much. The shop was open until ten so he had heard about the fire but not seen anything till after he'd locked up.

'You know anything about the Old Chapel, people breaking in there?'

'No.' He looked up as the door buzzer went and a woman came in. She picked up a copy of the *Sun*, asked for twenty fags, paid and left. Once they were alone again Rachel asked him about trouble in the area.

'What, like the shop being done four times in as many months?' he said.

'Your community policing team–'

'Is a fucking joke,' he interrupted, 'and you lot couldn't catch a cold.'

'I'm sorry you feel that way but I'm dealing with a major incident.' Before he could moan any more Rachel said, 'We'd like to talk to two individuals who wear matching hoodies, eighty-eight printed on the back and a picture of an eagle.' Something like dislike slithered through his eyes, the Celtic knot at the base of his throat rippled. 'The Perry brothers,' he said, 'twins.'

'They live around here?'

He nodded. 'Beaumont House, the tower block.'

'They trouble?' Rachel said.

'The community policing team will tell you all about it.' She gave him a grin.

'They don't come in here,' he said, 'they're banned.'

'How come? They nicking stuff?'

'Not that so much,' Liam Kelly replied, 'threatening people, nutters, idiots the pair of them.'

'How old?'

'Nineteen, twenty,' he ventured. 'Look,' he gestured to a stack of boxes, crisps and fizzy drinks, 'I've stuff to sort.'

'Nearly done,' Rachel said. 'You got that tape?' He fetched it for her and she was about to leave when she heard a door out the back being unlocked and then a slam. A black woman with dreadlocks, wearing combat pants and a green vest, came in, saying, 'Liam, that stuff's still out there, shall I chuck it?'

'Give him another hour, then take it to the food bank.'

The woman glanced at Rachel, able to tell she wasn't just a passing customer or a rep pushing confectionery. 'Feeding strays,' she explained.

54

'Dogs?' Rachel said.

'No – people.' The woman laughed. She had a missing tooth. 'But I think it's only Rick that takes it.'

'Stuff past its sell-by date,' said Liam Kelly.

'I don't know if it's a good thing or not,' the woman said.

'Better than giving him money to piss away on booze,' he replied.

'Softy at heart.' She punched his arm.

'Get off.' But there was affection in his tone. 'Police, about the murder,' he gestured to Rachel. 'This is Mels.'

'You see the fire?' Rachel asked.

'Some. I was doing cash and carry,' Mels said, 'got back and it was all going up. You think it's a drug thing? They say he was shot.'

'We don't know what's behind it yet. But if you do hear anything, I'd really appreciate it if you got in touch.' She handed over her card.

The chippy was busy. Rachel ignored the queue and the muttered complaints as she barged to the front and spoke to the Chinese woman serving, telling her she wanted to talk to her about the incident at the Old Chapel.

'OK.' She called out something Rachel couldn't follow and her husband, Rachel assumed, came out from the back and took over at the counter so Rachel could talk to Mrs Lin, who spoke reasonable English.

They were working until eleven but their son had told them about the fire. They'd no CCTV and she had no idea who might have been involved in the murder or the fire.

'What about other trouble?' Rachel said. 'In the shop?'

Mrs Lin pulled a face, shook her head. When Rachel referred to the spate of break-ins next door, to the other arson attacks, all she said was, 'Kids. It's kids, yes. Very bad.'

Questions about the Perry twins were met with quick, vehement shakes of the head as if she was barely listening to what Rachel was saying. The husband's approach to serving was heavy-handed, slamming chips on to trays, shovelling fish on top, banging the parcels on the counter top for the customer.

'I wanted scraps,' the person at the front of the line said loudly.

The man barked something in Chinese and his wife pulled another face. 'Finished?' she said to Rachel.

Rachel briefly considered asking for chips and curry sauce but thought it best not to give the locals anything else to grumble about. 'For now.'

'You here about that murder?' a woman at the back of the queue called out.

'That's right,' Rachel said. 'Can you help?'

'Me? No.'

'If anyone can,' Rachel said, addressing them all, 'there will be a mobile incident van setting up in the area any time soon. And if anyone is aware of a person missing from home please let us know.'

Coming out of the chip shop, Rachel saw the lad on the stunt bike who had been among the crowd at the fire, cycling his way on the wrong side of the road. Numpty.

'Hey,' she called out as he mounted the pavement, braked and slung his bike down. 'You want to watch that, get yourself killed.'

'Fuck off,' he said and spat on the floor.

'Charming,' said Rachel. She showed him her warrant card. 'DC Bailey, Manchester Metropolitan–' Before she completed the sentence, he snatched his bike and was riding over the roundabout and off along Tanners Back Lane.

Rachel went after him. He was faster than she was and he knew the area so she expected to lose him. But then as he reached the junction with Derby Fold Lane an HGV roared past. The boy didn't have time to stop, maybe his brakes weren't working, so he pulled the bike up to do a wheelie and went over backwards, skidding across the road with the bike on top of him. The lorry drove on oblivious.

Rachel caught up to the boy and pulled the bike off him. He scooted to the side of the road, swearing repeatedly and rocking in pain. His arm was skinned, elbow to wrist, and his cheek cut and bruised.

'Why did you run?' Rachel said, crouching down.

''Cos you were chasing us,' he said.

'Not until you scarpered, I wasn't.'

He winced, twisting his arm over to look at the damage.

'Nothing broken,' Rachel said.

'You a bleeding doctor?'

'No, but I'm a trained first-aider. Just watch the attitude,' she said.

'Huh?' he grunted. He pulled himself up. 'You nearly got us killed.'

'That's not on me. You ought to do your cycling proficiency. Rules of the road. You get a certificate,' she teased him.

A twitch that might just have been a smile.

'What's your name?'

He squinted at her, blue eyes alert. 'Connor.'

'Connor who?'

'Connor Tandy.'

'Right.' She stood up. 'I'm investigating the murder of a man found in the remains of the Old Chapel after last night's fire.'

'So?'

'So. You were there,' she said.

'I was not!' he said, shocked.

'Not there, there,' she said. She pointed. 'You were watching the fire, last night.'

'So. It's not a crime, is it?'

'Did you see anything? Do you know anything?'

'Like what?' He studied his injury again.

Rachel sighed. 'Anything suspicious?'

'No.'

'You heard any rumours?' she said.

'I'm not a fucking grass.' He touched his cheek, gingerly.

'So you have heard something?'

'No.' He got to his feet, limping slightly.

'Can you wiggle your toes?' Rachel said.

He just glared at her and bent for his bike.

'Any idea who he might be, the man who was killed?'

He shook his head.

'How old are you?' Rachel said.

'Sixteen!'

'I can check.'

'Fourteen.'

'Not in school?'

'Off sick,' he said.

'How's that then?' Rachel said.

'Hurt my arm.' He showed her the fresh scrape, beaded with blood.

She fought a smile. *Cheeky little bastard.*

'Where d'you live?'

He sighed. 'Manton Road.'

'You know it's an offence to lie to a police officer?'

'It's God's truth,' he said, outraged again.

'And you not knowing anything about the murders, that true?'

'I told you,' he said, 'you fucking deaf?'

'Oi!' she said sharply. 'Stop swearing. What

about the Perry twins? You know them?'

'No.' He spat on the floor.

Rachel thought he was lying, maybe not about the rest but about the twins. If they were as much trouble as Liam Kelly had implied, then every scrote, every scally on the estate, would know exactly who they were. And would either be nervously in thrall to them, or scared shitless and steering well clear.

'Go on, Bradley Wiggins,' she said, 'on your bike.'

He jumped on and cycled off. Rachel couldn't be certain but when he turned off into the estate the hand gesture he made looked suspiciously like he was flipping her the finger.

5

At the end of the day the team reconvened and Gill led them systematically through the different strands of the inquiry. As senior investigating officer, everything had been fed through to her and now needed to be shared with her detectives.

'First off, where are we on ID? Kevin?'

He tapped his pen against his notebook. 'Three possibilities for marriages with those initials on that date, one in Oldham, one in Bury and one in Manchester. John Smith and Ruth King, Judith Smith and Richard Kavanagh and Jennifer Simpson and Robert Keele.'

'Any bells?' Gill scanned the room to see if any of those names had come up in the course if the day. When no one responded she said, 'Kevin, keep on with that, see if you can eliminate anyone.'

'Yes, boss.'

'OK,' she said, 'updates on forensics at the crime scene. As expected, the accelerant has been identified as petrol.'

When Mitch groaned, Gill said, 'I know – ubiquitous but we may be able to be more specific. Meanwhile talk to petrol stations in a ten-mile radius, any cans filled in the days before the murder.'

'Could be siphoned off,' Pete said.

'Yes,' said Gill, 'we should look at that as well. Access to and from the building looks to have been gained from the rear where there is a hole cut in the chain-link fence.'

'Spoke to the current owners,' Mitch said. 'The site was last checked eight months ago. They've had the fencing up for three years, after a spate of break-ins and vandalism. Fairly quiet since. They want to sell but they're sitting on the property until there's an upturn in land values.'

'Round there?' Rachel snorted. 'They'll

have a long wait. Manchester prices have stayed steady, if I owned anything–'

'Hey,' Gill said, 'save the *Homes under the Hammer* drivel for your own time. Focus. Now, at the other side of the building from the breach, steps lead down to a basement door. It's a storage area under the anteroom with steps up into the main part of the building. That's how our killer gained entry. Persons of interest, Noel and Neil Perry.' Gill nodded to Rachel.

'Twins,' Rachel said. 'They were in the alley on Wednesday night, watching the fire, I saw them. They wear these American baseball-style hoodies, Class of 88 and an eagle printed on the back, and an eyewitness saw them in the grounds of the chapel that night.'

'Independent? Reliable?' Gill said.

Rachel nodded. 'Bit doddery though, not got twenty-twenty vision.'

'Brilliant – you bring me Mr Magoo.'

'The sweatshirts,' Lee said, 'it's a fascist thing. Eighty-eight stands for Heil Hitler.'

'Seriously?' Kevin said.

Gill felt a kick of adrenaline, the case was growing legs, taking shape. 'Anyone remember Terence Perry?'

'Rapist,' Pete said.

'That's right. A nasty shit-bag of a man by all accounts. And these are his kids. He died in prison – poisoning, been brewing his own hooch apparently, recipe went wrong. This

62

was in 2004. Since then his sons have come to the attention of our colleagues on numerous occasions. Spent eighteen months in a young offenders' institution for arson. Were they interviewed for the other recent fires, the mosque and the school?'

'Interviewed and released, nothing to put them there. Alibied by a family member, the grandmother, Eileen Perry,' said Mitch.

'Terence's mother,' said Pete, 'she'd swear black is white to cover for the family. Odds on she'll alibi them this time.'

'Liam Kelly, the newsagent, he banned them,' Rachel said.

'Do we know why?' Gill asked.

'Causing trouble, violent, nasty. And Mrs Lin at the Chinese didn't want to talk about them, gave me the bum's rush.'

'Flagged up by the community team as well,' Lee said. 'Affray, disturbing the peace. Word is the mosque fire was down to the EBA, English Bulldog Army, a spin-off from the English Defence League. Where the worst of the nutters go, to use a technical term.'

'Are the Perrys members?' said Gill.

'It's a fluid organization,' said Lee, 'all the dregs, raving racist loonies who are too openly violent even for the EDL, end up there. The twins could well be, judging by their clothing and reputation. We'll make some inquiries.'

'So we can agree the Perrys have un-savoury political views,' Gill said.

'Is the EBA a banned organization?' Janet asked.

'Not yet, there hasn't been time, but I believe it's under consideration,' Gill said. 'Have the Perrys any history of firearm offences?'

'No,' Mitch said.

'Connected?' she asked, thinking about the criminal fraternity.

Mitch shook his head.

'Right,' Gill said, 'once we've more hard evidence we'll have a word with the Chuckle Brothers. Who are the main players on the estate? Who's causing us grief on Manor-clough these days?'

'Most of the drug traffic is believed to be controlled by Marcus Williams,' Mitch said. He'd been talking to the neighbourhood policing team and to the drug squad. 'Wil-liams stepped up when Keith Grant was busted. Been in charge ever since. A can-nabis farm closed down in January was believed to be his. Steady business, handles the lot, Class Bs, some Class As.'

'Except he doesn't handle anything,' Gill said.

'That's right, hands free.' Mitch showed his palms. 'There's even talk of him stand-ing for the local council.'

'You're kidding,' said Janet.

'The lure of respectability,' Gill said.

Mitch smiled.

'Anyone picked up for the cannabis farm?' Gill said.

'Suspects are awaiting trial, no one's talking,' Mitch said.

'So who is our victim? Has he started a turf war? Is Williams the trigger-happy type?'

'No. Things been very quiet on that front,' Mitch said.

'Is Williams into any other business, prostitution, loan sharks?'

'Concentrates on the drugs,' said Mitch. 'Known associate, Stanley Keane, a bruiser, he's probably Williams's enforcer.'

'We park that information,' said Gill. 'If we find any link between Williams and company and our victim then we'll come back to it.'

'Maybe it's been set up to look like a hit when it's actually a domestic,' Kevin said. 'The wife or whoever has had enough. Hires a hitman.'

'Thinking on an empty stomach, Kevin, never a good idea,' said Gill.

'It happens,' Kevin said.

'Thinking?' This from Rachel.

'Hired hitmen,' Kevin said.

'Rarely,' Gill said. 'If you're right I'll buy you a pint. And a pot to put it in. OK, what else ... nothing as yet to indicate the body was moved to the site post-mortem. Good start,' she wound things up, 'get some kip.

See you tomorrow.'

Gill was surprised to find Sammy at home when she finally got back after ten. 'Thought you were going to your dad's,' she said, surveying the empty pizza box, the baking tray in the sink, and half a dozen dirty mugs and glasses on the counter.

'We rearranged,' he said.

'How come?'

'Just did.' He opened the fridge.

'Hey, this lot first, dishwasher and paper bin,' she said, nodding at the mess.

'I was,' he said.

She laughed. 'Hardly.' She wondered who'd rearranged. Had Sammy put his dad off? She could see why he might. Dave wasn't great company these days. His love nest with the whore of Pendlebury and their spawn had disintegrated and Dave was now back living with his mother. Not a good look for a man in his fifties. Sammy liked his grandma but was of an age where a handful of visits a year would suffice. But for all Dave's failings, and they were legion, Gill still thought it best that Sammy maintain regular contact with his dad. It'd help Dave too, she reckoned, to know there was still somebody who loved him. A solid relationship that wasn't going to go tits up when a younger model rolled along. Did Dave still see his second child? She'd never asked. It wasn't her business, anyway. Dave was an adult, fact. Despite his sometimes childish behaviour. He could handle the fallout from his midlife crisis by himself. Why the hell should Gill concern herself with it?

Sammy put the crockery in the dishwasher and took the carton outside to the recycling bin while Gill fixed herself an omelette.

'I need a suit,' he said as he came in, 'for the prom.'

'What's wrong with the one you've got?'

'Too short.' He went back to the fridge, opened it. The light shining out on him. Like a shrine, Gill thought, where he worships. He can't eat enough. Eighteen and still growing.

'You sure?'

'Yes, it's halfway up my legs. I look like a knob.'

'Well, I think your dad'll have to take you,' she said, forking up the last of her food.

'Why can't you?'

'Because I've just started an investigation. I'm not going to have time to draw breath.'

He sighed heavily, brought ham and cheese out of the fridge.

'Or take Orla,' Gill said.

'Cool.' Shopping with his girlfriend obviously appealed more.

'Revision?' she said.

'Done some.' He'd three more exams to sit, then his schooldays would be over.

'Orla's being nominated for prom queen,'

he said.

'Is she now?'

'Yeah. I think Daisy Tuttle will get it, she's more popular.'

'We never had any of that sort of thing,' she said, 'proms.'

'You had a party, though, didn't you?'

'Of sorts. Smuggled in vodka to mix with fruit juice, crammed into the school hall. Smelled of sweaty trainers. Disco – that was our lot. No limos, or kings and queens. If anyone had worn a suit they'd have been laughed out of court. The only people who wore suits were teachers and squares.' She laughed.

'Sounds rubbish,' he said.

'It was brilliant,' she said. 'We were free, school's out, all that business, we burned our ties. None of this American tosh.'

'And you knew then you wanted to join the police?'

She studied him for a moment. 'I did. Never thought about doing anything else. With Grandma and Grandpa in the job, although Grandma left when she married.'

'Why?' he said. He took a huge bite of the sub sandwich he'd made.

'That's how people did it back then. Married women weren't supposed to work, a man was expected to support the whole family. Guess it was in my DNA, the police.'

'And mine,' he said with his mouth full.

'Lot easier to join then.'

'You keep saying that, like you want to put me off,' he said.

'No, I don't. But it is important you know how tough it will be.'

'I do know. I've got to get more experience. I've applied to join the special constabulary, so I can start that as soon as the exams are done, and I've got my driving licence. Once I've done some time volunteering with them I can try for the police community support officers and the police proper after that.'

'Yes, but who knows how long there'll be a freeze on police recruitment,' she said.

'You still think I should have gone to university.'

She chose her words carefully. 'I think it might have given you more options. You'd have a degree, which is a valuable qualification, in the police as much as anywhere else. If there aren't any openings in the police, if you don't get in, then what?'

'Go abroad, Australia or somewhere.'

'Seriously!' She had never imagined him emigrating. Felt a squirt of panic but then thought about his future, his life. 'That would be amazing,' she said. 'I could come and visit.'

'How? You're always at work.'

'When I retire. Not all that long now.' She could barely imagine it. Work, the job, had shaped her life over twenty-eight years. What on earth would she do without it? Maybe there'd be space as an adviser, a specialist. Retired officers did sometimes keep their hand in, working as consultants.

The force had changed almost beyond recognition in Gill's time. Advances in science and technology had perhaps made the biggest impact. Everything from DNA profiling and CCTV coverage to mobile phones, the internet and a plethora of software systems provided tools for the detection of crime. There had been improvements in prevention as well: the police advised on secure building design, for example, features that reduced the opportunities for crime, neighbourhood watch schemes. Crime was falling as a result. How much more would change in Sammy's lifetime?

But beyond all those tools, the most important resource was the staff themselves. Trained, monitored, mentored, assessed. There was no space for slackers or the mediocre in the service. God knows how Kevin Lumb had got through selection. Officers had to be highly motivated, intelligent and personable, able to work with others and show initiative. Sammy was all those and then some, but she was biased, she was his mother and there'd be another hundred kids like him all vying for the same sweet spot.

Gill caught the local television news, saw a picture of the blackened chapel with the briefest of reports. She cleared up and emptied the kitchen bin. Outside it was a clear night, cool, with pinprick stars over the moors.

She wondered about their victim. Was someone missing him tonight? Would DNA lead them to find him or his killer on the police database?

Gill noticed the top of the blue wheelie bin was open. Drawing close; she could see Sammy had just stuffed the pizza box in without squashing it down, so the lid wouldn't shut.

As she went to remedy the situation, a dark shape slithered from the bin and shot off into the dark. 'Jesus!' Gill started, felt the hairs on her forearms prickle.

She went back to the door and called out, 'Sammy?'

'What?'

'Here. Now.' He could bloody well sort out the bin himself. She should have called him in the first place. Perhaps an encounter with a rat would be more effective than any amount of nagging from his mother.

'Test me, Mum.' Taisie burst into the sitting room, script in hand. She'd obviously heard Janet arriving home. Janet stifled the impulse to groan and said, 'Two minutes, let me get my breath back.'

'Where?' Taisie said. 'Dad's watching TV.'

'Here then.' Janet found half a bottle of white in the fridge and poured, herself a glass. Cut some cheese. In the breadbin she found the heel of a French stick, not quite stale. She sat down, ate a few mouthfuls and drank some wine.

Taisie chattered on, a few mmms and yeses the only input required from Janet.

'Genevieve missed three rehearsals, right, three and so Miss said Polly could do her part and then Genevieve came back and she said she'd had flu, right, and so Miss said Polly would be stand-in again and Polly burst into tears and Genevieve was all like, "I'm so sorry," all gushy, yeah? And Miss said if Genevieve was off any more then she'd lose the part but we think they should take turns. And 'cos we said that, right, now Genevieve isn't talking to us. Except in the play.'

'Mmm,' said Janet.

'But Miss said no, and that is so tight. Polly was bare good too.'

Bare, Janet knew, was the current slang for very.

'And if you want tickets, I need the slip and money by Friday.'

'Tomorrow!' said Janet.

'Duh,' said Taisie.

'Where's the slip?'

'I gave you it,' Taisie said.

'No,' said Janet.

'I did – I left it on here.' She rapped her knuckles against the table.

'Well, I didn't see it.'

Taisie gave a huge sigh.

'Look, can't you just get the tickets if I give you the money?' Janet said.

'OK.' Crisis averted as quickly as it had erupted. Taisie was all drama. 'Go on,' she said, nodding at the script.

'Your hand Leonato; we will go together,' Janet read the cue.

'Benedick, didst thou note the daughter of Signior Leonato?' said Taisie.

They'd almost got through to the finale, Taisie word perfect, when Elise came in. 'Did you talk to Dad?' she asked Janet.

'Shut up,' Taisie yelled, 'I'm doing my lines.'

'This is important,' Elise sneered.

'What – a stupid party?' Taisie said.

'Just 'cos you're too young to go,' said Elise.

'So are you, isn't she, Mum? Tell her.'

'Elise,' Janet said, 'let us finish this.'

With ill grace Elise leaned, arms folded, against the counter, a derisory look on her face, and Janet knew she was trying to unsettle Taisie. She suspected that Taisie was made of sterner stuff and was proven right as her younger daughter finished her part faultlessly.

'Brilliant!' Janet said. 'Perfect!'

'Finally,' Elise complained.

Perhaps it was healthy, this antagonism between the sisters, an indication that they felt secure enough to bicker and spat. The solidarity, the drawing together there'd been when Ade had left, now easing with the reinstatement of the status quo. The girls no longer relying on each other while the grown-ups messed up. And if/when they got divorced, if the house was sold? Janet felt a shiver, a sour taste in her mouth.

Taisie rolled up her script and skipped off.

'I haven't spoken to your dad yet,' Janet told Elise, 'I've only just got in. Weren't you supposed to be getting some more details?'

'I have. It's Matthew Planter's party, it's at his house and we're invited because his brother is in our year and he's allowed to invite people.'

'Where do they live?' Janet said.

'Middleton Road and we can get a taxi home to Olivia's and we have to be back for one o'clock.'

'Come on,' Janet said and they went through to the lounge.

'This party,' Janet said.

Ade paused his programme, something about the Pharaohs.

'Tell him,' Janet said.

Elise rattled off the facts she'd given Janet.

'And who's supervising?' said Ade.

'His parents. God! It's like you don't trust me.'

'It's not you we don't trust,' Janet said, 'but we've been there, we know what can happen. People drink too much and take stupid risks or they do daft things and end up regretting it.'

'Please?' Elise said, her voice aching with frustration.

We should trust her, Janet thought. It's the only way she'll learn. She nodded at Ade, who gave a shrug of resignation.

'All right then but a taxi back by one, promise?' Janet said.

'Yes!' Elise began texting on her phone. 'Thank you so much.' Suddenly sounding far too young for what they had just agreed to.

Sean was hunched over his laptop, the sports channel on the box, men in shorts running around on grass on both screens and the smell of fried onions thick in the flat. Rachel lit up and, as an afterthought, opened the window.

'Chill Factor,' he said, 'Saturday, or maybe Sunday. Could do WaterWorld an' all maybe. Stay over somewhere.'

'What?' She'd had too many fags today, the first drag failed to deliver the kick she craved. Instead it just made her mouth feel rancid.

'You, me and Haydn,' he said, 'skiing or

snowboarding? He's here this weekend.'

Oh, joy. Rachel had nothing against the kid; he was harmless enough. A mini Sean, interested in anything that involved balls or sticks. Or food. 'No can do,' she said. 'We picked one up, man in that fire in Manorclough.'

'That yours?' he said.

'Yeah.'

'I'd better book for two then, unless you want to wait until another time.'

The thought that Sean was worried she might be disappointed at missing out on the trip was both touching and plain daft. 'You go ahead,' she said. Relieved that she had a rock-solid reason not to be around for more than a few hours' kip over the weekend. Sean and Haydn could do their male bonding, father–son stuff and welcome to it. She didn't want to intrude, or maybe she just felt ill-equipped.

Had her dad ever taken Dom anywhere? Doubtful. Not like her dad would be much use at entertaining the kids. Could barely feed and clothe them. It was Rachel who dragged Dom off to the cinema on the rare occasions when special vouchers meant they could afford it, Rachel who would cheer him on when he played football. Her mum gone by then, Dad taken up residence in the pub to all intents and purposes and her sister Alison working all hours as the sole breadwinner.

76

Her dad had gone now, as in dead. Ashes blowing in the wind. His liver finally packed up. It had been two weeks before the smell alerted his fellow residents at the doss house to his demise. And now her mum was back.

Which might or might not be a good thing. Rachel was still waiting to see. Sharon had been penitent at their reunion, an occasion engineered by Sean, who was keen to see the family reunited. Then she had been pissed at the wedding, made a right tit of herself, acting like a slapper. Sean said it was just nerves. A wedding wasn't a wedding without someone having one over the odds, at least there hadn't been a scrap. No one bared their fists. Quite an achievement considering.

It was Her Maj being there, seeing her mother, that had made Rachel so uneasy. Alison had hated it too. Alison wouldn't entertain Sharon, was not at all interested. Made things a bit awkward between Rachel and Alison; they always seemed to be taking different sides with family stuff. Alison wouldn't play nice with Sharon and yet she used to make time for their dad, trying to help him out when she could. And it was Alison who visited Dom in prison the first time round, even though Dom had always been closest to Rachel. Rachel hadn't been able to stomach seeing him there. Not back then when the twat had been done for armed robbery and certainly not now when he was in for twenty-eight years. Twenty-eight years for murder. But Alison did.

She couldn't think about it. She finished her fag and shut the window.

'Get us a beer,' Sean said, busy typing on the laptop.

Get your own fucking beer. She bit down on the thought. What was wrong with her? What did she want? Him to say please? Oh Christ, was she going to turn into one of those women who try to improve the manners of their loutish husbands?

She got his bottle, helped herself to wine, stared at the TV screen for a few minutes.

Sean kissed her on the cheek. 'Happy?'

'Yeah,' she said, 'course.'

Day 2

Friday 11 May

6

Kevin, on the hunt for a surviving spouse, had traced and eliminated Ruth King, who had died in a car crash along with her husband, John Smith. He had been unable as yet to find Jennifer Keele, née Simpson, but Mrs Richard Kavanagh, née Judith Smith, was at an address in Rhyl.

Godzilla told Rachel and Janet to take the ring and see if Mrs Kavanagh could identify it, and whether her husband was missing. 'If the other facts fit: height, age, ethnicity, then advise her of the death and see what she can tell us.'

Rachel had booked the ring out from Pete, who was handling exhibits. It was important to keep the chain of custody unbroken for all items, any of which might form part of the evidence presented at trial. They were almost out of the door when Her Maj called out, 'And Janet...'

Janet turned.

'Potted shrimp wouldn't go amiss,' the boss said.

'Not rock then?' Janet said.

'No, shrimp.'

'Got it.'

They were mates, the boss and Janet. Like Janet and Rachel. Not a trio though, never that. Janet in the middle. Godzilla spent half her life racked off with Rachel – they had a professional relationship at best, boss and junior officer – but Janet and Gill went way back.

It was a dull day, layers of cloud, thick and grey, threatening drizzle. A contrast to the past couple of days of fine weather.

'Richard Kavanagh's not come up on the MisPers database,' Rachel said. She was driving. It was a straight run so Janet didn't need to navigate, and once they got close to the seaside town the satnav would guide them to their destination.

'Could be reported missing in Wales but not got on to the system yet. They'd wait forty-eight hours anyway,' Janet said.

Rachel looked at her own wedding ring. 'Forty years. Can you imagine it? Mind you, you and Ade have done twenty-six now.'

'Not sure we'll make another year,' Janet said.

Rachel glanced at her swiftly. 'That bad?'

'Whatever there was – that sparkle is long gone.'

'Sparkle?' said Rachel.

'OK, not sparkle, but that attraction. And what comes after, comfort, companionship, happy to be raising a family together. Even that's not the same any more. I feel like a nun,' Janet said.

'A nun?'

'Celibate. What if that's it, Rachel? The end of my sex life.'

'Don't be daft,' Rachel said, 'you'll meet someone else.'

'How, where?'

'At work maybe?'

'And that went really well last time,' Janet said dryly. Meaning Andy.

'Dating sites, then,' Rachel said.

'No way!'

'Some of them are all right.'

'And what if you end up with some nutter who's got a thing for spanking?' Janet said.

'You don't like a good spanking?' Rachel kept a straight face. 'You and Ade never–'

'Shut up.'

'As long as you agree a safe word you're fine,' Rachel said.

'How do people ever pick those?' Janet said. 'How do you choose something you might not say anyway?'

'Have to be something daft, like pine-apple.'

'Pineapple?' Janet laughed.

'Or a weird phrase, "It's foggy in Paris".'

'Too long,' Janet said, 'sounds like a spy novel. The kids had a safe word when they were little. If there was a change of plan and someone had to pick them up, someone they weren't expecting, then they'd have this password. It was Pikachu for a while, then Ariel. And Taisie went through this phase when this girl was sort of stalking her. Wanted to be friends, dead clingy, and Taisie didn't like her but didn't want to be blunt so I'd get these phone calls: Maria wanted her to stay over, Maria wanted her to go back after school, and Maria was going ice skating, could Taisie go. She'd get herself that wound up and we were always trying to find out what Taisie really wanted to do, knowing that this girl was there listening. In the end we worked out this code. We'd say something like "How you feeling?" or "You up to it?" and if she said "Fine" then off she'd go. That was usually because there were a group of them going. But if she didn't want to, she'd say, "I think I'm getting a migraine."'

'Does she get migraines?' Rachel said.

'Does she heck. That meant "Come get me now". We'd ride to the rescue and no feelings were hurt.'

'Did this friend get the hint?'

'No. But they ended up at different secondary schools. Never seen her since. So, you and Sean, what's your safe word?'

Rachel laughed. 'You must be joking. No way does he get to tie me up and hit me. Other way round maybe.'

'Dominatrix,' Janet said.

'You should try that with Ade, long black

84

boots, fishnets–'

'Shut up! We're way past that.'

'You're blushing,' Rachel said.

Janet just narrowed her eyes and pointedly put the radio on.

It started to rain as they entered the town; a mist of fine drops speckled the windscreen and blurred the view. The address they had was a few streets back from the seafront. Pale-blue painted walls and a stripy awning over the front door. *SAT TV, Wi-Fi* and *Vacancies* signs in the window. A B&B. One of many. All with vacancies, from what Rachel could see.

The woman who answered the door was in her sixties, on the fat side and wore denim trousers and a navy needlecord shirt with a small print of birds on it. Her hair was brown, dyed, Rachel reckoned, cut fairly short. Practical, easy to look after.

'Judith Kavanagh?' Janet said.

'Yes?'

'I'm DC Janet Scott from the Manchester Metropolitan Police and this is my colleague DC Rachel Bailey. Could we come in for a minute?'

The woman pulled a face, half-wry, puzzled to find the police on her doorstep but not alarmed, which was a more common reaction. Was she hiding any consternation? Probably not fair to cast her as a potential villain on first sight but Rachel understood that most victims were known to their killers. Though picturing Mrs Kavanagh with a gun and a can of petrol took some doing.

The property was bigger than it looked from the outside. 'We'd better go through to the back,' Judith Kavanagh said. They passed a residents' lounge, dining room and kitchen and then went through a door marked private and into what served as her own living room. 'Can I get you a drink?' she said once they'd sat down. A slight Welsh lilt in her accent.

'No, thank you,' said Janet. 'Can I just check, you are married to Richard Kavanagh?'

'Yes. Why?' Worry was creeping into her expression.

'I'm sorry, I need to check a few more details,' Janet said. 'You married on the twenty-third of April 1972?'

'Yes.'

'Could you please give me your date of birth.'

She did and Janet noted it. 'And this is your usual address?'

'That's right.'

'And your husband lives here?'

'No, we're separated,' she said.

That makes things slightly easier, thought Rachel.

'We're investigating a major incident and I

wonder if you could look at an item of jewellery to see if you recognize it,' Janet said.

Judith Kavanagh coughed, increasingly uneasy. 'Yes of course,' she said.

Janet took the ring in its sealed evidence bag and handed it to Mrs Kavanagh. The awkward smile faded from her lips, her posture altered, her shoulders sank. 'It's Richard's ring, his wedding ring.'

'Thank you,' Janet said. 'Please would you describe him for us.'

'I'm sorry, I don't understand.'

'How tall is he?' Janet said.

'Six foot two.'

'And he was born in 1952 so he would be sixty years old now?'

'That's right,' Judith Kavanagh said.

Rachel looked around the room, saw family photos of a wedding, not Mrs Kavanagh's, a son or daughter's perhaps?

At Rachel's insistence that their own wedding be simple and planned with a minimum of fuss, she and Sean had not had a professional photographer, but he had arranged for a mate of his to take photos of them before everyone got half cut and Sean had got one printed and framed.

Mrs Kavanagh's other photos showed a couple with a baby, a young man in a gown and mortar board. None of the man who was their victim.

'What's this all about?' Mrs Kavanagh set

the bag containing the ring down on a side table.

'Mrs Kavanagh, I'm so very sorry to tell you that the body of a man was recovered from a building in the Manorclough area of Oldham, near Manchester, on Wednesday night,' said Janet. 'We believe that man to be your husband. I'm sorry to have to tell you that he is dead. We will be doing all we can to make a positive identification but the man was of the same age and height as Mr Kavanagh and he was wearing that ring.'

'Oh, my God,' she said, colour draining from her face.

She was shocked but not overly emotional, which Rachel was thankful for. When they were sobbing their hearts out it was hard to get the information needed to push on with the investigation. It was common to have to go away and come back later. Often as not, grieving relatives would be tranqued up to the eyeballs by then and hard-pressed to remember left from right, let alone their loved one's movements over the previous days and weeks.

'If you feel up to it we would like to ask you some questions. Could you tell us when you last saw your husband?' Silence. 'Mrs Kavanagh?' Janet prompted.

'1999,' she said.

'1999?' Janet flicked her eyes at Rachel, who pulled a face. If they'd been estranged for thirteen years they might not learn much from Mrs Kavanagh.

'Yes, we separated. We were already separated then but that's the last time I saw him.'

'And where was that?' Janet asked.

'In Bury,' she said, 'we lived in Bury, we ran a shop there. Had a shop. Until...' she sighed, fisted one hand and gripped it with the other. No wedding ring, Rachel saw. '...he drank it away,' she said, 'the business, the marriage, everything. In 1999, I told him the kids didn't want to see him again, and neither did I. Not unless he sorted himself out.'

'He left the family home?' said Janet.

'Yes, about two years before.'

'Where was he living in 1999?'

'In his car,' Mrs Kavanagh said. 'The children, they dreaded his visits.'

'Was he violent?' said Janet.

'No,' she said hastily, 'no, never that. Maudlin, weepy, or sometimes the opposite, laughing when things weren't funny. It was too much for them to handle. He tried to stop a few times, the drinking, but it never lasted. You know, I thought he was probably dead already, his health ... but you said a fire?'

'Mrs Kavanagh, I'm sorry to tell you he didn't die of natural causes. We're treating his death as suspicious.'

'Suspicious?' Frown lines deepened on her forehead.

'We've launched a murder investigation,'

Janet said. 'The man who we believe to be your husband was shot and killed and left in the building, which was then set on fire.'

'Shot?' she said, her brow creasing.

'Yes,' Janet said.

'Why on earth would anyone shoot Richard? He'd never hurt a fly.' She looked bewildered.

'To your knowledge, was Mr Kavanagh ever involved in any illegal activity?' said Janet.

'No,' she shook her head. 'He wouldn't have a clue, anything like that, people would run rings round him. He was – he could be gullible, trusted too easily.'

'He lied about his drinking?' Rachel knew how it went, alkies, addicts – lying and secrecy came with the territory.

'Badly,' Judith Kavanagh admitted. 'He was a painter.'

'Decorator?' Rachel said.

'No.' She gave a sad smile. 'Artist, oils. Barely anyone makes a living at that so we had the shop: art supplies, photocopier back in the days before everyone had a printer at home. We made enough to live on, I worked as a receptionist for an optician. Then,' she sighed, 'he'd be off to the pub at lunchtime, or after work, or he'd have a bottle under the counter. He started losing control, messing up the orders.'

'You never divorced?' Janet said.

'It didn't seem important and then, as time went on, I wouldn't have known where to find him. We moved here later that year, '99. My dad had died and left me some money and I put it into this place.'

'And the children, how many?' Janet said.

'Two, Karen and Barry. Both flown the nest – though they've not gone far.'

'And to your knowledge neither of them has resumed contact with your husband?'

'No, they'd have said. It's not like I'd forbidden it or anything. They...' she paused, '...they were quite bitter about it, and they couldn't understand why he chose drink over them.'

That's how it works, Rachel thought, an image of her dad swaying down the street and Rachel, hating him and embarrassed, darting into an alley so he'd not see her.

'Could you tell us who his dentist was when living in Bury?' said Janet.

She nodded. 'Henry Sharples. On Fortins Rd.'

'The dental records will help establish beyond any doubt that this person is Richard,' Janet explained.

'Poor man,' she said, shaking her head slowly.

'Mrs Kavanagh, do you have a photograph of your husband?'

'Somewhere,' she said, 'in the basement.'

'Please could you have a look?' said Janet.

'It'll be years old.'

'Yes, that's fine.'

She left them and Rachel heard the sounds of the door to the basement opening, the snick of a light switch and footsteps going downstairs.

They didn't talk while she was out of the room. Rachel checked her messages and Janet wrote in her notebook. Outside seagulls shrieked. Rachel thought maybe her family had holidayed in Rhyl, back when holidays were possible. They'd always stayed in caravans, not B&Bs.

Mrs Kavanagh came back. Her hand shook as she handed two photographs to Janet. 'He always had his hair long,' she said, a catch in her voice. 'He was a mess when he got into drinking but he was harmless. Who on earth would do that?' She froze. 'He *was* shot first?'

'Yes,' Janet said. 'There's been a post-mortem, it's standard with any sudden or suspicious death.' Her voice was level, quiet, slow, reassuring. 'And from that we could tell the shots were fired before the fire was started. It would have been quick,' she said.

Mrs Kavanagh nodded, her lip trembling. 'Thank you.'

'Can you write down contact details for your son and daughter – we'll need to talk to them as well,' Janet said.

'Yes, of course.'

Mrs Kavanagh reached out for a small

92

address book on the side table and copied out the details. She handed the note to Janet.

'And are there any relatives on your husband's side who might have kept in contact with him?' Janet asked.

Judith Kavanagh shook her head. 'His parents are dead. He had a sister, she emigrated, met a South African, a Methodist preacher. As you can imagine, Richard's drinking went down like a lead balloon. They didn't even exchange Christmas cards once the parents had died. What will happen now?'

'Our inquiries will continue,' Janet said. 'We will confirm identity and let you know. While the investigation goes on, Richard's body will be held by the coroner. The release of the body will be at their discretion. You appear to be next of kin so the body will be released to you when the time comes.'

'Yes.' Her face flickered with emotion, tears stood in her eyes but she sniffed loudly, rubbing her forearm with her other hand.

'I'm sorry, Mrs Kavanagh,' said Janet. 'It is a very difficult situation. Is there anyone you'd like me to contact, anyone you'd like to be with?'

'No, thank you, I'll be all right.'

'Thank you for your help. Please can we take a short statement from you now, confirming what you've told us?'

The woman nodded and cleared her throat and they began.

Karen and Barry Kavanagh still lived in Rhyl. Rachel and Janet spoke to Karen at the restaurant where she was a chef and to Barry at the local high school. Both confirmed the information that Mrs Kavanagh had given them. While each of his children were shocked to learn of Kavanagh's death, neither of them seemed particularly upset. And why should they, Rachel thought, they'd not seen him for years, only remembered the chaos he'd caused.

She snatched the chance to smoke as they walked to the front, in search of potted shrimp. The place was more or less deserted, just a few tourists wearing raincoats and carrying brollies, but in the amusement park most of the machines stood idle, there was no queue at the ice cream van. The tide was up and the grey water empty save for some seagulls.

They stopped at a café for a cuppa and a bite to eat.

'Staying long?' the bloke in the café asked.

'No, just passing through,' Rachel said. 'It's quiet.'

'The weather, and money, people watching their pennies. First thing to go, holidays and that, luxuries. Sometimes I wish they'd gag the weather forecaster. You hear it's going to be unsettled again, you'll not be eager to come down here.'

94

'He kept the ring,' Janet said, on their way back to the car.

'Probably couldn't get it off,' said Rachel.

'What?'

'His fingers got swollen, his knuckles. The only reason an alkie down on his luck wouldn't part with a piece of gold like that is because he'd have to cut his finger off to get at it.'

'You are such a cynic,' Janet said.

'A realist.'

'He could have had the ring cut off.'

'Not easy if it's really tight. And most jewellers won't let someone like that over the threshold.'

'I think you're wrong,' Janet said. 'I think he kept it because it was all he had left to remind him of what he'd had, what he'd lost.'

Rachel stared at her. 'Cue the violins.'

'Harsh,' Janet said. 'So where has he been since Bury in 1999? What was he doing on Manorclough?'

'Rick!' Rachel exclaimed, making Janet jump out of her skin.

'What?' she said.

'Hang on.' Rachel looked back through her notes, eyes running across the pages, flipping paper over then back. 'Not written it down.'

Janet tutted. 'Naughty.' *Write it down,* a mantra the boss drummed into them.

'Can we stop on Manorclough?' Rachel said. 'Something the woman at the newsagent's said. A tramp they gave handouts to, called Rick.'

'Brilliant,' Janet smiled. 'Let's go see, shall we?'

7

The misty rain at the coast had turned, to a steady downpour back in the Pennines. The shop was busy, a bunch of rowdy kids in uniform, buying sweets and fizzy drinks. The air peppered with 'fucks' and 'knobs' and 'slags'.

'Ten Lambert & Butler,' one of the kids said. Liam Kelly's eyes flicked towards Rachel.

'Proof of age?' he said.

'Come on, Liam,' the lad complained.

Liam Kelly simply shook his head. The lad wheeled round, arms raised in exasperation.

'One twenty-nine,' Liam Kelly said, pointing to the snacks.

'I need some fags.'

'Against the law, I could be prosecuted,' Liam Kelly said. 'That's right, isn't it, DC Bailey?' The kids looked at Rachel and Janet. The hubbub quietened.

'That's right,' Rachel said. 'And this is DC Scott.'

'Aah!' the lad who'd been refused service groaned. 'The dibble.'

'Cagney and Lacey,' someone called out.

'Is it about the murder?' said a girl with teeth covered in braces and a narrow face like a shrew's. 'That fella what was shot and burned alive?'

'If he was shot, he wouldn't be alive, thicko,' the first lad said.

'Depends where they shot him,' she snapped back, shoving the boy for good measure.

'It is about the murder,' Rachel said, 'and if anyone here knows anything that might help, you can call at the mobile incident unit up the road. In complete confidence,' she added.

'Not very confidential if everyone can see who's going in,' piped up a very small boy with a brutally shaved head. He had a point.

'You can ring in,' Rachel said.

'You ever shot anyone?' This from the shrew girl.

'Don't tempt me,' Rachel said.

'You're not armed,' said the small lad. 'Only special units carry guns.'

'Now we'd like a word with Mr Kelly...' Janet said.

'Ooh!' a voice called out.

'A threesome, eh?' the shrew girl said.

A bout of laughter.

'Who's got the handcuffs?' More laughter

as they spilled out on to the streets.

Liam Kelly raised his eyebrows, shook his head.

'Your partner,' Rachel said, 'she mentioned someone yesterday, hadn't been round for his food parcel?'

'Rodeo Rick, yeah.'

'Seen him today?'

'No,' Liam Kelly said.

'Where's he live?'

'He's homeless, dosses where he can.'

'Can you describe him?' Rachel said.

'Tall, on the skinny side, long hair.'

'White guy?'

'Yeah.'

'How old?'

'Hard to say, fifties, sixties.'

'You know his full name?' Rachel said.

He shrugged. 'No. Goes by Rodeo Rick, wears check shirts, an old cowboy hat.'

Rachel looked at Janet, who nodded her agreement.

Rachel picked out the best photo from Mrs Kavanagh. 'Could this be him, when he was younger?'

Liam Kelly took the picture. 'Yeah,' he said. 'It's not...' He looked at Rachel, his shoulders sagging. 'You think it's him?'

Rachel pulled a face. 'Sorry, yes. Was he dossing in the chapel?'

He frowned. 'Could've been. God, I never thought...' He shook his head. 'He didn't say where he stayed, best to be cautious.'

'How do you mean?'

'Well, some places, he could be done for trespassing. But he liked to be off the streets, out of sight, come dark. He'd get a bit of aggro, people having a go.'

'How long had he been in the area?'

'Few months. Found him going through the bins before Christmas, told him he'd no need, we'd give him out-of-date stuff.'

'Ever hear of him mixing in bad company?' Rachel said.

'Never. Kept to himself. He was on the drink. That's all he could be bothered with. He'd beg now and then if he had to,' said Liam Kelly.

'Any enemies?'

'Not that I know of.' He shook his head, rubbed at his forehead. 'Poor old sod.'

The confirmation of identity represented a significant breakthrough, dental records putting the seal on what already seemed to be the case. Gill called the syndicate together for an update.

She was about to speak, the room quiet, when Pete leaned over and muttered something to Mitch.

Gill caught the words, *better defence* and *injury time*.

'Do I look like Sir Alex frigging Ferguson?' she said.

Pete straightened up, a sick look on his face. 'No, boss.'

'José Mourinho? Arsène Wenger?'

'No, boss.'

'Then why are you talking football twaddle in my briefing? You in the wrong job, Pete? Want to go try out for the Latics?'

'No, boss.'

'Mitch?'

'No, boss.'

'OK, we have a lot to get through,' she began, 'and it doesn't involve dribbling or fancy footwork. Our victim is Richard Kavanagh, aged sixty, separated from wife Judith in 1997, last seen by her two years later, when she told him not to visit again. Shopkeeper, artist, husband, father in his glory days. Alcoholic, rendered destitute. Known locally as Rodeo Rick on account of his liking for flannel shirts and a leather cowboy hat. He'd been sleeping rough for several months on Manorclough. No one reporting any criminal behaviour, he has a clean sheet and not known to be involved with any illegal activity on the estate. So why does he end up shot and set on fire in the Old Chapel?'

'Mistaken identity?' suggested Pete.

'Possibly. If so, mistaken by who, for who?' Gill said. 'Talk to people, see if we can find out anything more about him, his movements, contacts, any possible enemies. This man so far has no reputation for violence.

Test that out. Had he any drinking buddies who can tell us more? Was he known to homeless charities or hostels in the area?' Nine times out of ten, building a profile of the victim led you to their killer. Usually someone close by. Who'd been close to Richard Kavanagh?

She turned to the notes on the whiteboard. 'Two elements we are investigating, firearms and arson. Firearms first. The lab reports the bullets are both from the same gun. The gun was used in 2007 in a post office shooting in Stockport – not a million miles away. Perpetrators were arrested, charged and are currently enjoying Her Majesty's hospitality at Strangeways. We'll have a chat with them, see if they'd like to earn some Brownie points by telling us what happened to the weapon. Did they sell it on, give it to someone for safekeeping?'

She saw Rachel roll her eyes. 'You'd like to contribute, Rachel?'

Rachel seemed skittish. Gill knew the young officer had been through the mill in the last few months, but dared to hope that settling down with her bloke would help stabilize her, ground her. When Rachel had turned her brother in, revealing his involvement in the death of sleazeball barrister Nick Savage, Gill had stood up for her. She had sung her praises at the subsequent hearing with the top brass. And she meant every word she said: Rachel was a great asset to the police service, had huge potential and had already done excellent work on a number of major investigations. Gill believed Rachel had nothing to do with any revenge attack on the barrister. She'd shown great self-control in not going after him when he escaped prosecution for trying to have Rachel herself killed to save his own skin. Corrupt and venal was Nick Savage, and with the connections he had he'd been able to evade the law, while Dominic Bailey felt its long cold grip all too swiftly. But marriage hadn't mellowed Rachel, she still seemed impatient, volatile. Perhaps she just needed more time to process what had happened.

'Well, it's not likely, is it?' Rachel was saying. 'They've taken the fall, banged up, they're not gonna cough now.'

'So we don't bother?' Gill said. 'We close down that line of inquiry? Take our bat home?'

'I'm not saying that,' Rachel argued.

'Good,' Gill said. 'It is our job to be thorough, to be meticulous, and to go where the evidence takes us, even if that turns out to be a complete waste of time. Yes?'

'Yes, boss,' Rachel said, fingers twirling her pen like it was a marching baton.

'Kevin, see about making a prison visit,' Gill said.

'Yes, boss.'

'Arson – the same accelerant, petrol, was used in the previous arson attacks at the mosque and the school.' Gill summarized what they had from the fire investigation officer. 'What more do we know?'

'No joy so far on the garages,' Kevin said. 'Also following up on two incidents of theft from vehicles. Siphoning.'

'Whereabouts?' Gill said.

'One Royton, one Middleton.'

'Bit risky,' Janet said, 'you could be caught by the owner, seen by neighbours.'

'Yes, but you won't be on CCTV like you would if it was station forecourt,' said Kevin.

'Good point,' Gill told him and almost wished she hadn't when he started to preen. She indicated the boards. 'And the Perry twins?'

'They attended an EBA, Bulldog Army, meeting earlier in the month,' Lee checked his notebook, 'at the George Inn on Sunday.'

'Yes,' Gill said, 'where talk was heard about "sending a message".' She wiggled quote marks with her fingers.

'We know this how?' Janet said.

Gill smiled, raised an eyebrow. 'I could tell you but then I'd have to kill you.' Intelligence from infiltrators was a double-edged sword. You couldn't reveal a source without jeopardizing an ongoing investigation and risking an informant's safety. Sometimes that informant would be a CI, a community informant, someone willing to risk spying on friends and neighbours for a regular few quid to help get by. The other informants were officers in deep cover. Gill couldn't think of anything worse than pretending to be a low-life or a fascist or a fanatic. And sometimes infiltration went horribly wrong, with officers going rogue or crossing the murky lines into deeply unethical territory, as had happened with those policemen who'd infiltrated various protest movements, sleeping with the activists, fathering children. Disastrous.

Janet caught on soon enough. 'Classified?' she said. 'We're treading on someone's toes?'

'We might be,' Gill said, 'except we are going to focus our attention on the machinations of the far right, neo-Nazis, only in so far as it relates to the murder of Richard Kavanagh.'

'This could be a hate crime,' Lee said. 'Homeless people are at increased risk of violence, seen as other, dirty parasites.'

'Possible,' Gill said. 'The Perry boys are still our only leads. We've not found any more evidence on them so I think rather than hang on we arrest them on suspicion, tomorrow morning.'

'Do we need an armed response unit?' said Mitch. 'They may still have the firearm.'

'Yes,' Gill said, 'wear your protective vests. Good work,' she addressed them all. 'A reminder, we use our victim's given name, we accord him the same dignity and respect as we would any other person. I don't want to hear talk of tramps or dossers or winos or hobos, or Rodeo Rick. He is Richard Kavanagh. Clear?'

They nodded.

'I am happy. You should be too. Goodnight.'

Rachel nearly walked straight back out again. Her mother there, at her flat, on her sofa, making jolly with Sean and Haydn. Nachos and dips and a bottle of tequila open.

'Rachel,' Sean beamed, 'get a glass, there's lemon on the side.'

'Mexican night. Olé,' Sharon raised her glass, smeared with pink lipstick, and winked.

Rachel felt her palms tingle, her throat tighten. This was her place, private, separate from work, from family. No one came here without an invitation and hardly anyone got an invitation. Sharon sure as hell hadn't. She couldn't fuck off for twenty years and then expect to be welcomed with hugs and kisses and Sunday bloody lunch.

'Thought you were going away?' Rachel said to Sean.

'Early start tomorrow,' he said, 'slot's at half nine. We're going to nail it, aren't we, Haydn?' Sean held up his hand and the kid high-fived him.

'Bottoms up,' said Sharon, having another swig.

Rachel felt irritation trembling under her skin. It was a matter of weeks since she'd met Sharon again and the only way she could cope with it was by taking it very slowly, by having some sense of control so she didn't feel overwhelmed, railroaded by the woman who'd fucked off and left them to it.

Sharon had changed, she said, she wanted to make amends. At their first meeting she'd explained how hard she'd found it to be a parent looking after three kids as well as a wastrel of a man. How she couldn't cope. *And us?* Rachel kept coming back to that. *Alison, Dom, me? We had to cope. We had to fend for ourselves, one eye on Dad in case he kicked off.*

Even so, Rachel had determined to give Sharon a second chance, but that did not mean Sharon could muscle in on Rachel's life. 'She's a user,' Alison had said, but then it was Alison who'd had to pick up the reins, back then, drop her plans for college, find work to support the family and take over the parenting role.

'Aren't you staying? Come on,' Sharon said, patting the sofa.

'Sean, here a minute,' Rachel said. His face fell, he must have noticed the edge in her voice. She went into the hall and he followed. 'What's she doing here?'

'Sharon?'

'Yes, Sharon. Why, have you any other women stashed away? Of course, Sharon.'

'She just popped in,' he said.

Popped in. 'Popped in? Did you invite her?'

'No!' He was affronted.

'Why did she pop in? I was at work,' Rachel said.

'Well, I told her you'd probably be back before long.'

'You told her to wait?' she said.

'Sort of.'

'What the fuck for?'

He looked uneasy. 'It's what families do, Rachel.'

'Not mine, not me. I don't want her coming here. Not unless she's expressly asked,' she said.

'You're meant to be getting to know each other,' he said.

'Maybe. But I'm not having this. It's too much, too soon. She pops round again, you don't invite her in. Got it?'

'OK.' He didn't try to argue though he didn't look all that pleased about it.

Rachel went back to the living room. 'I've got a really early start, Sean too, so...'

Sharon looked, nodded. 'Course. I'll get out from under your feet. Adios!' She laughed. 'I just wanted a quick word.' She pulled on a cream leather jacket, tugged a cigarette out of her pack. She'd been at the fake tan, dark stains in the creases on her neck made her look like she hadn't washed for weeks. She'd silver eye shadow on and thick black eyeliner and what looked like false lashes. Her hands were decked with rings and chains, mainly gold coloured. Rachel doubted there was any real gold in any of it. Her lipstick had bled into the fine lines around her lips. She wasn't that old but she looked well worn and dressing like a teenager didn't help. Rachel felt like a bitch. Wished she could switch off the critical commentary in her head. Accept that Sharon was doing her best, that it couldn't be easy for her, the clumsiness of trying to rub along after all that had happened. But going at it like a bull at a gate, rushing it, was not helping.

Sean called Haydn and they disappeared.

'Your hair's nice,' said Sharon, 'you done something different?'

Oh, for fuck's sake. 'No,' Rachel said. 'Look, I'll be working late a lot the next few weeks so I'll get in touch, you know, when I've more time. Yeah? No point in you coming round and we're all out. Wait to hear from us, yeah?'

'Right.' Sharon laughed again, fiddled with her lighter. 'I'll get off then. Just wondered if you could see your way to lending me a few bob, I wouldn't ask but...'

Rachel's heart sank.

'...I don't want to get into arrears and I

can pay you back soon.'

Rachel just wanted to stop her talking, hated the bright anxiety in her voice, hated that she didn't believe her. 'Here.' She took sixty quid from her purse.

'You're a star.'

Rachel smiled, edged Sharon towards the hall, the door, the outside. Willing her to go. Just go.

'You really are, you're a star.' Sharon paused on the threshold. Outside it was dark, murky and damp.

And you, Rachel thought, *are a fucking nightmare.* She shut the door after her mother and leaned back, her eyes sore, too long a day, heaviness in her chest making her throat ache, sad, as though she'd lost something but she didn't know what it was.

8

Gill was dreaming, being chased, her legs rubbery, fire licking at her heels, when she was woken by the sound of a car crossing the gravel outside the house. She sat up. Her heart gave a kick and she felt a moment's dizziness. She wasn't expecting anyone. It was far too late for social callers. Or business. Late and dark. Sammy was staying at Orla's and Gill no longer got romantic fleeting visits from Chris Latham. He'd met someone else and had the guts to be straight with her about it before disappearing from her life.

She was holding her breath, head cocked to one side. The engine cut out. She heard the car door open, footsteps.

Climbing out of bed, she pulled on her dressing gown, drew the curtain back a fraction but could see nobody. The car had stopped at the side of the house, near the door, but her bedroom looked out over the front. They were isolated, on the edge of the moors, the nearest neighbour along the road out of sight. Certainly out of earshot. The farmhouse over the fields visible in the distance from the front windows but too far away to help. *The house has good security,* she reminded herself. Security lights, alarm, top-of-the-range bolts and mortise locks. The burglar alarm was connected to the police station.

Should she go and look out of Sammy's window? What if they saw her and realized she was alone? Footsteps crossed the gravel, the sound changing as they reached the flagged path that skirted the house. Her pulse was jumping, her throat dry.

Would they go away once they got no response? They couldn't get in unless they smashed a window. A determined man with a lump hammer could crash his way through the reinforced glass eventually. Gill thought of bus stops, the shower of glass in drifts around them.

And if they got in? How long till the police responded? It was a nine-minute drive from the nearest station – if they left as a matter of urgency.

Violent banging on the door jolted her into action. She grabbed her phone and pressed 999, her heart in her mouth.

The doorbell went, long and shrill, then more banging. A pause. A crashing sound, *something breaking?* The alarm would sound if the windows broke, she was sure that's what they'd had set up. More banging, *whump, whump, whump.* Strong enough for her to feel the vibrations.

'Emergency, which service do you require?'

'Police,' Gill said quickly, knowing there was no need to elaborate to the switchboard, who could only redirect her call.

Thud, whump. She heard a roar of rage which curdled the contents of her stomach and made her tremble.

'Police, can you tell me the nature of your emergency?'

'My name is DCI Gill Murray, I'm at Shaw and an intruder is trying to break into my house.'

'Are you alone in the house?' the operator said.

'Yes.'

111

More shouting downstairs, still outside. Then fast banging, blows raining on the door.

Gill felt a lurch of fear.

'Do you know how many intruders there are?'

'No. One, I think.' She'd heard only one voice, one set of footsteps. Had she? The prospect of more than one of them made her knees weak, her head spin.

'Please stay on the line. Is there anywhere in the house you can lock yourself in?'

Another shout, she caught some of the words. '...fucking door, Gill, I'm warning you.'

She froze. *Dave!*

'Are you there, caller? The car will be with you soon.'

Gill moved quickly out of her room and into Sammy's, overlooking the side of the house. She could see the car, the BMW that Dave drove. Relief drenched through her and with it came a wave of rage so intense she thought she'd explode.

'I think I know who it is,' she said to the operator.

She ran downstairs, the house shaking with each great thump on the door. Gill glanced out of the side-light beside the door and could see Dave, illuminated by the security lamp, his face contorted as he staggered back then launched himself at the building.

'It's my husband,' she told the woman.

'Any history of violence in the marriage?'

Not yet, Gill thought, seething, *but you just bloody wait.* 'No,' she said. 'I'm fine. I don't need the response car. I'm fine, really. I'll be fine.' Much as she'd love to heap humiliation on Detective Chief Superintendent Dave Fuckwit Murray by having him cuffed and chucked in a cell for the night, she still had sense enough to think of the wider ramifications. The fallout for Dave and his professional standing, which was already a damn sight wobblier than hers, the embarrassment for Sammy, the whole frigging mess. *Bollocks!*

But of course, they couldn't cancel the call-out, she could hear the siren already, nee-nawing along the valley. The stupid dream had left her muddled, panicking, when if she'd only gone and checked from Sammy's room in the first place...

Gill turned off the burglar alarm and waited for Dave to move. He'd settled into a rhythm. A thump then he swayed back again and readied himself. As soon as the next blow fell, Gill slid back the bolt quick as a flash, twisted the key in the lock and snapped off the Yale. She threw open the door just as he charged again.

He fell headlong, feet tangling over the door sill, pitching forward so fast he'd not got time to brace his fall. It didn't help that his reactions were severely hampered by the amount he'd had to drink. A big man, tall and solidly built, he landed heavily with a great cry, banging his head on the hardwood floor, and the air was knocked out of him. Gill hoped he'd broken something. He groaned, lay dazed. The siren grew louder and soon blue revolving lights flashed into the house and swung round Dave's prone body.

While Dave sat on a kitchen chair, bleary-eyed, wiping blood from his nose and chin, Gill apologized for wasting their time. She could tell there was some scepticism politely masked in the eyes of the female police constable, who no doubt suspected domestic violence and was unconvinced by Gill's protestations. 'I'd no idea it was my ex-husband, he hadn't phoned to tell me he was coming,' she said. Could they tell he was pissed? Off his tits? Would they do him for drunk driving? Oh, how she longed to drop him in it. But she buttoned her lip and made nice and apologized and behaved calmly and it seemed to pay off.

The fact that she was a DCI and several ranks up the food chain helped. The service still expected officers to respect and be unfailingly obedient to senior staff.

When their tail lights finally disappeared over the brow of the hill, she imagined they'd be dissecting the call-out, speculating how long Chief Superintendent Murray had been knocking lumps out of his lady wife. And whether to report the incident. Domestic violence accounted for a substantial amount of violent crime and new guidelines meant the crime could be reported even when the victim did not wish to press charges. The fact that Gill had been demonstrably sanguine and untouched and it was Dave who was injured might have persuaded the coppers that this was a misunderstanding and not a case of abuse. Or perhaps they thought Dave was the victim and Gill's call had been some mind-fuck to avert suspicion. While men were a far smaller proportion of victims of domestic violence, they were even more reluctant to report the attacks than women were.

Bound to be rumours, she thought. Police officers were the worst gossips and there was always plenty to gossip about, normally who was shagging who – and who'd found out. This would make even juicier material.

Dave's car was unlocked, the keys still in the ignition. She removed them and put them in her pocket. He was going nowhere, but she was tempted to make him sleep in the summerhouse in the garden. Freeze his balls off overnight.

He tried to sit up straight as she came back into the kitchen. 'Gill, you and me, Sammy,' he slurred, 'you and me and Sammy–' Blood crusted his nostrils, he'd a scrape on his chin.

He wore a suit, a shirt, both creased and stained, his hair was dishevelled, the smell of booze coming off him and sour sweat.

'I'm going to bed,' she said.

He leered.

'That is not a fucking invitation. You can sleep on the couch. There's a sleeping bag in the utility room.'

'We need to talk.' He leaned forward, one hand spread open, imploring her.

'You got that right. In the morning. We will. I'll talk, you listen. You–' She bit off the rant.

'Gill,' he chided her.

Sudden tears, tears of anger, pricked her eyes. She clenched her teeth at Dave and his sodding mess.

'In the morning,' was all she trusted herself to say.

Day 3

Saturday 12 May

9

Dave was on the lounge floor when Gill came down at half five. No sign of a sleeping bag. She made coffee, ate porridge with brown sugar and crème fraîche. Felt halfway human. She'd barely slept, too busy rehearsing her speech to Dave, then meandering off-track into a parallel universe where it didn't matter what befell him, where she could exact revenge, see him ridiculed, demoted, gone, with no messy repercussions for either her or Sammy. Fantasies.

She kicked his foot. 'Wakey-wakey.'

He groaned, didn't even open his eyes. She kicked him again, his shin, harder. 'Get up. Now.'

He yelped, and this time his eyes flew open. She saw the confusion in them: he didn't know where he was, how he'd got there. He blinked a few times, raised himself on one elbow, coughed.

'Coffee in the kitchen.'

'It's not six yet.' He was staring at his watch. 'If you want to go–'

'I'm going nowhere, not until we've talked. And we're going to talk now. Not later or tomorrow but now. Got it?'

He sank back, hand over his eyes. 'Yes,' he muttered.

When he joined her he'd washed his face, not that it had improved anything much, just made the edge of his hair wet. He sat down at the table where she'd left him a mug of coffee. She was opposite him, leaning against the work surface, arms folded.

'Do you remember last night?'

'Course.' He gave her a smile. Grotesque. He was lying.

'Do you? The accident, the arrest, me coming to bail you out?'

He looked alarmed, tried to cover it with a laugh. He'd not a clue.

'Thought not,' she said. 'Let me tell you what happened, Dave. You were drunk. That probably goes without saying except it actually needs saying, loud and fucking clear. You were completely rat-arsed and you got into a car and drove. A criminal offence under section 4 of the 1988 Road Traffic Act. You attempted to hammer your way into my house, scaring the shit out of me. In fear for my safety I put out a 999 call. Officers attended the scene.' She watched his face blanch. 'I didn't press charges. God knows I'd have liked to, you could argue that as a serving police officer I had an ethical duty to but I felt it was important, for the sake of our son, not to have you splashed all over the *Oldham Chronicle,* looking like a dick.'

He rubbed his face, winced as he touched his nose. 'You hit your nose,' Gill said. 'I wish you'd broken something. What was it all in aid of? Can you even remember?'

'I wanted to see you,' he said.

'Why?' She was genuinely mystified.

'To … just to see you.'

'You were drunk,' she said.

'I'd had a couple–'

'No! Just listen to yourself. It's out of control. You're out of control. You need help.'

He barked a laugh, humourless.

'I don't want you coming here, drunk. If it happens again, I will press charges.'

'Bitch,' he said.

White-hot rage flooded through her. It took every ounce of self-control not to fly at him, knock him off his chair. Wordlessly she took his car keys from the drawer, dropped them on the table. 'Get out.'

'Look, we can–'

'Get out,' she repeated, 'get the fuck out and don't come back.'

Janet felt weighed down, her movements hampered by the protective vest. They waited in cars parked outside Beaumont House, the tower block where the Perry twins lived.

Rachel yawned, which set Janet off.

'Keep you awake, did he?' Janet asked.

Rachel gave her a dead stare.

'Pardon me for breathing,' Janet said.

Word came to move in and they filed up the stairs, following the trained firearm unit in their Darth Vader outfits. Janet and Rachel stopped on the fifth-floor stairwell while the specialists went up to the next level.

They heard the thumping of the ram on the door, then the shouted instructions. 'Police, police, get on the floor, on the floor. Lie down. Now. Hands on your head.'

A woman was yelling. 'What's going on? Leave them alone. Get your fucking hands off me.'

'The mother?' Janet said.

Once the suspects were restrained and a sweep of the flat had been done to check for booby traps, hazards and other occupants, Janet and Rachel and the search team were able to enter.

In the living room, Noel and Neil Perry had been cautioned, cuffed and were flanked by uniformed officers. They were identical: pale-blue eyes, golden-blond hair cropped close. Large square heads, bulked-up bodies. Not particularly tall, maybe five foot nine, but strong looking. They both wore striped boxers and vests. They had matching tattoos on their forearms, words in a fancy script that Janet couldn't decipher. Pictures inked on the side of their necks.

Neither of them said a word, faces set, eyes gazing into the distance. But their mother, clad only in a sheer nightdress, was filling the silence. And then some. 'You need a warrant,' she said. 'You can't just come in here like the SAS, like a fucking militia and take people away.'

'Mrs Perry,' said Janet, 'DC Janet Scott.' She showed her warrant card. 'I am here to arrest Noel and Neil Perry and I have a warrant to search the property.'

'Looking for what?' Noreen Perry said. She had thin, greasy brown hair. She was overweight and her complexion was pale, doughy.

'As you'll see from the warrant,' Janet said, 'we are pursuing evidence connected to the murder of Richard Kavanagh at the Old Chapel on Wednesday.'

'Murder?' Mrs Perry said. 'You're off your fucking trolley.'

'Any objects removed will be itemized and listed,' Janet said.

'You're wasting your time,' Mrs Perry said, 'they've done nothing wrong. This is harassment.'

'If you wish to make a complaint, please do feel free.' Janet was tired of the woman's knee-jerk loyalty, the blanket defence, the rabid hostility.

Neither of the twins spoke at all.

'Get them some disposable suits to wear and take them down,' Janet told the officers escorting the suspects.

Once they had left, Mrs Perry shook her

head, a bitter expression on her face, then eased herself into an armchair.

'Perhaps you could tell me where Noel and Neil were on Wednesday evening?' Janet said.

'Perhaps you could fuck off.'

'Hey,' Rachel said, 'watch the language.'

Janet nearly laughed, Rachel swore like a trooper.

'You can't say where they were?' Janet said.

'Here.'

'All evening?'

'Yes.'

Rachel gave Janet a knowing look.

'They never went out?' Janet said.

'They were here all night,' said Noreen Perry.

'You do any washing since?' Rachel said.

'Machine's broken,' Noreen Perry said.

'We'll check that,' Rachel said.

'Launderette then?' This from Janet.

Noreen Perry shook her head.

'We're going to execute the search warrant now,' Janet said.

Assisted by four other officers, the search was thorough. Janet and Rachel began in the bedroom that the twins shared. The space was dominated by a large flat-screen TV and games console in front of the window, the floor a tangle of wires and controllers. The lighting was dim, the curtains closed. Janet drew them back to let in some natural light.

Cobwebs and dead flies littered the window sill.

Six floors up and the view was extensive, out over the estate. Janet could see the ruins of the Old Chapel down below, the canal a glinting, line between the buildings, the traffic streaming along Shuttling Way, the roundabout, the parade of shops, the roofs of the houses. Another damp day, the sky bruised and mottled.

Twin beds, each with a headboard and side table, were positioned to face the TV. High-energy snacks and power drinks littered the tables, and there was a mobile phone on each. A laptop lay on one bed. A set of dumb-bells sat in the corner. The walls were decorated with posters, a naked woman draped over a Sherman tank, a bulldog wrapped in a Union Jack. A large St George's Cross flag had been pinned up, and close by hung a pair of ceremonial swords in fancy sheaths. Janet shuddered to think of the twins wielding them.

Wearing latex gloves, to prevent contaminating any evidence they might find, they went through the bedding first, checking under the mattresses and inside the pillowcases. In the side-table drawers were condoms, knuckle-dusters, batteries, and lots of plastic baggies containing drugs: cannabis, white powder that was probably cocaine, yellow pills with a stamp of a palm tree on and some coloured capsules in plastic containers. Janet showed the capsules to Rachel.

'Steroids, be my bet,' Rachel said.

On a folding canvas chair, Janet found the hoodies and held them up.

'That's them,' Rachel said, 'Class of 88.'

They took pictures of the items they were seizing, in situ, and then secured them separately in evidence bags, clearly labelled. The laptop was taken, along with the phones. As well as the discarded clothes from the chair they removed shoes and trainers from the room and garments from the laundry basket in the bathroom.

The search team continued to look in all the usual places for the weapon or ammunition: the airing cupboard, cistern in the bathroom, under the bath panel, in the freezer, bread bin, cupboards, fridge and microwave, behind pictures, inside lampshades and cushions, up chimneys, under drawers, behind radiators. They examined the pots on the balcony outside.

They found no handgun, no bullets and no stash of petrol.

On the dot of ten, Gill got a call from Trevor Hyatt, the fire investigator. 'Morning,' she said, 'we've got the Perry brothers in the cells, awaiting solicitors, will let you know soon as–'

'I wasn't ringing about that,' he said. 'We've

had another fire. The big warehouse on Shuttling Way. Been burning all night. Tenders are still there, getting it under control but we'll not be able to go in for some time. Several floors, very hazardous environment.'

'Is it arson?'

'Extremely likely. Once we do get in, we should be able to check the seat of the fire and establish whether accelerants played a part,' he said.

'And if they match,' she followed his train of thought, 'could be the same person or persons?'

'Yes,' he said, 'geographically close, about a quarter of a mile apart, both buildings disused. Looks like a pattern.'

'OK, keep me posted. The questioning of our suspects will be confined to the murder and the Old Chapel fire at this stage. Can't go fishing.'

'Understood,' Hyatt said.

'Janet, you take Noel, Rachel – Neil,' Gill said. 'Solicitors have arrived. Gunshot residue tests on the suspects' hands came back negative.'

That was disappointing but not unexpected, thought Janet. Three days since the murder and the residue was easily washed away.

Once in the interview room, Janet had done the preamble, explained to Noel why he was being interviewed and what his rights were. Then she asked him to tell her what he had done on Wednesday evening.

'I was at my nan's,' he said.

'Where's that?'

'Langley, 43 Perkins Close.'

'And how long were you there?' she said.

'Stayed over.'

'What time did you get there?'

'About five.'

'Anyone else there?' Janet said.

'Neil was.'

'Right. What did you do while you were there?'

'Watched telly.' He stretched and scratched his ribs, making the disposable suit crackle. Indifferent: a good act or was he actually unconcerned because he'd nothing to fear?

'What did you watch?' Janet asked.

He shrugged. 'Dunno, can't remember.'

'Did you go out at all that evening?'

'No.'

'You're sure? Maybe to run an errand?' she said.

'No.' That same vacant nonchalance.

'If I told you that someone had seen you in the vicinity of the Old Chapel that evening, how would you explain that?'

'They're wrong.'

'They are sure it was you, you and your brother,' Janet said.

'Can't have been.' The dull expression in

his eyes hardened into something more intense, more acrimonious.

'Did you know Richard Kavanagh?'

'No.'

'He looked a little like this.' She passed him a photo, one created using software to age the original image and show how the subject would appear when he was older. 'I am now showing Mr Perry exhibit PR31.'

'No.' He shook his head several times over.

'You might have known him as Rodeo Rick. He wore a leather cowboy hat.'

'Never seen him.'

According to Liam Kelly, Richard Kavanagh was a familiar figure, walking around in all weathers, sometimes begging. Anyone who lived in the area would know him by sight.

'You were charged with arson and spent time in a young offenders' institution, that right?'

'Yes,' he said.

'And in that incident an accelerant was used to spread the fire. The same method as was used in the Old Chapel this week.'

'You can't put that on us.'

It was common for Mancunians to use 'us' instead of 'me'. *Leave us alone, get off us.* But Janet suspected from his last words that Noel was talking about himself and his twin. It was important to focus on him and him alone, even if it messed with his mindset.

Important from a legal standpoint.

'Even though a witness saw you there?'

'They're lying,' he said. He stared at her as if he'd stare her down. Janet smiled, deflecting his attempt to threaten her. The ideal situation in an interview was to try to create a bond, forge some connection, however unlikely that seemed. Given time and her skills, it was usually possible. But she'd a sense it might elude her with Noel Perry.

'Tell me about your jacket,' she said, 'Class of 88. Where did you get it?'

He hesitated a fraction, then said, 'Online, they make 'em to order. You tell 'em what you want.'

'So they're unique?'

'I suppose,' he said, frowning slightly. Realizing perhaps that unique might not be so great when it came to witness identification.

'What website are they from?'

'Don't remember,' he said.

'We can check on your computer,' Janet said. 'Have you ever been in the Old Chapel?'

'No.'

'What about in the grounds, the land around it?'

'No.' He scratched his side again.

'You possess a firearm, a gun?'

'No,' he said, a smile tugging at the corners of his mouth. He felt comfortable, cocky about the weapon. Why?

'Tell me what you did earlier on Wednesday.'

'Just in the flat,' he said.

'Doing what?'

'Gaming, with Neil.'

'And the day before, Tuesday?'

'Same,' he said.

'You're unemployed,' Janet said, 'signing on?'

'Yeah,' he nodded.

'When did you last sign on?'

He took a slow breath, pulled a face, screwed up his eyes. 'Monday,' he said, eventually. 'Last Monday.'

He was slow-witted, Janet saw, maybe a side effect of his lifestyle: drugs, steroids messing with his concentration. Or by nature. He was definitely on the slow side.

'Thick as pigshit,' Rachel said to Janet in the custody suite, 'mine was. Starved of oxygen or inbred or something.'

'Keep your voice down,' Janet hissed, flaring her eyes at Rachel, aware of a solicitor passing by on the way to the next call of duty.

He'd sat there, his big head reminding Rachel of a teddy bear, those old-fashioned ones, stuffed with straw or whatever, and he'd answered her in monosyllables. Saying the minimum. Less you said, less you could make a mistake. His longest reply in response to a question about his tattoos. He'd read out quotes on his forearms, 'It is not truth that matters but victory,' and 'If you want to shine like the sun then first burn like it.' Nodded and added, *Mein Kampf.*' Then pointed to his neck. 'That's a lion and that's a unicorn.' Rachel thought they looked like meerkats. Said nothing.

'Not thick enough to admit being there, being involved,' Janet said when they were alone. 'But they're both giving their nan as their alibi. Meanwhile Mam's saying they were with her. Story's all over the place. If they are our killers they've really not thought it through. Same old, same old,' Janet said, gesturing to the stairs to indicate that they should go out for a bit.

'I know,' Rachel agreed. Most of the crimes they dealt with were sad, savage and often pointless. The culprits similar. Grubby little arguments leading to loss of life. Families riven by violence and raised on crime. She thought fleetingly of Dom, twenty-eight years. Pushed it away.

Rachel only had chance for half a fag, Janet keeping her company, before Kevin came down to find them. 'Boss wants us all.'

'Now?' Rachel said.

'If not sooner.'

10

Upstairs in the briefing room, Godzilla was looking perky, eyes sparkling, back ramrod straight, zinging with energy. We've got something, Rachel thought, must be. Something's turned up. The weapon?

'Neil Perry's mobile phone,' the boss said, straight in, no messing. One good thing about Godzilla, she never bothered with chit-chat or anything, it was all about the job, the case. Rachel got that, wanted to do it like that if she ever made it as far as SIO.

'Chock-a-block with text messages. Many run-of-the-mill, to his very limited number of contacts. One of particular interest to an unregistered number last Monday evening, *Tomorrow 830 Bobbins* and to the same number the next evening, *Here now*.'

Bobbins was a pub in Coldhurst, known to the police who regularly attended when customers fell off their perches and started knocking lumps out of each other, or the fixtures and fittings. A series of managers had tried all sorts: home-cooked meals, family room, quiz night, disco, sounds of the 80s, pool table, large screen, but nothing seemed to change the quality of the clientele.

'We want CCTV from the pub that Tuesday evening. Who was Neil Perry making arrangements with? Rachel, Janet,' Godzilla turned to them, looking expectant, 'initial impressions?'

'Cautious,' Rachel said, 'but not that bright.'

The boss nodded. 'I'd say leaving all your messages on your phone backs up that observations. Sandwich short of a picnic.'

'We should check out the alibi, the gran,' said Lee.

'Where are we on the search, the forensics?' Janet asked.

'Nothing else of interest at the property, forensics have fast-tracked the hoodies, the jeans and trainers with them,' Her Maj said.

'We know the alibi is false even before we see Grandma,' Rachel said. 'I saw them and Mr Hicks saw them near the chapel, we know they're lying about that.'

'But if that's all we have,' Janet said, 'we've nowhere else to go. They sit there swearing blind they weren't around and we say the opposite. But if we can find another piece of solid evidence...'

'Janet's right,' Godzilla said, 'all we have at present is a sighting in the vicinity. We have nothing that puts them in the chapel, at the scene of the murder, nothing that puts a gun in their hands, nothing that connects them to this particular fire. Until we get that next step, we wait to interview them again. Let them twiddle their thumbs or whatever else.' She grimaced. 'Strike that image.'

Rachel couldn't face the idea of kicking her heels so she spoke up. 'Boss, can I go to the grandma? Me and Janet?'

Janet gave a little nod, happy to go.

'Fine by me,' Her Maj said. 'Get the CCTV from Bobbins as well.'

'One thing,' Janet said, 'when I asked Noel about the gun, he was ... confident. Like he knew that was safe.'

'You've got a gun,' the boss said, 'you've commissioned a crime, you live in a tower block. You've not hidden it at home. Where'd you put it?'

'Gran's,' said Kevin, which earned a laugh.

'Or you get rid,' said Rachel, 'give it to someone to look after.'

'That's common practice in the gangs,' Lee said.

'Except Tweedledum and Tweedledee aren't affiliates as far as we've been able to tell,' the boss said, 'nor do they have a wide social circle, judging by their phone book contacts and Facebook pages.'

Janet groaned.

'You may well groan,' the boss said, 'a load of racist, homophobic codswallop with photos of this pair as avenging warriors. And atrocious punctuation. Gives new meaning to the fact that we are all descended from apes.'

'We know they're pally with the EBA,' Mitch said, 'they could have associates there to take the weapon.'

'Or they flog it,' Rachel said.

'It could be an urban myth,' Kevin spoke up, 'but some of the kids are saying the Perrys set fire to a cat.'

A collective moan went up from around the table.

'On that cheery note,' the boss said, 'I'll leave you to get on with it.'

As expected, Eileen Perry, the grandmother, was insistent that her grandsons had been with her on Wednesday evening. She was a tiny woman, with crooked teeth, oversize specs and arthritic hands, the knuckles swollen like spring onion bulbs.

'They was here,' she said, arms folded in the hallway. Janet noted that she'd allow them over the threshold of the small terraced house but not any further.

'What time did they arrive?' Janet asked.

'Teatime.'

'Which is when?'

'Five,' she said, 'around then.'

'And when did they leave?' Janet said.

'Thursday.'

'What time?'

'Don't know. I was at work.'

'You work?' Janet said.

'Cleaning,' she said flatly.

'Did they go out at all?'

'No.' Eileen Perry sighed.

'What did you do?'

'Watched telly,' she said, with a note of disbelief at the question – what else would anyone ever do of an evening?

'What about Tuesday, the day before, did you see them then?' Janet asked.

'Yes,' she said, 'they were here then and all.'

Wind it up and it walks, thought Janet. 'Thank you, Mrs Perry, if you think of anything else, if there's anything you remember,' she stressed the word, just the right side of polite, 'do get in touch.' She held out her card.

Mrs Perry stared at it for long enough, then unfolded her arms and took it between one distorted thumb and finger. It'd be in the bin before they reached the pavement.

'So she's learned her lines and trots them out on cue,' Janet said to Rachel as they got in the car. 'Any date we care to mention, they were here. All night, she never slept.'

'In fact they live here,' Rachel chipped in, '24/7, never leave the house, never leave her sight.'

'If these two turn out to be our shooters we could do the whole family for attempting to pervert the course of justice,' Janet said.

'Three generations.'

Bobbins, originally Bobbins Hotel, still had its old pub sign, showing a mill worker standing at a loom. There hadn't been a working mill nearby for decades.

Snug and *Taproom* read the stained-glass windows either side of the entrance.

A handful of drinkers were scattered around the snug, a pair of men played darts in the taproom. The central hallway led past the rooms either side to a general lounge bar. There was a corridor off to the left near the bar, a sign pointing to toilets. The rooms were small, with low-beamed ceilings. Nothing like a gin palace, more like a cottage turned into a hostelry.

The woman behind the bar was reading a magazine. Janet noticed her nails, great long talons painted with an elaborate red and black design which, on first sight, looked like they'd been spattered with blood. *I've been in this job too long,* Janet thought.

Rachel explained what they wanted and the woman rang the manager, who said to go ahead – the tapes from previous days were in the office.

'Were you working then?' Rachel asked as the barkeep unlocked the office door and they edged in. The place was piled with cartons and folders and bits of broken furniture. The woman threaded her way through to the green metal filing cabinet.

'Yes, five till twelve.'

'You know the Perry twins?' Janet said.

'Twins?' She looked up, the tapes in her hand. 'No.' No fear in her eyes, Janet saw, more curiosity. Perhaps this wasn't one of their locals, it'd be a fair way to come from Manorclough and they didn't have a car, as far as the police had established.

'They may have been in here that Tuesday. Identical, five foot nine, bulky, blond, tattoos,' Janet said.

'I don't remember any twins. Here you are.' She found Tuesday's tape and retraced her steps.

'You just sign this, here.' Janet passed her the form, describing the item they were removing.

'What's it all about then?'

'The man found in the Old Chapel, Manorclough, Richard Kavanagh,' Rachel said.

'Oh, yeah.'

'You heard anything?' Janet said.

'People talking about it.' She shrugged.

'Saying what?' Janet said.

'That he must have crossed someone, to be shot like that.'

'He ever come in here?' Rachel said.

'Don't think so. There's some say it could be suicide.'

Janet stared at her. 'He shot himself,' she

said, 'twice?'

'Exactly,' the woman laughed. 'That's what I said but they won't have it. Mental.'

Back at the station, Rachel and Janet viewed the tape. The CCTV was split screen, recording feeds from one camera outside the pub and three inside, covering the snug, the taproom, and one in the general bar area which also caught the corridor to the toilets.

The twins appeared outside the pub at eight twenty-five.

'Behold,' said Janet, her heart skipping a beat. The pub was busy, a game of pool in progress in the taproom, a large family group in the snug, a row of drinkers in the general bar. They could see the woman they'd met serving alongside a man, presumably the manager.

The twins spoke to each other and one of them pulled out his phone (Janet guessed it must be Neil), thumbs working over the keys, then nodded to his brother and went into the pub. Cameras picked him up at the end of the general bar area where one of the drinkers, phone in hand, turned and moved away from the bar, pocketing the phone as he walked to the gents. Neil Perry followed him.

'Sex?' said Rachel. 'Drugs?'

'I've seen that guy before.' Janet frowned.

'Give us a clue?'

'Wait.' Janet watched the film. Neil Perry emerged and left the pub, making a small fist, a gesture of celebration, as he reached his brother. The pair walked off camera.

Seconds later, the other man came out of the toilets and resumed his place at the bar, took up his paper and finished his drink. Then left. Speaking to no one.

'I know that face,' Janet said again.

'Show Pete,' Rachel suggested, 'he worked on Coldhurst for a bit, didn't he?'

Pete watched the footage, closed his eyes in thought, and then said, 'Tandy. Gary ... no, Greg. Bit of a fixer in his time.'

'I know the name,' Rachel said, 'spoke to a lad called that on Thursday.'

'So what was he fixing for Dick and Dom then?' Janet said.

Pete opened the database and typed in the name.

The man's face appeared, and his charge sheet. 'Out on licence,' Pete said. 'Just served five for possession of firearms, intent to supply.'

'That's where they got the gun,' Janet said. 'Brilliant. So where is it now?'

'Maybe he's got it back,' Rachel chipped in, her eyes glinting. 'What's the address?'

'Manton Road,' Pete said.

'Middle of Manorclough,' Janet said. 'This gets better and better.'

Gill considered the situation. 'OK, we discuss this with our guests. Don't let on, at this stage, that we're aware of Tandy's reputation as the go-to man for firearms but tell them we will be speaking to Mr Tandy, to hear his side of things. Tandy is a known associate of Marcus Williams. Perhaps there is some link between Williams and the events of Wednesday night. Mitch, see what the current intel is on Tandy and Williams, will you?'

He nodded.

'Anything I've missed?' Gill said.

'No, ma'am,' they chorused and returned to work.

11

Rachel sat opposite Neil Perry. 'Can you tell me where you were on Tuesday the eighth of May, that's last Tuesday, at eight thirty in the evening?'

He hadn't been expecting this question. He didn't speak for long enough, some slow process churning away behind clouded eyes.

'My nan's, I think,' he said. Default reply.

'You think?' Rachel made it a question.

'Yes.' There was a little sore at the corner of his mouth, deep red, and he kept licking and picking at it.

'Do you recall going to Bobbins, a public house in Coldhurst, that evening?'

'No,' he said.

'Less than a week ago.'

'I never went there,' he said.

'Are you sure?' Rachel said.

'I only go to the King's or the George or the Black Pig.'

'But that Tuesday you went to Bobbins,' she said, 'you and your brother.'

'We never.' He gritted his teeth and rocked slightly and she could sense a growing aggression in him.

'I am now showing Mr Perry a CCTV recording, exhibit JS18.' She had lined up the footage so it began with the two men arriving outside the pub. She set it running and paused it before Neil Perry went inside.

'That is you and Noel, am I correct?'

'Yes,' he said tightly.

'And can you read the date and time at the bottom right-hand side of the screen?'

'Yes,' he said, sounding offended, as though she was casting doubt on his ability to read. *Well – you never know.*

'Please would you read them out to me?' Rachel said.

'Why should I?'

'For the recordings.' She nodded at the machine recording the interview, the camera in the corner. 'And so we can be sure that you understand my question and what I am suggesting.'

'Eighth of the fifth,' he read the date, then the time, 'twenty twenty-five.'

'Which was last Tuesday at twenty-five past eight, you agree?'

'Yes.'

'At this point you make a call on your mobile phone. Who were you calling?'

'A mate.'

'With no name in your contacts list on your phone?' Rachel said.

A spike of something in his eyes, understanding perhaps that they had gone through his phone. *Well duh.* 'Which mate?' she said.

'Don't remember,' he back-pedalled.

'Let's see if we can jog your memory,' Rachel said. She pressed play. The film showed Greg Tandy with his phone, making eye contact with Neil Perry, standing up from his barstool. 'Which mate?' she said.

'Don't know him.'

'You just rang him,' she said.

'No, not him.'

'Who then?' Rachel said.

'Can't remember, I told you.'

'How come you followed him to the gents?'

'I didn't follow him. I needed a slash,' he said, his eyes flinty, a spasm twitching across his forehead. He rubbed at the sore on his mouth.

144

'Why did you arrange to meet this man?'

'I never.'

'For the benefit of the tape I am now showing Mr Perry a screenshot of the text from his mobile phone, item number PR46. Will you read it out, please?'

His face darkened. It was getting to him. Rachel eased back in her chair a little. This wasn't about getting him riled up, no need to provoke. Just the steady, relentless presentation of evidence, exposing lie after lie.

'Tomorrow 830 Bobbins,' he said.

'I put it to you that you set up a meeting with the man in the CCTV film, that you used your mobile phone to alert him to your arrival at the bar and that you then met him in the men's toilets.'

'No comment.'

'That man's name is Greg Tandy,' Rachel said. 'Ring any bells?'

'No comment,' he said.

'We'll be talking to Mr Tandy later, perhaps he'll be able to tell us what you were meeting him for. Was it drugs?'

'No comment.'

'Several different illegal substances were found in your room. Were you dealing?'

'No comment.'

'I'm interested in what business you'd have with another man in a pub toilet,' Rachel said. 'Were you meeting for sex?'

He sprang to his feet. 'Don't you fucking

say that.'

'Neil, Neil,' his solicitor said, 'sit down.'

'Fucking libel, that is,' spit flew from his mouth, 'fucking bitch.' He sprang at her, face contorted, the tendons on his neck taut like wires.

His fist connected with her shoulder, spinning her round, throwing her to the floor. He came after her, the solicitor shouting.

Neil Perry kicked at her, she dodged the blow, scrabbled up, not far from the wall. Rachel threw an arm back, connecting with the alarm rail, the bell sounding shrill.

'Fucking lezzer,' he yelled, 'you take that back, take it back!' He was enraged, Roid Rage, giving him both strength and aggression. He caught her wrists, his hands rock hard.

'Let go,' the solicitor shouted, 'Neil, Mr Perry.'

'You take it back,' he said, froth at the corners of his mouth.

'Get your fucking hands off me,' Rachel said. 'Assaulting a police officer, you want that adding to the charge?'

'You calling me a fucking queer?'

You'd rather be called a Nazi. 'You could clear it up, fuckwit,' she said. 'What were you doing in the toilets with Greg Tandy?'

He grabbed her throat, his eyes glittered, she saw the crude drawings on his neck ripple and twitch. She could smell his sweat and another high chemical scent a bit like bleach. Behind him the solicitor ran to the door and opened it, calling out above the alarm.

Rachel, feeling the blood sing in her, temples, raised a foot, and stamped down hard on Neil Perry's. He grunted, but tightened his grip and moved closer, pinning her against the wall so she had no leverage to ram her knee into his balls. His breath was hot and meaty in her face. If he got any closer she'd bite his frigging nose off.

Her instinct was to claw at his hands, try to peel them away from her neck, but her training and experience had taught her that, especially with someone so strong, it would be futile. She needed to distract him from choking her by going for something soft and vulnerable – eyes, nose, groin. She saw dots dancing at the edge of her vision, felt the force crushing the cartilage in her throat, the pressure mounting in the back of her skull. She raised her hands, fingers bent like talons, and grabbed at his face. He reared back and his grip loosened slightly. Then he moved sharply, whipping her head forward then back, like a rag doll. Rachel's head smacked against the wall, a wave of nausea washed through her, saliva thick in her mouth.

She went limp, deliberately, letting her body weight drag her down, him with it. He lost his balance slightly and had to let go. Rachel kicked out hard, her heel connecting with his kneecap, and Perry yelled in pain and staggered back.

'Fucking bastard toe-rag,' she said, her voice dry, grating.

She was up and swung out her other leg, catching the back of his foot and tripping him up. A burst of triumph gave her fresh energy as he landed heavily.

'Knobhead.' She drew her foot back, ready to kick him, to kick his face in, to turn his head to pulp, as several officers piled in and were on him.

Rachel stood panting. 'That's all on record,' she said, clearing her throat, trying to make herself heard above the din of the alarm. 'You've been framed, pal. You'll not be getting the fifty quid, mind. What a spectacle.' Neil Perry gave her a look of contempt but Rachel didn't care, the case against him was growing and she was beginning to think they'd be able to nail him and his scumbag brother for Richard Kavanagh's murder.

She turned to the solicitor, who looked shaken, close to tears. 'Break?' And then to the men hoisting Perry to his feet. 'Put him back in the cell, will you. And turn that bloody alarm off.'

Mitch was on the phone reporting back to Gill: no response at Greg Tandy's address on Manton Road. According to probation records, Tandy was living there with his wife and son.

'Try again in the morning,' Gill said.

There was suddenly a crashing sound in the outer office and raised voices.

'Night,' she ended the call and flung open her office door. 'What the fuck is going–'

Dave. On his hands and knees trying to pick up the contents of Kevin's desk, by the looks of it. Lee bending over him. Dave threw up an arm, holding a fistful of papers, released them on to the desk. Then saw her.

'Gill.' He practically dribbled the word. 'I just wanted...'

She just wanted ... to die. There and then. To disappear.

'All right?' Kevin stood at the door from the landing, coffee in hand, bemused.

'Kevin, Lee,' she said briskly, 'I've got this.' No introductions needed. They both knew Chief Superintendent Murray.

'Shall I get a first-aider?' Kevin said. 'Or the paramedics?'

'No need,' Gill said.

'Give you a hand,' Kevin said, 'my desk, don't mind.'

Fuck off and die. 'Kevin – thanks. No. Leave. Now. See you in the morning.' The messages hit their target. Kevin stopped, Lee nodded, grabbed his jacket and left. Kevin trotted after him.

She could just imagine the conversation. The humiliation.

'Get up,' she told Dave, though maybe he'd be safer on his hands and knees. She couldn't lift him. He was half her weight again. Probably more these days.

He levered himself upright using the desk as ballast. 'Sit there,' she pointed to Kevin's chair, 'and stay there.'

She went for coffee, praying that no one would come in meanwhile, no cleaners or any of her syndicate. Rachel and Janet were still interviewing. No one else was due back. She might get lucky. Lee and Kevin had seen the floorshow and although Lee might be tactful, respectful, Kevin was a gobby little git. He struggled at work and she'd ridden him hard and he'd probably see this as his chance for payback: *Lady Muck reckons she's got it all under control, never puts a foot wrong, but her old man is a pisshead.*

She went back upstairs with the drinks. Dave was where she'd left him. He smiled inanely when he saw her. She gave him a coffee. Told him to drink it.

'Why are you here?' She intended to be calm, to try to reason with him. Get him to understand the boundaries.

'Sorry,' he slurred. He reeked. 40 per cent proof in his veins instead of blood. 'To say sorry, sorry for last night.'

'Sorry? Look at you now.'

'Got a taxi,' he said, 'not the car, no car.' As though that made everything all right.

'You come here, you barge into my office in front of my colleagues, you can't even see straight, you stink like a brewery and you call this some sort of apology.'

'Sorry,' he said again.

'You can't do this, Dave. You are not part of my life any more.'

'Just friends.'

'No.' She shook her head irritably. 'Not friends. Not even that. Not anything. You left me, Dave. It's over. It's dead and buried. I've moved on and you need to do the same. And this, getting pissed out of your head, have you any idea what people think? Word gets round – and it will – you'll be suspended.'

'OK, OK.' He waved his hands to shut her up.

'You are out of control,' she said, 'sort it.' She felt her temper rising, warmth in her face.

'You don't understand–'

'You've got that right. And you need to understand...' she said hotly, '...you need to understand that you are making a complete prick of yourself. You could lose everything.'

'I already have,' he said.

'Oh, spare me the bloody melodrama.'

She began to clear up the stuff scattered over the floor, papers and pens and Post-it

151

notes. Kevin's in-tray, his Man United trinkets. Arranged them roughly on the desk.

'Get up,' she said. 'I'll drive you home.' She didn't want to say 'to your mother's', didn't want to rub it in.

'I can get a cab,' he offered.

'No.' She didn't trust him not to just head off to some pub or off-licence. At least if he got into the house he might sleep it off. God knows how his mother was coping with it. But that wasn't Gill's concern.

Dave went to stand up, failed, tried again and made it.

There was a dark patch round his crotch. Oh God, he'd pissed himself. He wasn't even aware he'd done it. She felt her stomach drop, a moment's sadness. This had gone way beyond the occasional bender. He had been a proud man, a vain man who thought he was cleverer than he really was. Sometimes a stupid, weak man, particularly where women were concerned. Now he was a wreck. How could he not see that, sense her disgust, want to stop it?

'You come here again,' she said, 'off your face and I will have you escorted from the building and inform professional standards.'

12

Noel Perry requested a break after an hour and a half of denial and stonewalling. Janet went up to the incident room. She switched her phone on. Elise had replied to Janet's earlier text which had read *Money in jar 4 taxi. Take extra £20 in case. Have fun xxx.* Elise's reply: *LYSM.* Love You So Much. Did Rachel know that one? Janet liked to test her every so often.

Rachel was still in with Neil Perry but Gill had disappeared. No Lee or Kevin either; it was getting late but they always worked late on a murder. Kevin had left his desk in a right mess. There was a stapler on the floor nearby and a whiff of booze in the air. Had someone been spicing up their brew with a drop of the hard stuff? If Gill found out, they'd be off the syndicate so fast their feet wouldn't touch the floor.

Janet drank some juice from the carton she kept in the fridge and checked her e-mails. She couldn't recall the last time she'd been totally alone in the office. It felt spooky. Like the *Marie Celeste*. Tired, she told herself, that's all. She logged off and washed her cup. The tap made a clanking sound which startled her and brought a rash of gooseflesh to her arms.

When her phone rang, she was halfway downstairs, her footsteps echoing in the empty stairwell. *Elise*.

'Hi,' Janet answered. Only ten o'clock. Had they not been able to find the party? Had they had enough?

'Mum.' Elise's voice was high with panic. 'Mum, it's Olivia. I don't know what to do. I can't wake her up. Mum, please.'

Shock riveted Janet to the spot. She could hear noises in the background, voices, more distantly the thud of a bass line. A shout of laughter.

'Where are you?' Janet said.

'At the party.'

'What's happened?'

'Olivia's collapsed. I can't wake her up.'

'Why's she collapsed?'

'I don't know,' Elise said wildly, 'I don't know, she just ... she just fell down.'

'Call an ambulance–'

'But–'

'Elise, listen, call an ambulance and tell them exactly what happened. Stay with Olivia. Do whatever they tell you. Yes?'

'Mum–'

'I'm coming. What number is it?'

'Sixty-four,' she said, beginning to cry.

'Elise, hang up and call the ambulance. Call them now.' The line went dead.

Janet ran downstairs, heart in her mouth. She told the custody sergeant she was leaving, a family emergency, and to inform Noel Perry's solicitor to attend the following morning at 9am for a 24-hour superintendent review. At that point, all being well, they'd be granted another twelve hours to talk to the Perrys, and if they needed yet more time then they'd go to court to apply for a further thirty-six hours.

Thankfully the lights were with her all the way as she drove as quickly as she dared to the address Elise had given her. Reaching the avenue – a development of upmarket three- and four-bedroom modern houses, with open-plan gardens – she saw the ambulance was already there and a patrol car as well. People outside the house, partygoers, Janet assumed, were drifting away in small groups.

The front door was ajar, all the lights on, inside more young people, and an atmosphere she recognized: the drained, worried faces, the stunned silence or muted comments.

'Where's Olivia Canning?' she said to a couple sitting on the stairs. They both held bottles of Spanish beer, slices of lime wedged in the necks.

'Through there,' the girl said, nodding at a door towards the back of the house.

As Janet reached it, the door swung open

155

and a uniformed cop came through. Behind him she glimpsed the high-vis jackets of paramedics.

'Olivia Canning,' Janet said.

'You her mother?' said the cop.

Janet shook her head. 'My daughter's with her. I'm DC Scott.'

He blinked, reassessing her. 'They're bringing her out soon. Taking her up to A&E.'

'Do we know how—' Janet began but he apologized, 'Sorry, I need to get names and addresses.'

Janet stared at him.

'She's unresponsive,' he said. He didn't say any more. Janet swallowed, fought the fears crowding behind her breastbone. She went into the room.

'Mum.' Elise broke away from a group of teenagers huddled to the left of the room and came to Janet, who hugged her. Olivia lay on the floor on a stretcher. The paramedics had put an oxygen mask over her face, a cellular blanket around her.

'Can you get the door?' the nearest paramedic said.

Janet released Elise and pulled the door open.

'Cheers,' he said. They lifted the stretcher, releasing the wheels that turned it into a trolley, and guided it slowly through the entrance hall.

'Which hospital?' Janet asked.

'Oldham General.'

'Did you ring Vivien and Ken?' Janet said to Elise.

Elise looked wrung out, puffy red nose, swollen lips, mascara smeared black under her eyes. She pressed her lips together and more tears came. 'They're away for the weekend,' she said.

'But you were staying... Oh God. Away where?'

'Edinburgh,' she squeaked.

'They need to know, now!' said Janet.

'I don't have their numbers.'

'Christ!'

'I'm sorry, I didn't mean to–'

'What? Spin me some story?' Janet had almost rung Vivien to check she was happy about the arrangements. But she had trusted Elise. She took a deep breath. 'Never mind about that now. We need to get to the hospital and get Vivien's number from Olivia's phone. She's never collapsed like this before, has she?' Janet studied her daughter's face.

'No.'

'What was she drinking?'

'Just cider.'

'Just cider,' Janet said. 'How much cider?'

'Not much,' Elise said.

'Did she take anything?' Janet was vaguely aware of people in the room clearing up cans and dirty glasses.

'No,' Elise said. Too quickly. Janet looked

at her; Elise wouldn't meet her gaze 'What did she take, Elise?' Janet lowered her voice, repeated the question, 'What did she take?'

'It was legal, Mum.'

'What?'

'They call it Paradise.'

'Paradise,' Janet said. 'Did you take it as well?'

'Yes. It's supposed to just give you more energy, a bit of abuzz.'

Janet felt like screaming.

'Did you tell the paramedics?'

'Yes.'

Thank God for that. 'Come on.' Janet, her blood boiling, frightened and furious, led her daughter out into the hall.

They were stopped at the front door by the police officer. 'I need your name and contact details,' he said to Elise.

'Elise Scott,' she said. She gave her address and her mobile phone number.

'And you rang the ambulance?' he checked.

'Yes.'

'You accompanied Olivia to the party?'

'Yes,' Elise said.

As they got into the car and Janet started the engine it struck her that she'd seen no other middle-aged adults at the house. 'Where are the boys' parents?' she said. 'Weren't they supposed to be supervising?'

'They went to the theatre,' Elsie said. 'They'll be back later.'

'Bloody hell, Elise, was there anything else you lied about?'

Elise began to cry. *Christ*, Janet thought, *just let Olivia be all right, please. Let her be OK.*

Janet's phone rang again while she was parking at the hospital. Unknown number.

'Hello?' she answered.

'Janet, it's Vivien Canning,' her voice shook, riddled with fear, 'we've just heard from the hospital. Have you seen her?'

'Vivien, I'm so sorry, we've just got here,' Janet said. 'We'll try and find out what's happening.'

'They say she took drugs,' Vivien said.

'Yes, some sort of legal high, apparently.'

'Ken is going to get a hire car, there are no flights at this time of night. Oh God, Janet.'

It could've been me, Janet thought, *Elise on the stretcher.*

'Please, anything you hear, anything at all–'

'Of course,' Janet said, 'I promise.' Even with the best driving in the world it would take four hours to travel from Edinburgh.

Elise had her eyes closed. Janet shook her, a rush of terror that she was having the same reaction. 'Are you all right?'

'Just dizzy.'

'I'm going to ask them to look at you,' Janet said.

'I'm fine.'

Janet glared at her.

'OK,' Elise said, close to tears.

At the Accident and Emergency reception, Janet first asked after Olivia.

'Are you a relative?'

'Loco parentis,' Janet said, 'our daughters are friends. I've just spoken to Olivia's mother, they'll be here as soon as possible, coming down from Edinburgh. I was looking after Olivia while they were away.' As an afterthought Janet showed her warrant card. This would mean that she was CRB-checked at least – fit to work with children. That seemed to be enough. The clerk looked at the screen. 'She's in Resus.'

Janet's stomach turned: resuscitation was not good. Resus meant that Olivia was critically ill, that her life was in danger, that they were trying to revive her.

'She's going to be all right, though?' Elise said.

'We are doing everything possible,' the clerk said.

'My daughter,' Janet said, 'she's taken the same drug. Would it be possible to have someone check her out?'

'Any symptoms at the moment?'

'Just dizzy,' Elise said, 'and I've got a head-ache.'

'Fill this in with your details.' She passed them a form.

Janet helped Elise complete the form and Janet returned it, then she got Elise a drink of water from the fountain and stepped outside to call Vivien. It was tempting to wait for more news, better news, but Janet knew that they would be absolutely desperate for every morsel of information. It would be cowardly not to ring her now and tell her.

Vivien must have had the phone in her hand, she answered immediately. 'Janet?'

'We're at the hospital,' Janet said. 'Olivia is in resuscitation.'

'Oh God.'

'We haven't seen her yet, but she's young, she's strong.'

'Yes,' Vivien said.

Janet felt her eyes prick. She sniffed. 'I'll ring you as soon as we know anything else.'

'Thank you.'

Elise kept nodding off, reminding Janet of when she was a little girl and would fall asleep at the dinner table or in the shopping trolley. Elise complained she was hot but when Janet felt her she was clammy. She made her drink more water, wondering whether they should ask again about seeing a doctor.

Janet rang Ade, speaking with a calmness that belied her true state. Telling him the minimum – not that there was much more to tell.

'Good God, shall I come down?' he said.

'No, stay with Taisie. I'll ring you when we know what's happening.'

'What the hell was she doing taking drugs?'

he said. 'She's fifteen.'

'Not now,' Janet said.

'Do you need me to do anything?'

'No, thanks, we'll see you later.'

Elise's name was called and Janet went with her. The triage nurse took her pulse, blood pressure and temperature and listened to her heart. She made a note of the circumstances.

'Your pulse is quite high and your temperature too but I don't think we need to give you anything at the moment. Something like this, we've no idea what's in it so we don't have any antidotes and we don't know if other drugs will create an adverse reaction. So, plenty of fluids and don't go to sleep. You are staying here?'

'Yes,' Janet answered.

'If there's any sudden change, let someone know,' the nurse said.

Janet sat with Elise, bone weary, stomach fizzing with acid. New casualties arrived, those with minor ailments waited. Some stepped outside for a cigarette, ignoring all the signs forbidding smoking anywhere near the building. Janet fleetingly wished she smoked, something to break the tension of waiting, a salve for the stress.

Dark-haired and fine-featured, Olivia was Elise's firm friend, had been for years. She was a gymnast, would challenge Taisie, the sportier of Janet's girls, to cartwheel competitions on the rare occasions when Elise let Taisie tag along with them.

An ambulance pulled in and there was a rush of activity. She heard someone say RTA. A road traffic accident. Someone else's world suddenly brought to a halt by a twist of fate.

This time last year, near enough, Janet had been waiting for news of her mother, who was undergoing emergency surgery. But it had all turned out OK, Dorothy was fit and well again now.

It was another hour before someone came to Janet, asked her to come through to a room along the corridor. Elise grasped her hand, stayed close.

A middle-aged, softly spoken man with shiny brown eyes the exact shade of Maltesers greeted them, and invited them to sit.

'When Olivia arrived at the hospital she was suffering from serious heart failure. We attempted to revive her using emergency procedures, but I am afraid there were complications.'

Elise yelped, letting go of Janet and covering her face with her hands. Janet pulled her close, held her with one arm around her back and one hand stroking her hair.

'I am very, very sorry but...'

Janet had said the words herself, dozens of times, *so sorry, so very sorry to tell you, to tell you, dead, died, your wife, sister, friend, son, mother, brother, daughter, so sorry.* In living rooms and kitchens and hallways and work-places.

Janet's vision blackened and she felt a fist of shock clutch at her own heart as he said, '...I have to tell you that Olivia died as a result of the problems with her heart. There was nothing else we could do.'

Elise began to sob, her face pressed into Janet's chest, the vibrations travelling through Janet's body.

'Her parents?' Janet said, almost a whisper.

'They will be informed as soon as they arrive. I am sorry,' the doctor repeated, 'please take as long as you like in here. I will put a sign on the door so you will not be disturbed.'

Janet closed her eyes. She heard the clunk of the door as he closed it. She felt the heat of Elise's tears, the way her body trembled, listened to her cries, raw, guttural sounds that tore at Janet's heart.

It was a loss of innocence for Elise, Janet knew. One of those moments when the world slips and everything you understand, all you are, changes. Leaving you older, wiser, tainted, and less open, less trusting. The enormity of what had happened kept hitting Janet afresh. She was no stranger to sudden death, it was the staple of her work, but the fact of Olivia dead, so young, such a random thing, the thought of Elise's future unravelling without her best friend, of that absence going on and on for ever, seemed unreal and ridiculous.

'Can we go home?' Elise looked at her, face stark with misery, hair tangled, salt traces on her cheeks where her tears had dried.

'We need to stay here, see Vivien and Ken.'

'I don't want to,' she said shrilly, frightened. 'I don't want to see them.'

'I know, but we can't just run away,' Janet said.

We have to wait. No matter how tired and stressed they were, they had to wait to see Vivien and Ken. To be there, bear witness.

They stayed in the little room. Janet went for drinks, coffee for herself and hot chocolate for Elise. They sat and drank them in shell-shocked silence.

When Elise began to cry again, quietly and shielding her eyes, Janet went and sat next to her and let her cry. Eventually Elise's breathing altered, became slow and shallow and Janet felt the tension in her body ease. She slumped into her mother. The nurse had said to keep her awake but that was hours ago now and Janet didn't believe she was going to choke on her own vomit sitting upright next to her.

Janet's phone rang, horribly loud in the boxy room, and Elise stirred. Janet checked the display – *Vivien* – and let it ring until her voicemail kicked in. What else could she do?

Answer and lie about how Olivia was? Answer and tell Vivien and Ken that their daughter was dead? Not the sort of news you gave over the phone to someone who was driving in a desperate hurry. She set her phone to vibrate only. Didn't listen to the voicemail.

There was a knock at the door. 'Sorry, cleaning,' the man, an African, said. He used a mop to wipe the floor. Then went on his way.

Some time later another knock and the doctor was back with Vivien and Ken. Janet saw that they had already been told, Vivien, white-faced, a look of utter devastation on her face, Ken, pale and trembling.

'I'm so sorry,' Janet said, standing to embrace Vivien. 'I am so, so sorry.'

'Olivia,' Vivien was in shock, 'Olivia,' repeating her daughter's name over and over again as if she'd call her back.

13

Alison answered the door to Rachel. 'You all right?'

'Fine, brought your bag back.' Rachel twirled the clutch bag this way and that. Not her style but she'd needed it for the wedding and Alison had asked her a few times since if she could return it. 'Have you lost it?' she'd said the last time, getting suspicious. 'No, I just keep forgetting,' Rachel had told her. Now Rachel moved her head and winced, feeling the bruises Neil Perry had inflicted on her.

'What?' said Alison.

'Nothing,' said Rachel, 'stiff neck.'

'You coming in?'

'Five minutes,' Rachel said.

'He waiting for you?'

'No, he's away.'

'Away?'

'I've not got him chained to the house,' Rachel said. 'He's taking Haydn off, skiing and that.'

'Skiing?'

'Snow, slopes, long shiny planks strapped to your feet?'

Alison rolled her eyes. 'Tea?'

'No, ta.'

'How come you've not gone?' Alison said.

'Work – that man who was shot and set on fire on Manorclough.'

'In that order, I hope,' Alison said and shuddered. 'So, skiing.'

'And WaterWorld,' Rachel added, 'staying at a Travelodge.'

'WaterWorld!'

'Why are you doing that?' Rachel said.

'What?'

'Repeating everything.'

Alison swallowed, set down the kettle. 'I went to see Dom yesterday.'

'Oh.' Rachel's guts turned cold.

'I know you don't want to go and I understand why, I really do, but I need to be able to talk about him. I can't be minding what I say.'

'All right,' Rachel said. Though it felt a long way from that. 'How is he?' she managed. She could imagine. All too clearly. Last stretch he'd done, he'd been a bum boy for the older, more powerful cons. Had to be to get by. It wouldn't be any different this time. Except he'd gradually turn from a twenty-nine-year-old to a fifty-seven-year-old in the course of his sentence. If he lasted that long. She couldn't bear to think about it.

'Doing his best,' Alison said. 'It's hard, of course. He's a bit down. He's asked to see the psychiatrist, see if he can get some medication.'

Rachel stared at the fridge, kids' drawings up there, houses, rainbows and stick figures with smiley faces. Happy fucking families.

'He understands,' Alison said. 'Your job, when you knew what he'd done, where he was going, you had to report him, he gets it.'

The room was airless, the space too small. If he'd only understood in the first place that beating someone so badly he broke their back and they died was totally wrong.

168

'Why he ever thought, even for a second, even in his wildest dreams that I'd want that–' Rachel's eyes hurt.

Alison looked as wretched as she felt. 'He doesn't think,' Alison said, 'he never has.' She turned back and made her drink. The clock on the wall ticked. Rachel rubbed at the back of her neck, the tension there making her head ache.

'Maybe in time, when you're ready,' Alison said, 'you could go see him. That'd help.'

'Help who?' Rachel snapped.

'Both of you,' Alison said. 'You're not settled with this, even if it was the only choice you had, and you're bound to feel guilty about it.'

'Am I?' Rachel said. 'You know, do you?'

'Rachel, don't,' Alison said wearily.

'Like he's gonna want to see me.'

'He does, he said, he always... Oh, never mind.' Alison shook her head, picked up her cup.

'What about Sharon?' Rachel said. 'Will he want to see her?'

Alison snorted. 'Yeah, right. Even if he did, why would she go? He's no use to her in there, no money, no possessions, she wouldn't even be able to tap fags off him.'

'Maybe she'd just like to see him, like she did me, you if you'd let her,' Rachel said

'Bollocks.' Alison was not giving an inch where their prodigal mother was concerned.

'I'm off.' Rachel picked up her car keys.
'Thanks for the bag.'
'No problem.'
'You'll have to come round,' Alison said at the door, 'you and Sean and Haydn. When you're off work.'
'Sure,' Rachel said, trying to sound vaguely enthusiastic.

It was raining hard now and she hurried to the car. Heaved a sigh of relief at escaping without getting into a full-on barney with her sister. She'd go home, have a drink and watch whatever she could find on the box. Please herself. No Sean. Her heart lifted at the prospect. Just miss my own company, time on my own, she told herself, that's all.

She thought of the Perry twins, always together, like having a clone, someone to reflect your every thought, share your every deed, understand you completely. Weird, really weird. Having someone in her flat day in, day out was strange enough but to understand another person so completely – Rachel couldn't imagine it.

Day 4

Sunday, 13 May

14

'Forensics have a present for us,' Gill began, then broke off. 'Where's Janet?'

Rachel shook her head.

Peculiar. If Janet was ill or delayed she always let Gill know.

'Rachel, you brief her when she's in. So – chemical analysis of trace material on the footwear of Noel and Neil Perry shows the presence of an accelerant.'

Mitch grinned, Kevin raised a fist and Lee nodded, smiling.

'And it gets better – the composition of the accelerant is compatible with the accelerant used in the Old Chapel. Petrol, and specifically Shell petrol as established by an analysis of the additives in the composition. Traces on all four items. So, Rachel, we go after them for that. Yes?'

'Yes, boss.'

Gill hoped that by acting as though nothing untoward had happened the previous evening, in effect burying the fact that her knobhead ex-husband had come crashing into her incident room, as welcome as a fart at a funeral, Lee and Kevin would share her amnesia.

'Superintendent review at nine and I'm optimistic we'll get our next twelve hours' detention, given the new evidence. More to talk to our suspects about. You all right, Rachel? Up for another bout or you want reassigning?'

'He's not getting shot of me that easy.'

'A testing situation and, having seen the recording, I don't think we'll have any problems though you could have been more careful with your language. Might be construed as verbal abuse.'

Rachel's mouth dropped open.

'Fucking ridiculous,' Gill added, 'don't know what the twats were thinking of but you know the rules.'

'Pillocks,' Kevin said. From somewhere Kevin had acquired an old-fashioned maths compass and was using the point to pick at his nails.

Gill stared at him, stopped speaking. Gradually the rest of them followed suit.

Kevin continued his efforts, head down, mining away for several seconds until he noticed the shift in atmosphere. He looked up quickly at Gill then his eyes flickered round the room. 'Boss,' he said weakly, perhaps thinking Gill had asked a question and was waiting for the reply.

'Good of you to rejoin us, Kevin.'

'I was just–' He dried up.

'Away with the fairies?' Gill said. 'Listen,

Slack Alice, you want a French manicure and polish you do it in your own time.'

'I was listening.'

'I'm not arguing the toss with you, sunshine. I expect your undivided attention. Got it?'

'Yes, boss.'

Kevin set the compass down then pushed it slightly further away, which Gill reckoned was a wise move. With the attention span of a gnat he would soon forget and if the thing was in reach it wouldn't be long before he picked it up and started chiselling away at his nails again.

'Meanwhile,' she said, 'I want Greg Tandy. Rachel, you go with Mitch.'

'Yes, boss.'

'What more have we got on Richard Kavanagh?'

'More of the same,' said Lee. 'No reports of him ever causing bother and no reported connection with criminals or criminal activity. People in the area generally tolerant. He spent some time in the hostel in town, they tried to get him into a programme with the *Big Issue* but he didn't take it up. Hospitalized last winter with pneumonia, discharged himself before treatment was completed.'

'Why?' Gill said.

'No booze on the ward?' Rachel said.

Lee laughed, 'In one.'

Gill felt a ripple of embarrassment, coughed and adjusted her notes while she recovered her composure. 'We have any timeline for his last day?'

'Near enough,' Mitch said. 'Sightings on Wednesday at eleven am and one-thirty pm walking round the estate. Latest sighting was four pm when he buys two tins of cheap lager from the Big Booze Bonanza. He was a regular there.'

'Get that charted up and cross-referenced with any sightings we've got of the Perry twins,' Gill said, 'find any overlap.'

'Already made a start,' Mitch said. 'Problem is people are a lot less forthcoming about seeing the Perry brothers, widely regarded as hard cases, sort of people who would break your face if you looked at them the wrong way. We do have them in the precinct mid-afternoon and on Low Bank Road which leads to the Old Chapel at twenty past seven.'

'Reliable witness, that last one?' Gill said.

'Yes,' Mitch said, 'local councillor. Martin Bleaklow. Runs the car repair place further down Shuttling Way. Keen to improve the area.'

'And those sightings fit with the one we already have from the resident, Mr Hicks, and from Rachel,' Gill said.

'Were they carrying anything?' Rachel asked.

'Possibly,' Mitch said. 'Bleaklow thought

one of them was carrying a bag.'

'With a can of petrol in it, bet you,' Kevin said, smiling.

'Excellent,' said Gill. 'So, bring me Greg Tandy, then let's find out how the Perrys explain their clothes being awash with Shell FuelSave unleaded.'

Rachel tried Janet before she and Mitch left but it went to voicemail. Janet was probably driving in, couldn't answer the phone, well – wouldn't answer the phone – conscientious to a tee. The result of having a schoolteacher for a mother, Rachel reckoned, instead of a ... the word *slapper* came to mind. Rachel felt a tinge of guilt. Sharon wasn't exactly a slapper, or a slag or a tart, all names her dad threw about once Sharon had gone off and left them. Likes a good time, that's all. Was that fair? Rachel was sick of thinking about it.

Greg Tandy's address on Manton Road was a couple of minutes from the Manor-clough precinct. To get there they took a turning just after the warehouse on Shut-tling Way, fire engines at work there.

'It's not still burning?' Rachel said to Mitch.

'Probably be there as a precaution. You can get secondaries, somewhere cinders smoulder then they get going again. Could be an insurance job, the developer went bust last year. No one's going to take it on in this climate.'

'What was he developing?' Rachel said.

'Luxury housing,' Mitch said.

Rachel snorted. 'On Manorclough? They'd need bloody high fences, watchtowers and sub-machine guns to keep the lowlifes out.'

'Concierge, gated. Even so, the demand's not there. Places sitting empty in Manchester, aren't there?'

'Left after the bridge,' Rachel said. 'You don't think it's the Perrys, then, the warehouse?'

Mitch shrugged. 'No idea. Maybe someone wants us to think that. Opportunistic.'

She could imagine them doing it though. Revved up after the murder and burning the chapel, wanting to see a bigger, fiercer fire. In the back of her mind a note of caution sounded – they hadn't got proof yet that the Perrys had shot Richard Kavanagh. They were still only suspects. 'Listen to your instincts but follow the evidence,' that's what the boss always said.

Tandy's house was the end terrace, there was room to park close by. The place was in reasonable repair, clean net curtains at the windows, UPVC windows and doors, unlike those at some of the neighbours' who still had wooden frames with peeling paint.

Mitch's press of the doorbell produced a swift response. A woman with curly red hair, freckled complexion, smoker's lips and crow's feet answered. She'd a jacket on, bag in hand, as if she'd just got in or was about to leave.

'Yes?'

'Mrs Gloria Tandy?' Mitch said.

'Yes?'

'DC Ian Mitchell and this is DC Rachel Bailey, Manchester Metropolitan Police. Is your husband in?'

Rachel caught the look, disappointment followed by resignation dulling her eyes. A slow blink. 'No,' she said.

'When are you expecting him back?'

The woman took a breath, her nostrils flaring. 'Don't know.'

'Where's he gone?'

'Don't know.'

A brick wall, thought Rachel. See no evil, hear no evil, speak no evil. Or any good for that matter.

'We're anxious to speak to him as soon as possible,' Mitch said.

'Course you are,' she said sarcastically.

'Perhaps you have a mobile phone number we can reach him on?' Mitch was unruffled.

She moved abruptly, opened her bag and pulled out her phone, reeled off a number which Rachel entered into her own handset. The phone number which she had given them was not the same as the one that Neil Perry had used to call Greg Tandy. Tandy probably used a separate phone for anything illicit. Many criminals did, often throw-aways, unregistered, dumped as soon as they'd served their purpose.

'If your husband does come in before we manage to contact him, please ask him to get in touch.' Mitch handed her his card; she took it without reading it.

'You're probably wondering what all this is about,' Rachel said, because the woman hadn't asked, hadn't shown the slightest curiosity or made the usual gabby demands and defences that they heard so many times when talking to suspects' families.

'I'm not interested,' she said bitterly. 'Whatever it is, it's between you and him.' Not quite wifely solidarity.

There was a sound upstairs, footfall, and Rachel glanced quickly at Mitch.

'Someone upstairs?' Mitch said.

There was no shock or guilt in Mrs Tandy's face as she said, 'Our lad.'

Connor, Rachel remembered. The kid she had chased on Thursday, the gobby one with the bike. Knowing the kid was Tandy's son made sense of his attitude when Rachel had first confronted him. The kid would've grown up with his father in and out of prison, mistrusting authority, with a bloody great chip on his shoulder about the police. Rachel was the law, the filth, the dibble, five-oh.

'Perhaps we could see him?' Mitch said.

Gloria Tandy waited a moment and Rachel could almost smell the resentment. She wasn't obliged to comply. All these families knew their legal rights, forwards, backwards and upside down. But Mrs Tandy, rather than telling them to fuck off, cooperated, called, 'Connor, come here a minute.'

Movement and then the boy, bare-chested, in bare feet, jeans hanging low, boxers visible, trotted downstairs. The scrape on his arm and the cut on his cheek scabbed over.

'What?'

'We're looking for your dad,' said Mitch.

'Not here,' the boy said.

'You know where he is?' Rachel asked.

A shrug, 'No.'

He didn't give a toss, Rachel thought, then she saw the bravado of his gaze slip momentarily and she realized he was un-nerved, scared. She decided to push him.

'I'll ask you again, Connor, do you know where your dad is?'

'No,' he said hotly, 'I told you.'

His mother intervened. 'He doesn't. I don't. That's the truth.'

Something off-key, Rachel thought. What? Do they really know where he is?

Mitch obviously picked up on the atmosphere too. 'You won't have any objection to me checking that Mr Tandy isn't in the house?'

'You calling us liars?' Connor said.

'Connor,' his mother said sharply, 'leave it! Go ahead,' she said to Mitch.

Rachel followed and they scanned each room upstairs and down, finding no other occupants.

'Look, I have to get to work,' Gloria Tandy said.

'Thanks, we're done here,' Rachel said.

'There's pizza in the freezer,' his mother told Connor. 'Here,' she got money from her purse, 'get some milk.'

She dithered for a moment, uneasy about leaving them with the boy. So Rachel nodded to Mitch and they made a move outside. Mrs Tandy got into her own car, a tatty-looking Ford, and turned the engine over several times before it started.

Connor emerged on his bike. He hesitated for a moment at the pavement's edge then bounced his front wheel up and down.

'What do you want him for anyway,' he said, squinting a little. The sky was bright, the sun struggling to break through the clouds.

'Just want to talk,' Mitch said.

'He might be able to help us,' Rachel said.

'About that murder?'

'You heard anything about that?' Rachel said.

'I'm not a grass,' the boy said quickly.

'So you have?' He looked down at his bike, twisted the handlebars this way and that.

'You picked someone up, it said on the telly. Is it the Perrys?'

The names had not been disclosed but it must have been easy enough for Connor to guess the 'two twenty-two-year-old men' were the twins, given their reputations and previous conviction for arson.

'Why would you think that?' Rachel said, seeing if he'd let something slip.

'A friend of mine, she seen them being arrested. Everyone knows it was them. It is, isn't it?'

Neither Mitch nor Rachel replied.

Connor sniffed, ducked his head and hawked on the pavement. *Nice.*

'How come people think the Perrys are involved?' Rachel said.

He jerked his shoulders up and down in a quick shrug. 'My dad goes up the King's on Wednesdays.'

When he's not inside?

'Right,' Rachel said. Was he trying to give his dad an alibi? Did he think he needed one? Did he imagine they wanted Tandy for the murder itself? 'We just want to talk to him, you tell him when he gets back.'

As they watched Connor speed off over the cobbles, Rachel said to Mitch, 'Greg Tandy, he's only been out nine days and already he's back in the life.'

'Doesn't know anything else,' Mitch said.

'That lad'll go the same way most likely, in

his father's footsteps.'

'That's it, look on the bright side,' Mitch joked.

She looked over to the ruined warehouse, across the strip of canal with junk floating on the surface.

What bright side? she thought. *Buggered if I can spot it.*

Close to dawn, Janet had gone back with Elise to Vivien and Ken's. Ken, in the kitchen on the phone, had begun to alert the wider family to the tragedy. His deep voice rumbled in the background.

Vivien was agitated, exhausted too. Circles under her eyes, hands shaking. Her mother was on her way, their son, away at uni, was getting the first train.

We all want our mothers, Janet thought, when something like this happens. That comfort, that unconditional love.

'She just collapsed?' Vivien said, uncomprehending.

Elise looked at Janet. Janet nodded – tell her.

'Like she had a fit,' said Elise. 'Her eyes went back in her head and she was jerking about.'

'You were out?' Vivien asked Janet. Her face crumpled with incomprehension.

Out? 'Still at work,' Janet said, 'Elise rang me at ten thirty.'

'What about Adrian?' Vivien said.

'He was with Taisie at home,' Janet said.

'And the girls? Olivia was sleeping over.'

Janet's heart sank. Elise closed her eyes, tensed her mouth, fighting tears.

'We thought Elise was staying at yours after the party,' Janet said. 'We didn't know you were away.'

'What party?' Vivien said.

Oh Christ. It just gets worse and worse. She should've checked, she should have rung and spoken to Vivien, she should not have taken Elise's word for it. *I trusted her. I trusted her and now this.*

'I'm sorry,' Elise said, 'I'm so sorry.'

It was mid-morning when Janet finally got Elise home and rang Gill.

'All right,' Gill answered breezily, 'it'd better be good.'

A beat of silence, Janet thinking, *Oh God.* 'Elise's friend, Olivia, there was a party last night. Olivia died.'

'Middleton Road,' Gill said, quick as a flash, 'drug-related.'

'You heard?'

'Division's got it. Oh, Janet, I am so sorry. How's Elise?'

'You can imagine. So I probably need to stay with–'

'Of course. Don't even think about doing anything else. High profile,' Gill said, 'could get kicked up to MIT.'

185

'I know,' said Janet.

'We couldn't take it, I don't think,' Gill added, 'not on top of everything else. If we did you wouldn't be anywhere near it.'

'I know that.' A conflict of interest. With Elise a potential witness and Janet being close to the victim and family, and official involvement by Janet could prejudice the inquiry.

'Legal high apparently. Fucking drugs, eh?' Gill said. 'The family have been informed?'

'Her parents, yes, still people to contact,' Janet said.

'OK. I'll let everyone know the situation.'

'Thanks, Gill.'

Gill put the phone down, thinking of Elise, of the dead girl. All that promise, a whole life snuffed out. She thought of the lectures she herself had given Sammy. People equated legal with safe. But the drugs were anything but. Horse tranquillizers, plant food. A cocktail of chemicals untested and with unpredictable effects. The police, the law, were constantly playing catch-up, banning those substances linked to death or serious side effects, but it was always too little, too late. The manufacturers could take the same recipe, tweak it, alter one ingredient or the proportion of others and hey presto it was legal again. Potentially deadly.

Her phone rang. She sat up straighter and

answered, 'Gill Murray.'

'Rita in forensics. Good news.'

'Go on.'

'As you know, there was no gunshot residue on the swabs from the two suspects, however–'

'I love that word, *however,*' Gill said.

'However,' Rita laughed, 'we did find gunshot residue particles on the right-hand wrist cuff and sleeve seam of Neil Perry's hooded jacket and on the right wrist cuff of Noel Perry's jacket. The wrist is ribbed and particles were trapped there.'

Gill knew the physics. The act of firing a gun generated a powerful cloud of dust that settled on hands, forearm and the front of the person using it, but the residue was heavy and soon dropped off unless the structure or design trapped it. For that reason cuffs, pockets, seams, zips and buttons were all places worth examining. And if the suspects put their hands in their pockets they could transfer GSR there from the hands.

'Of course, we can't give you a time frame,' the forensics woman said. 'But it tells you they each fired a weapon at some point recently.'

'Perfect,' Gill said, 'absolutely bloody perfect.'

15

Rachel began with the weapon. 'Do you own a gun?'

'No.' The sore by Neil Perry's mouth was bigger, more inflamed. She imagined him picking away at it all night in his cell.

'Have you ever fired a gun?' she said.

'No.'

'Think carefully,' she said.

'No, I haven't.'

'You sure about that?' Rachel said.

'Yes.'

'I am now showing the suspect document 15. This is a report from the forensic science lab. Tests were carried out on your clothing. The report notes gunshot residue on your hoodie. Can you explain that to me?'

There was a light in his eyes. He was enjoying it, the fucking toe-rag. Most of the scrotes she interviewed, there was resentment or rage, derision, but behind that there were flashes of fear and anxiety or horror at what they'd done. But with Neil Perry there'd been no whiff of that. It went beyond cocky. Something missing, Rachel reckoned, something wrong with his wiring.

'No idea.' He gave a slow shrug.

'Not something you're likely to forget, firing a weapon. Noisy, deafening actually. You still don't remember?'

'Nothing,' he said.

She wanted to wipe the smile from his face. It seemed like the tighter the corner he was boxed into, the more he relished it.

'This report also analyses the distribution of the gunshot residue particles. The greatest concentration are on the cuff of your right wrist, inside and out, and in the stitching of the lining up to the elbow. The only way you get that pattern of dispersal is when you fire a weapon. How do you account for that?'

'Dunno,' he said, 'weird, innit?'

Rachel moved the report to one side, took a slow breath in and out then another. She placed a second report on the table.

'I am now showing Mr Perry document 19. This is another report from our forensics lab, detailing trace materials found on your clothes. Tests found traces of accelerant, namely petrol, on your trainers and your jeans. How did that get there?'

'I don't know,' he said.

'There were splashes of the petrol on the front of your jeans. According to the forensic investigators, this pattern is consistent with what would be found when someone was throwing petrol from a container in order to start a fire. Is that how it got on your jeans?' Rachel said.

'Could've been a barbecue,' he said.

'What do you mean?'

'The petrol, maybe we used it to get a barbie going.' He shrugged.

'Did you?'

'Don't remember.' A slack smile on his face.

He was pratting about but she knew she mustn't let him get her back up and interfere with the agreed strategy for the interview. 'Did you know Richard Kavanagh?' Rachel said.

'Who?'

'The victim of the shooting in the Old Chapel.'

'No.' He shook his head.

'You might have known him as Rodeo Rick.'

'Didn't know him,' he said. Still the denial.

'Tall man, long hair, wore a cowboy-type hat.'

'I don't know no manky dosser, they eat crap out of bins, full of fleas, in't they. They eat roadkill.' If Kavanagh had been anything like Rachel's father, food would be an incidental, an add-on to be considered once the savage need for a bevvy had been attended to.

'A quantity of illegal drugs were recovered from your room,' Rachel said. 'Can you tell me where you obtained them?' They had debated whether to introduce the drugs or

190

not. Godzilla thought they should. The possibility of a drugs war, robbery or a deal gone sour could still give them motive.

'But we've nothing to put Kavanagh next to drugs,' Rachel had argued.

'Yet,' the boss said. 'Could be a dead end but we go down it and have a good root around and find out instead of just ignoring it.'

Neil Perry laughed and scratched again. Hope he's got scabies, Rachel thought, and felt her skin prickle in response.

'Was it your intention to supply drugs to others?' she said.

'No, personal use only,' he said.

'Excessive amounts for personal use.'

'Bulk buy,' he said, 'like with the cash and carry, makes sense.'

So he'd cop for possession but Rachel wasn't interested in that, she wanted him for murder.

'Tell me about Wednesday,' she said.

'Went to my gran's.'

'We have an independent witness who saw you on Low Bank Road at twenty past seven in the evening,' Rachel said.

'Can't have,' he said, 'I wasn't there.'

'We also have an independent witness who can place you in the grounds of the Old Chapel ten minutes later, at half past seven that evening.'

'They're lying.'

So it went on and on, round and round until Rachel felt dizzy.

Gill was preparing notes in support of the application for a warrant of further detention. The court, specially convened as it was a Sunday, would want to know what inquiries had been made and why more time was needed.

She sketched out her summary of the evidence, the narrative she would present.

She started with the eyewitness sightings of Noel and Neil Perry: Councillor Bleaklow placed them in the centre of Manorclough on Low Bank Road at twenty past seven, Mr Hicks in the chapel grounds at half past seven and Rachel had seen them in the alley at twenty past eight. All those sightings contradicted the alibis given by both mother and grandmother, which in turn contradicted each other.

However, Gill drummed her nails on the desk: eyewitness testimony rested to a great extent on the clothing worn by the suspects. And although the jackets were distinctive and had to be ordered specially online, they might not be the only ones in existence. But then what were the odds of two people, identical in height and weight, within five hundred yards of the Perrys' flat and the scene of the murder, wearing similar jackets?

Next was the preparatory act, the meeting

with Greg Tandy, a man out on licence after serving a sentence for firearms offences. That still begged many questions, not least what the meeting had been about. While the police suspected Tandy of supplying the gun to the brothers, it was only a suspicion, no hard evidence to support it.

Much stronger was the forensic evidence: gunshot residue on the clothing of both suspects indicated the use of a firearm. No time could categorically be given as to when the gun had been fired but Gill was sure that they would be able to secure expert opinion that, taking into account the amount of particles found, the incident had been recent, a matter of days rather than weeks or months.

The presence of petrol traces, in significant amounts, on the jeans and trainers of the brothers, petrol containing the same additives as in that used to start the fire, while not conclusive was persuasive evidence. They shared everything, she thought, the gunshots, one each, taking turns, chucking the petrol about. In it together.

What was still missing was motive. No known link between the parties. Could it be a stranger murder? They often occurred as a result of fights, fuelled by booze, testosterone and rampant stupidity. Men were twice as likely to be the victims. Or predator killings. Was this one of those? She would talk to Lee again about the psychology of the crime. He could do the next interview with Noel if Janet was still off. Focus on that line of questioning for a while.

Gill stretched her arms, reaching up towards the ceiling, flexing her fingers. She checked the time, texted Sammy that she wasn't sure when she'd be home and not to save her any casserole, then she began to type up her report.

Rachel was on the doorstep, looking slightly sheepish.

'I wasn't sure whether to come,' she said. 'If now is not good–'

'No, come in,' Janet said, glad to see her.

'Sure?'

'Yes.'

Taisie bobbed out from the kitchen. 'Hi, Rachel.'

'All right. How you doing?' Rachel said.

Taisie adored Rachel, had a girl crush on her, and clung like a limpet whenever Rachel called round.

'I'm good.' Taisie nodded. 'I'm in the school play. And I got on the football team.'

'Get you!' Rachel said and Taisie beamed and blushed; all the mardy, awkward, bolshie side of her had disappeared.

'Who is it?' Janet's mum came into the hall from the lounge. 'Oh,' her voice fell with disappointment. If Taisie thought Rachel was the bee's knees, Dorothy thought she was a walking disaster.

'It's Rachel, Mum.' Dorothy just didn't get the friendship. Not that Janet did all the time. She and Rachel didn't always see eye to eye on things. They were at different stages of life, different backgrounds, but something just clicked.

'We're off to get some air,' Janet said.

'At this hour?' Dorothy said.

'They called it walking the dog in my day,' Ade grumbled from the living room. *In my day?* He talked like an old fogey sometimes.

'Won't be long,' Janet said, glancing at Rachel who looked lairy, wondering if she'd put her foot in it. Janet gave her a little nod, *it's OK*. Grabbed her coat.

'It's raining,' Dorothy, said.

'It's stopped, actually,' Rachel pointed out.

Dorothy rolled her eyes. Before there could be any more sniping Janet opened the front door and got them out of the house.

She took a gulp of air, cool, damp, and another.

'How is she?' Rachel took her arm.

'Asleep now. Oh God, I need a drink. Come on.' As they walked up to the junction where the pub was, Janet filled her in. 'You know Elise never puts a foot wrong, quick to point the finger, moral high ground and all that, then ... it's like she's fallen off a cliff, Rachel.' She thought of the look on Elise's face, the deep sadness but worse than that the shame. 'She lied to us about everything, about this party, she said there was a group going and everyone's parents had said yes. But Vivien and Ken, Olivia's parents, had gone off on a romantic weekend in Edinburgh thinking Olivia was having a sleepover at our house. Next thing they know, Olivia is dead. And of course Elise had told us she was staying at Olivia's.'

'That's an old one,' Rachel said.

'Yes,' Janet said. Her own teenage years had been disruptive in a very different way, the breakdown at sixteen had seen her in a mental hospital for several weeks. Recovering from that, supported by Ade, she'd never really had the wild teenage rebellion other people did.

The pub was warm and not too busy. Janet and Rachel got seats in one of the old-fashioned booths, benches with wooden panelling and frosted glass above which afforded them some privacy.

Rachel went for drinks. Janet asked for a double gin and tonic. She closed her eyes for a moment, images from the last twenty-four hours crowding in her head, the shocked tableau of youngsters at the party, Olivia on the stretcher, Elise sobbing when she learned about the death, Vivien alternately bewildered and frantic.

'Where did you get the drugs?' Janet had asked Elise when they got home from the hospital. Ade there, looking thunderstruck.

Elise had tugged at her hair, stalling.

Janet waited. Something she was used to, practised in. One of the tools of her trade as an interviewer. Patience, silence.

Ade opened his mouth to speak, Janet moved her hand, *don't*.

'This girl came to the party, she had them. She went round seeing what people wanted, I wasn't that bothered but...'

'Go on,' Janet said gently.

'Olivia really wanted to try something. She wanted me to buy some Ecstasy.'

'You bought them?' Janet said.

'I had the taxi money,' she said in a small voice. For the mythical taxi home. Except they'd intended staying out all night. And Olivia wouldn't have had extra cash with her parents unaware of the party plan.

'I wasn't sure about it,' Elise said, 'but the girl said she'd got some Paradise. Legal. It would be like taking an E.'

Ade's face drained as he heard the casual reference. Janet shot him a warning look.

'It was legal,' she said, 'that's why we picked it.'

'It was bloody stupid,' Ade growled, 'that's what it was.'

'I know that now!' Elise cried. 'But Olivia was so ... she really wanted to take something and everybody else was.'

'Who was this girl?' said Janet.

'I don't know. I've never seen her before.'

'Not in school?'

'No.'

'Was she there when Olivia got sick?' Janet said.

'No, she went, she wasn't there long, just while she was selling things. Will they arrest me?' She looked terrified, fists clenched together, mouth wide with panic. Shaking.

'No,' Janet said. She had moved closer and held her daughter by the shoulders. 'But they will want to talk to you and you must tell them everything, OK?'

'Bought you some crisps,' Rachel said, breaking Janet's train of thought. 'Keep your strength up.'

'They'll do the job,' Janet said sarkily.

'Be grateful,' Rachel said, 'or I'll eat them.' She studied her friend. 'Do they know what she took?'

'Not yet, probably some variant on meow meow. Elise described it as a small white tablet with a palm tree on, called Paradise. Sound familiar?'

Rachel nodded. 'Like we found at the Perrys'. Town's awash with it, according to the drug squad, it's new on the scene.'

'She kept saying it's legal. I said to her so's bleach and caustic soda and ground glass – it doesn't mean it's safe. They'd have been safer with something illegal. At least people know what to look out for, how to deal with it, and if there's a dodgy batch around word gets out.'

'Elise took it too?'

'Yeah, she felt weird,' she said, 'but you would, wouldn't you, when your mate–' Sudden tears robbed her of speech. 'I'm sorry,' she said eventually.

'Don't be daft,' Rachel chided.

'What's so awful is there is nothing, nothing Elise can do to make it right. It's final. And she'll have to live with that for the rest of her life.'

'It wasn't her fault though,' Rachel said.

'She lied–'

'Yes, but she didn't force Olivia to take the stuff, did she?'

'No, of course not.'

'She'd no idea it'd cause any harm, or she'd not have taken it herself,' Rachel said.

'OK,' Janet agreed.

'She got help as soon as she could, yes?'

'Yes, of course.'

'So, it was an accident, you have to tell her that. How could she have known? No-one could,' Rachel said.

'She's so hard on other people, she'll be the same with herself.'

'Can't think where she gets that from,' Rachel said.

Janet put her glass down. 'I'm not hard.'

'Sure you are. Principled, you'd call it, conscientious.'

'Fair-minded, maybe,' Janet countered.

'If you like. Keep my seat warm.'

Janet watched Rachel head off for a smoke. She was right. Horrible and tragic though Olivia's death was, it was an accident, but Janet didn't know how on earth she'd get Elise to accept that. Dorothy wasn't helping matters. She regarded drug use with the same unreserved horror others might have for bestiality or cannibalism.

'It's part of the landscape,' Janet tried to tell her. 'Everyone who tries it doesn't end up addicted to crack cocaine or turning tricks to fund a heroin habit.'

'Some will,' her mother had retorted. 'You never messed about with drugs, did you?'

'Only Librium and Mogadon,' Janet said dryly.

'Don't be flip,' Dorothy said. 'You were ill. I mean for kicks.'

'No, Mum, but these days I'd be a rare exception.'

Ade hadn't said much at all up to that point but he chipped in, 'She needs to take responsibility for her actions.'

'How exactly?' Janet demanded. 'She's torn apart with guilt, she's lost her best friend. How does she take responsibility for that?'

He had evaded the question, he was blustering, and she saw that. He was worried for Elise, felt terrible about Olivia, but he didn't know how to deal with it so he was talking rubbish. 'I never wanted her to go in the first place.'

'She's too young,' Dorothy had said.

'We're not doing this,' Janet had said. 'Hindsight is a wonderful thing but it gets us absolutely nowhere. They went. It happened.' Any further discussion was postponed by the arrival of Taisie, who had been sitting with Elise in a rare show of sisterliness.

Now Rachel came back into the pub smelling of cold air and tobacco smoke.

'Has she been interviewed?' she asked.

'In the morning,' Janet said.

'It's a lead story.' Rachel showed Janet her phone. The tabloid headline: LEGAL AND LETHAL. OLIVIA'S TRAGIC DEATH.

Janet looked at the photo, the face she'd known so well. It wasn't fair. That poor girl. Oh God. 'Tell me about work, tell me something else, distract me.'

'You don't want to go back home?'

'One more.' Janet drained her glass.

'Sure?' Rachel stood up.

Janet nodded. Gestured to Rachel's phone. 'Can I? Mine's charging.'

'Course.'

She bent her head and began to read, gritting her teeth together, determined not to cry.

Dave's mother answered the phone to Gill and went to fetch Dave without bothering to make any small talk.

The night before Gill had spoken to Sammy about his dad, tried to tread a careful line, not wanting to slag Dave off but needing to explain to Sammy that his father's drinking was out of control.

'How did he seem these last few visits?' she said.

He shrugged. 'Dunno. Why?'

'He's drinking more than he should be. Drinking in the day too. If you find him like that – well... He needs some help.'

'What, like rehab?'

'Yes,' Gill said.

Sammy nodded.

'You're not surprised?'

He wrinkled his nose. A look in his eyes. Guilt? 'What?' she said.

'Last time, he was off his face,' Sammy said. 'I went round and he was crying and apologizing and talking about how he'd messed everything up. So I left and went round to Orla's instead. Dad didn't rearrange on Thursday, I just didn't go. I couldn't face it.'

'Oh, Sammy, why didn't you say?'

'I don't know.' He gave a sigh. 'It creeped me out.'

'Look, you don't have to put up with that, nobody does.' She could imagine how distressing Sammy would've found it. His father sobbing and sentimental, full of self-pity and theatrics.

202

'I'll tell him you won't be seeing him again until he's straightened himself out if that's what you want?'

'Yeah,' he said. 'Are you OK?'

Oh, you lovely, lovely boy. 'Course I am,' she said. She could see the man he was becoming, not just his father's son or hers but his own person. See how the disaffection of the last couple of years was being replaced by engagement now he'd found something he wanted to do. Happy with Orla too. She was so proud of him. And she would not let Dave undermine all this. If it meant keeping them apart then so be it.

'Dave, I'm coming round, OK?'

'Sure, yeah.'

She couldn't tell if he was sober or not. 'About half an hour. See you then.'

'We could go out,' the first thing he said when he answered the door.

'I don't think that's a good idea,' Gill said, stepping inside.

They went into the living room. There was no sign of Dave's mother, which was a relief; the conversation Gill intended to have was best conducted in private.

'You want a drink?'

Seriously? 'No,' she said, sitting in an armchair. He sat in the other one. His eyes were slightly bloodshot but he had shaved, and she could smell aftershave. Sprucing himself up for her?

The room was tidy enough, no bottles or glasses half drunk.

'I'm sorry,' he said, 'about yesterday, your office.'

'You remember, do you?'

He stopped, disconcerted, but ignored her question. 'It won't happen again.'

'You've no way of knowing that.'

'You have my word,' he said, palm open, begging her to believe him.

'Worth precisely nothing,' she said.

He coloured. 'If you came here to insult me–'

'I came here to talk some sense into you. Your drinking is out of control, you are risking your job, your livelihood, never mind your health.'

'That's bullshit,' he said, 'it's just been a rough patch.'

'Hasn't anybody said anything at work?'

'I've a week's leave.'

'So what – this is your holiday? The lost weekend writ large? The bender of a lifetime? You need help.'

There was a pause. Dave stared at her, jaw working, temper in his eyes, then his expression softened. 'Look,' he said, 'I've made a mess of things – you, Sammy, Emma, the little one. I know I've let everybody down.' He took a breath. 'It was a mistake, Gill, leaving you. But I think if you and Sammy, if we could just try again–'

Aw fuck no. 'Stop there,' she said. 'I'm not going to waste my breath explaining to you all the many, many reasons why that is not going to happen. But it is never going to happen. It is over. Dead.' *How many times?*

His mouth tightened. 'You're here, aren't you?'

'I'm here because whatever else you are, you are still Sammy's dad and I don't want you to chuck that away.'

'I'm not chucking anything away.'

'Dave, he doesn't want to see you. You get pissed and emotional and it freaks him out.'

'You don't know what you're talking about–'

'He told me.' She fought to keep her voice level. 'You have a problem, accept it, and deal with it. You won't see him until you do.'

'You're giving me a fucking ultimatum!' He stood up, walked to the bay window, turned back to face her. 'I can stop, I can cut down. You're blowing it out of all proportion.'

'No,' she said. 'How long before you fuck up at work and have that meeting with HR? How long before your mother kicks you out and you end up sleeping in some B&B?'

'That's never going to happen, I won't let it happen,' he insisted.

'You won't be able to stop it, not unless you stop drinking. This murder I'm working, that guy had a business, family, the

205

works. He lost everything. He was living on the streets–'

'That's not me,' he said.

'Don't be an idiot, Dave. You're not that stupid. You've seen it happen, Willie Deason, Patrick Barker. Or what about Julia Dalloway?' Officers they'd both known, two of them dead from drink-related illnesses, the third a recovering alcoholic, a dry drunk back on the job. 'There's a million excuses,' she said, 'boozy lunches, a snifter at sundown, something in the morning coffee, something to celebrate, to commiserate, a good day, tough day, take the edge off. I like a drink as much as the next person but you are drinking way too much. You're off your face. Every day. Every time I see you.'

'Look,' he said angrily, 'if you've said your piece–'

'You pissed yourself,' she said quietly.

He glanced down. *Oh, sweet Jesus.* 'Not now. When you came to my office. You couldn't stand, you fell over and you pissed your pants.'

He shut his eyes and walked back to the chair and sat down. He didn't speak for long enough, his gaze lowered so she could not read it, and when he finally looked up she saw tears in his eyes. Gill's stomach flipped over. Her instinct was to go to him, comfort him, but she knew that would be dangerous and could be misconstrued. Used to buoy up Dave's fantasy of a second chance with her.

'It's all shit,' he said gruffly.

'That's the booze talking,' she said. 'Sort it, Dave, AA, rehab, whatever you decide but don't get in touch until you have. I mean it.'

He glanced at her then away, the tension in him gone, and an air of defeat in its place.

She left him sitting there. She could not judge whether anything she'd said had sunk in. Had no idea whether he'd heard the wake-up call or whether he had further to fall before he acknowledged his addiction and took action towards recovery.

Day 5

Monday 14 May

16

Gill was dreaming, more of a nightmare than a dream. Dave had moved back in with her, bringing the whore of Pendlebury and her spawn, and Gill was having to sleep on the sofa while they took the master bedroom. The smoke alarm was beeping but Gill couldn't find it. She ran upstairs and down again, Dave shouting at her to turn the bloody thing off but she couldn't see it. They'd all die in their beds. She came awake to find her phone ringing, the middle of the night. She picked it up. Trevor Hyatt, the fire investigation officer.

'Trevor?'

'Sorry to be so early but I knew you'd want to hear.'

'What?'

'The warehouse fire, Shuttling Way...'

'Yes?' She was expecting, if anything, him to say it was definitely the same accelerant or even that someone had seen the twins, but wouldn't that wait till morning?

'We found two bodies.'

Oh my God. Her heart rate doubled. She was wide awake now, mind spinning, trying to grasp all the ramifications.

'I'm on my way.'

She snapped on the light.

Two bodies. Two more bodies. What the fuck was going on?

The warehouse was a huge structure, five storeys high and extending for over a hundred yards alongside the canal. In its heyday it would've housed bales of cotton for transport by the waterway to the ports at Manchester and Liverpool. Lorries would've done the job latterly.

Surveying the scene in the first light of dawn reminded Gill of photographs from the Second World War, bombings in Coventry and Dresden, everything shattered, black.

Hyatt led her along a dedicated pathway to the building. He explained that it had last been occupied by a foam and furniture wholesaler who used part of the ground floor. Remnants of foam and pieces of furniture were left when the business moved out. These had fed the fire, making the blaze fierce enough to consume the floors above. The whole thing had collapsed in. She fancied she could smell the plastic chemical smell of the foam in the stink of burning that filled the space.

The bodies had, in effect, been excavated from the layer of ash and cinders. A few feet apart, opposite each other, they were crouched, curled, half reclining. Macabre in their positioning. Skulls bent forward, the skin stretched like scorched parchment tight over the skeleton. Here and there a glint of bone. Adults, Gill thought from the length of the leg bones, but beyond that it was impossible to tell anything.

'Sitting in chairs, we think. See the springs.' Hyatt pointed out the spiral of metal beside one of the bodies. As the seats burned, they'd collapsed back and the victims with them.

Shot? she wondered.

'I'd like the CSIs to take the bodies and all the debris around them,' she glanced at him, 'like we did at the chapel.'

He nodded.

'You're sure it's arson?' she said.

'Looks like it. The seat of the fire is here.' He pointed between the two figures where the floor itself had been eaten away. 'Looks like an accelerant was used and the foam on the chairs would also act to speed up the fire.'

'Petrol?' Gill asked.

'I don't think so. I want to do some more investigation here but this looks like a smaller initial ignition area, whereas with the Old Chapel we had petrol splashed around and when that goes up it's the vapour that ignites. This is more localized. And we've got melted glass.'

She looked as he indicated a shiny blob in

the ash. 'Could be innocuous, a drinking glass. But it could be a bottle.'

'Molotov cocktail,' she said.

'That sort of thing. We'll get an analysis done, we can do a headspace gas chromatograph; might be able to find out what it is.'

Gill knew the rudiments of the test, a way to identify and quantify volatile compounds. 'If it's not petrol then what is it?'

'Could be paint thinner, acetone or a kerosene-based accelerant,' he said.

'Kerosene?' Gill asked.

'You're looking at paraffin for heaters or lamps or lighter fuel, the sort of thing people use to light a barbecue.'

Neil Perry had made a comment about a barbecue when Rachel asked him to account for the petrol on his clothes. 'We only found petrol on the Perrys' clothing. No kerosene.'

'True. Of course a device can be thrown from some distance so you don't get that splashback effect you have when emptying a petrol can.'

'Light the blue touch paper and stand well back,' Gill said. 'Have you been doing any house-to-house yet?'

'We have, I'll get everything sent through to you. You'll merge the inquiries?'

'If it's murder,' she said.

'You think it is?'

'Don't you?'

He tipped his head in agreement.

'Let's see what the pathologist finds.' She opened her phone, ready to rouse all and sundry from their beds to get the investigation moving.

The post-mortems gave Gill a sense of déjà vu. The smell of charred flesh in the room, the blackened forms on the tables. The procedures were carried out on each body in turn. Gradually, methodically, Garvey built up a profile of the victims.

Victim number one was a woman, height five foot nine, evidence of historic injuries to the right arm and leg. Teeth showed poor dental care. African ethnicity. Age estimated between eighteen and twenty-five. Victim number two, male, height five foot ten, evidence of malnourishment with poor bone density. The same ethnicity and estimated age.

X-rays showed that both victims had been shot.

The woman had two bullets in her chest cavity.

The man had one in his chest and one in his head.

It was murder.

Nobody was grumbling about being pulled into work so early, certainly not Rachel. This was what she lived for. The court had granted them a further thirty-six hours to question the Perry brothers for the Kavanagh murder and Rachel reckoned that they nearly had enough to discuss going to charge with the CPS. Sometimes the Crown Prosecution Service were too cautious, bleating about insufficient evidence and letting people walk – that was the pits. When after all the work, all the hours they put in, gathering evidence, interviewing, carefully putting it together, the scumbags waltzed off, scot-free, a smirk on their face and a hard-on, no doubt: fucked the system.

Now this had blown up. Two more bodies, same neck of the woods, same MO. It was possible the twins would be looking at charges on three counts of murder, not just one. The boss had barely got her coat off and she was bringing them up to speed. They had drafted in extra officers to cope with the challenge of working three murder investigations.

'Fire investigation officers had already been speaking to the community when this was believed to be simply a case of arson,' the boss said. 'Summaries of those interviews, along with any significant intelligence, will be available within the hour. I understand that the Perry brothers are persons of interest but as yet we have not had any information putting them at the warehouse on Friday. What we have been hearing is that the premises were being used for drug-dealing in the last few months.'

No surprise there, Rachel, thought. An abandoned building was a magnet for junkies and other lowlifes. Off the radar, no water or electric but walls and a roof, somewhere to shelter. Attractive to dealers too, off the streets and out of sight, away from prying eyes. Though these days some of them were bold as brass, hanging about on street corners, and taking orders with kids on bikes to run the drugs. Students of *The Wire*.

'This could be a drug dispute?' Rachel said.

'Possible,' said the boss.

'Intel are still saying no known hostile takeovers,' Mitch said.

'Maybe this is it, just kicking off.' Rachel again.

'Could be our two victims were dealers then someone robbed them,' said Lee.

'If they've been dealing for some months they're going to be getting the supply from Marcus Williams,' Mitch said. 'Anyone mad enough to go after them must have a death wish themselves. Williams is still in pole position and he's vicious as a pitbull when he's crossed.'

'Allegedly,' the boss said, reminding them Williams had never been charged with any crime. 'And his lieutenant, Stanley Keane, allegedly, does the nasty when needs must. As I said, we have no ID for our two victims so that is top of the list.' Godzilla went on, 'The crimes look very similar except for one significant difference: the accelerant used was not the same in both cases.'

'Ballistics?' Rachel was wondering if the same gun had been used.

'They're busy with it now,' the boss said.

Kevin spoke up. 'The men in prison for the post office robbery–'

'In which the same weapon was used,' the boss said.

'Refused to comment,' Kevin said.

Fancy that, thought Rachel. 'Pretty safe bet they got it from Tandy.'

'You want a flutter, Rachel, get yourself down Paddy Power's. We need facts, not bets,' Her Maj said, 'and we need Tandy.'

'Not answering his phone,' Mitch said.

'Maybe he's left the area,' said Kevin.

'Why?' asked the boss.

'Because of the murder, he doesn't want to be taken down with the Perry twins,' Kevin said.

'Where would he go? Has he any associates elsewhere, family?'

'No,' Pete said, 'stays close to home when he's not banged up.'

The boss shook her head, irritated at their failure to find the man.

Without Janet available as acting sergeant, Her Maj asked for a volunteer to allocate actions and Lee volunteered. Rachel didn't.

She didn't want to be coordinating other people, she wanted to be back out there, finding the dirt on Neil and Noel Perry that would see them looking at life in prison.

'As we did with Kavanagh,' the boss said, 'talk to local organizations and residents, churches, charities, whatever. Do any of them recall a young, black couple? Of course this will be bad for public confidence and for our crime stats. The Chief Con and the reducing crime bods can worry about the statistics, we can't do anything about that. But what we can do, in terms of community morale and public relations, is put every ounce of energy into finding out who killed these people and bringing them to trial. Any questions?'

The room was quiet.

'Before you go, I need to make you aware that Janet Scott is taking some personal time. As most of you will know by now, the teenager Olivia Canning was a close friend of Janet's daughter. For the purposes of that investigation, Janet is a civilian. Should you acquire any information on that inquiry from our colleagues on division, those details shall remain confidential from Janet.' The boss swivelled her head this way and that, checking they'd taken in what she was saying. 'Regarding our friends in the fourth estate...'

Godzilla's phone rang, she broke off and

held up a hand for quiet.

'You're sure,' she said, 'both of them?'

Rachel could see light gleam in her eyes. Godzilla palmed her phone. 'Analysis on the bullets shows the same weapon used in all three murders. We've got a series. Now let's see what you can bring me. Quick as you like.'

The warehouse stood between the main road, Shuttling Way, and the canal. Derby Fold Lane bordered the plot to the west, leading from the dual carriageway and over the canal bridge. Where the lane descended from the bridge was the spot that the fire investigation officers had identified as the point of entry. The boards there had rotted away at the base and someone had smashed a hole big as a doorway to gain access to the site. So anyone going to the building would have to go along Derby Fold Lane. To the east was a small terraced row, Pocklington Street. Any view those houses might once have had across the yard to the building had since been blocked by high sheet fencing, so only the upper floors were visible. Rachel turned the map around and checked. The land at the far side of Derby Fold Lane was unoccupied scrubland. Which left Manton Street over the canal as the nearest houses likely to have seen any comings and goings. Manton Street, where Greg Tandy lived with his wife and son.

Rachel began there.

Connor answered the door, rolling his eyes when he saw who it was.

'Your dad back?' Rachel said.

'No.'

'You seen him since yesterday?'

'No.'

'What about your mum, she in?'

'Work,' he sniffed.

'The bodies of two people were recovered from the fire at the warehouse,' Rachel said, 'a man and woman, we're trying to identify them. Early twenties, both black.'

'Dunno,' he shrugged.

'Not seen anyone like that about?' Rachel said.

'They all look the same to me, niggers,' he said. Trying to wind her up?

'What about the warehouse, people coming and going there, you notice that?'

He pulled a face, shook his head. She didn't believe him.

'I've got to go,' he said.

'Where?' Rachel said.

'School.'

'You're late, aren't you?'

He didn't answer, rubbed his nose.

'Word has it the warehouse was used for drug-dealing. You know anything about that?' Rachel said.

'No.' Something altered in his eyes.

'You've not been there, buying stuff?'

'No,' he scowled.

'So, if we were to arrange a drugs test, you'd be clear?'

'You can't do that without permission, I'm only fourteen,' he said. 'Need an appropriate adult with me, too.'

'Been reading up on your rights, have you?' she said. 'Look, I just don't think you've been very honest with me, and that makes me think you might have something to hide. Maybe you do know where your dad is but you're not saying, maybe you know something about the drug deals but you're too scared to say.'

'I'm not scared,' he sneered.

'But you are concealing something and that would warrant us cautioning you and holding you for formal questioning. Your mum could be the appropriate adult if you wish.'

He set his jaw, the edges of his lips whitened with tension. 'I don't know where he is,' he said, 'I swear.'

Rachel didn't respond, she wanted more.

He cleared his throat. 'But I seen them about, the blacks.'

'You know their names?'

He shook his head.

'Come on Connor.'

'It's the fucking truth!' His face flushed red. 'Look, there's this girl, Shirelle, she used to hang with the bloke. Talk to her.'

'Shirelle who?'

He shook his head.

'Where will I find her?'

'She lives in Hawkins,' he said.

The high-rise, Hawkins Tower. Over a hundred flats. 'That really narrows it down,' Rachel said.

'That's all I can tell you.'

'What's she look like, this Shirelle?'

'Half-caste,' he said.

'How old?'

'Twenty?' he said uncertainly. 'I didn't tell you, and I'm no grass.' For a moment he sounded very young, scared. He bit his lip. How many times had he answered the door to the police already? His father not out five minutes and already looking at a recall. *Return to jail, do not pass go.*

'You ever done any boxing?' Rachel said.

'What?' He was thrown by the change of topic.

'Boxing. The gym in town. They do boxing, self-defence.'

'I can look after myself.' He bristled, probably thought she was calling him a weed.

'Not saying you can't. Bet you'd be a good bantamweight with the right training.'

'What's this? Olympics crap?'

The country was awash with promotional stuff for the London Olympics. 'No,' Rachel said. 'You should give it a go. There's five-aside too, table football. What else you going to do? Hang around here and end up getting into trouble?'

'You a social worker?' he said scornfully.

'Try it,' Rachel said.

'Fuck off.'

'I dare you.'

He looked askance.

'Bring the bike, we're building a stunt circuit. You can do stunts, can't you?'

He glared at her.

'Open three till ten every day. Doesn't have to be like this,' she said. Cursing herself as the words left her mouth, sounding all touchy-feely like Alison. He looked at her, raised eyebrows, a hint of humour in his eyes. Why did she bother? She'd tried this sort of thing with Dom and that had worked out really well hadn't it?

17

Janet sat with Elise and two detectives from division in the soft interview room at Middleton police station.

DC Goodman was doing most of the questioning. Young – well, young in Janet's eyes – and mild-mannered with a slight stutter, he had explained to Elise her rights, why she was there and that she was free to leave at any time.

His colleague, DC Khan, spoke to introduce herself, then kept notes and listened intently to Elise's answers.

So far Elise herself had been subdued, cooperative. No tears today, though she sometimes came close. There were tissues on the table, water and glasses.

'Then we went to get a drink in the kitchen,' Elise said.

'What did you have?'

'Cider,' she said.

'And Olivia?'

'Same.'

'And then?'

'We talked to some people there and then went in the living room. Someone was playing music, on decks,' she said. 'We got another drink, more people came and then this girl was going round, talking to people and selling things, drugs.' Her voice wavered. 'Olivia said we should try some, to have a laugh. The girl stopped by us and she said, "What are you after?" Olivia said, "Something for the party," and the girl held up some pills with smileys on. "Es," she said. I said, "No, it's all right." I didn't want to get them but then she said, "How about some Paradise?" We didn't know what she meant. Then she showed us these tablets, said it was legal, there was no law against taking it or buying or selling it. And that it would put a smile on our faces like E. I thought maybe she was making it up, but she said check it online if you want to, everyone's selling it, you go into Headspace in town and you can get it there. It just sounded better. So we said yes.'

'How much did you get?' DC Goodman asked.

'Two each, ten pounds altogether,' Elise said.

'And who paid?'

'Me, I did,' she said, glancing at Janet, her face clouded with misery.

'Can you describe the person who sold you the drugs?' DC Goodman said.

'She wasn't as tall as me, she had black hair, wavy. I think she was mixed race. I don't remember anything else.'

'Did you hear anyone use a name?' DC Goodman said.

'No.'

'What did she do after you bought the drugs?' he said.

'She carried on into the other room. Then she went,' Elise said.

'You saw her leave?'

'Yes.'

Home delivery, someone at the party knew a dealer to call on for the occasion.

'What happened then?' DC Goodman said.

'We took the stuff and we sat on the stairs

for a bit, just hanging out and erm ... Olivia said she felt dizzy, and I said...' Elise gulped.

Janet could feel the mounting tension in her.

'..."Isn't that the point?" We thought it was really funny and laughed but then she said she felt worse. She said she was cold but when I felt her head she was really hot so I said to get a drink of water. We went in the kitchen and erm...' a wobble in her voice, 'then she, then she had the fit. Some people thought she was messing about but she wasn't and then she wasn't talking or answering. And I rang Mum and then the ambulance.'

'You both took the drugs?' he said.

'Yes.'

'And you didn't expect there'd be any harmful effects?' DC Goodman said.

'No. We thought it would be fun.'

'Thank you. We're going to get your statement written up and then you'll be asked to check it, tell us if anything isn't correct or if you'd forgotten anything, and then you'll sign it. If you do that you are also agreeing to testify in court, if required.'

Janet had lost count of the number of times she'd said the very same words. Elise nodded vigorously. Janet felt a flicker of fear. If charges were brought against the dealer, Elise could be in a vulnerable position, people might try to prevent her from giving

evidence. Elise, naïve, sheltered, was unaware of this.

It might not get that far, Janet told herself,
and they might not need Elise as a witness.
Charges would focus on drugs banned by
law, there must be other youngsters from
the party who had bought illegal drugs, who
would be witnesses to that. If it did come to
a trial and they wanted Elise for some
reason, they could ask for special measures,
so she could give evidence anonymously
from a video link or from behind screens.

'Mum,' Elise said, while they were waiting,
'could we get a card for Vivien and Ken, is
that what people do?'

'Yes, if you'd like to.'

Elise gave a nod.

DC Goodman returned and Elise read
through the statement and signed it.

'What happens now?' Janet asked him, for
Elise's benefit rather than her own.

'We've some more inquiries to make. When
those are completed, we consult with the
Crown Prosecution Service as to whether
there are any grounds for bringing charges.'

'Like what?' Elise said.

'That would be up to them but in your
situation, you didn't break the law buying
the Paradise or giving some to your friend.
You had no reason to expect that the substance would cause harm, you took some
yourself. So I really can't see that any crime

has been committed.'

Janet agreed and was very grateful that the man had tried to reassure Elise. But the irony kept hitting home; if Elise had bought weed or cocaine then she'd be liable for prosecution and in all likelihood Olivia would still be alive. The law-abiding option had proved the most deadly.

Rachel called at the newsagent's first – to see if Liam Kelly knew the girl Shirelle's address.

He shook his head. 'I know who you mean but I've no idea which flat she's in, sorry.'

Rachel was leaving when he said, 'I hear you've arrested the Perrys.'

'No names at this stage,' she said.

He shook his head. 'That poor bloke.' Word had yet to reach the public that another two victims had been found.

Hawkins House was just across the way from the shops, beside Beaumont House, home to the Perry twins. A concrete pile with a buzzer entry system.

Rachel pressed a few buttons, a disembodied voice answered, 'What?'

'DC Rachel Bailey, Manchester Metropolitan Police.'

'He's not here,' the voice said, 'he's still in Strangeways. Don't they tell you anything?'

'Who am I speaking to?' Rachel said.

'The Wizard of Oz,' the woman said and

the line went dead.

Rachel peered inside through the safety glass and could see the lights on the lift shaft changing, someone coming down.

Rachel waited and watched as a young woman emerged dragging a buggy. She swung it round and headed for the door. The child in the pram was huge, fat-faced. Could babies be obese? Rachel had no idea.

As the girl came out, Rachel held the door, showed her warrant card. 'I'm looking for Shirelle?'

The girl blinked rapidly. 'Shirelle?' she repeated.

'Look, you can tell me which number now, make life that bit easier, or I can fart around getting her address from the DWP or the housing office, which would really piss me off.'

The girl seemed to be weighing up the options.

'Might be tempted to get the DWP to check you're getting the right benefits while I'm there,' Rachel said.

The baby began crying and kicking its legs. A grating, droning noise that made Rachel want to clamp her hand over its face. Perhaps the mother felt the same. The girl sighed and said, '311.'

Rachel stepped aside, letting her pass. She took the stairs, reckoned it might be better than the lift, but she still had to breathe through her mouth to minimize the stink of piss. The smell of skunk hung heavy in the building too, unmistakable.

She found 311 on the fourth floor, nothing but the numbers to distinguish the door from any of its neighbours. All painted a dark moss green, probably meant to look tasteful but it served to darken the gloomy hallways even more. There were recessed lamps in the ceiling, protected by cages, and in the one above Rachel a fat black fly buzzed about.

Rachel listened for a moment, heard the faint chatter from a television inside. Then she knocked. She heard footsteps. 'Who is it?'

'Police, can you open the door?'

A pause. 'Show us your ID.'

Rachel held her warrant card up so it was level with the peephole in the door. She heard a soft curse and the door was unlocked.

'What's it about?' the young woman said, arms folded, a frown creasing her forehead. She was petite, inches shorter than Rachel, with curly black hair pulled back in a ponytail. She wore close-fitting sports clothes, trainer socks, and a crucifix round her neck. Her face was peppered with patches of dry flaky skin.

'Shirelle?'

The girl nodded.

'Can I come in?' Rachel said. The girl didn't reply but moved back and once Rachel stepped inside Shirelle went ahead of her into the living room. Rachel glimpsed the kitchen as she passed. Quarry tiling on the floor, fitted cupboards in a high-gloss finish.

Not a junkie. Rachel could tell that straight away, the place would have been empty of everything that could be sold off to feed the beast. But Shirelle's flat was well furnished. Curtains in red matched the sofa and the chair, the furniture was upholstered, plump, looked brand new. There was a chandelier for the central light and a large telly and SkyBox. Sean was on at Rachel to get one for the sport.

Framed pictures on the wall were taken from old copies of fashion magazines, *Vogue* and *Harper's Bazaar*. Browsing the coffee table as she sat down, Rachel saw the buff envelope, addressed to Ms Shirelle Young. Something official.

'So?' Shirelle said.

Her legs were crossed tightly together and she was blinking more often than was normal. She was shitting it, not so obvious until you saw those little signs. She reminded Rachel of a dog, a greyhound, the sort that look like they are dying from stress, about to keel over, but will run like the wind given chance. Shirelle picked up rolling tobacco, pulled out a paper. Rachel's mouth watered.

'Two bodies were recovered from the warehouse on Shuttling Way today. A man and a woman of African descent.'

Shirelle's hand shook, she spilled some of the rolling tobacco.

'We're trying to identify those people. I believe you might be able to help us.'

'Who told you that?' she said.

'Can you help us?'

Shirelle pinched her lip with her fingers. Rachel wondered what the problem was, why would she hesitate? 'Shirelle?'

'Victor,' Shirelle said, 'Victor and Lydia.'

'Do you know surnames?'

'Victor Tosin and Lydia Oluwaseyi.'

'And what was your relationship to them?' Rachel said.

Another pause. 'I went out with Victor for a bit.'

'When was this?'

'Last Christmas. Just a few weeks.'

'I am sorry,' Rachel said, 'this must be an awful shock.'

Shirelle flinched, her face sharpening, as though the sympathy angered her.

'Can you tell me what the relationship was between Victor and Lydia?'

'They were together,' Shirelle said.

'A couple?'

Shirelle nodded. She was picking strands of tobacco off her clothes, placing them in the paper, trying again.

'So, was that a problem – you going out with Victor?'

233

'I suppose,' she said. 'That's why we stopped.'

'Whose call?'

Shirelle took a drag on her rollie before answering, 'Mine.'

'How come?' Rachel said.

'What does that matter?'

'I'm trying to get as much information as I can about Victor and Lydia to help us work out what's happened.'

'Lydia didn't like it and I didn't want to share,' she said.

Could this be a motive? Had something erupted between Shirelle and Lydia or Lydia and Victor? The triangle imploding in violence?

'Do you know why Victor and Lydia would have been at the warehouse?' Rachel said.

'They were squatting there.'

'Do you know their previous address?'

Shirelle shook her head. 'They're illegals.'

'Immigrants?' Rachel checked.

'Yeah.'

'Where from?'

'Nigeria,' she said. Slowly she rolled the cigarette paper, brought it to her lips and licked the gummed edge. Her hand steady until she used her lighter.

'Were they selling drugs?' Rachel said.

'No.' She glanced at Rachel then away. 'Couldn't they get out?' she said. 'Was it the smoke?'

'We're trying to establish exactly what happened but it appears they were killed,' Rachel said, watching her carefully. 'They were shot.'

A flare of surprise darted through Shirelle's eyes and her mouth dropped open. She composed herself quickly, dragging on her smoke, recrossing her legs, but it was enough to convince Rachel that although Shirelle was definitely hiding something, she had not known about the murders.

'Why would anyone want to kill them?' Shirelle said, her voice fraying. 'That's crazy.' She sucked in her cheeks, a frown etched on her forehead.

'Either of them been in any bother? Fights, feuds?' Rachel said.

'No.'

Shirelle's phone rang, a polyphonic burst of music, a snatch of vocals and heavy bass. She froze.

'Answer it, if you like,' Rachel said.

Shirelle shook her head. 'You're fine.'

I might be, Rachel thought, *but you're far from.* 'Had they made any enemies, was anyone threatening them?'

'No,' Shirelle said, 'I've not seen them for a while anyway.'

'You broke up with Victor when exactly?'

'End of January.'

Shirelle's phone blared again and the girl started.

'Answer it,' said Rachel.

'S'OK, I'll text,' she said. Her fingers flew over the screen, tapping lightly, then a trill of birdsong signalled the text had been sent

'Work?' Rachel hazarded a guess.

'No,' she shook her head.

'You got a job?'

'Signing on,' Shirelle said, taking a drag on her rollie.

'So you can see, we're concerned to try and find out who would have cause to harm Victor and Lydia. You sure you can't think of anything?'

Shirelle pressed her lips together, puffed out her cheeks a little. 'No. Sorry.'

'They were living in the warehouse,' Rachel said. 'What was that like?'

'Pretty grim,' Shirelle said, 'the place was in a state.'

'They were downstairs?'

'Yes, they had some old chairs and milk crates and pallets to put stuff on.'

'How long had they been there when you met them?' Rachel said.

'Not sure, a few weeks.'

'I hope you understand, as a matter of routine I have to ask you where you were on Friday evening,' Rachel said.

Shirelle stared at her, a look of incredulity spread across her face. 'What – you are not serious?'

'Where were you?'

'Here,' she said emphatically. She took a final pull on the fag and crushed it out in the cut-glass ashtray.

'Anyone verify that?'

'No. Yes. Pizza delivery.'

'What time?' Rachel said.

Shirelle shrugged. 'Can't remember. Some time around eight.'

'Which takeaway?' Rachel said.

'Gino's.'

Rachel made a note. 'Noel and Neil Perry,' she said, 'you know them?'

A look of dislike crossed Shirelle's face. 'A bit.'

'Did they know Victor and Lydia?'

'Was it them?' she said.

'Did they know Victor and Lydia?' Rachel repeated.

'Don't know.'

There was a sound from outside the flat, Shirelle glanced quickly at the door. Was she expecting somebody? She pulled her attention back to Rachel and said, 'If that's it...' Putting a brave face on but Rachel could tell she was shocked and upset. If Shirelle knew the couple squatted in the warehouse she must have realized they could have been killed in the fire, even if she hadn't known about the shooting. But she had not contacted anyone in authority to share her fears. All weekend she must have lived with that dreadful suspicion.

'Almost done. When the warehouse went up in smoke, why didn't you tell anyone there could be people inside?' Rachel said.

'I didn't know they were still there,' she said, her eyes darting round the room. 'Like I said, I've not been for ages.'

'Do you know whereabouts in Nigeria they came from?' Rachel said.

'Just Nigeria,' she said.

'Any relatives over there?'

'No idea.'

'Did Victor talk about Nigeria, why he'd come?'

'No. Just said it was a nightmare, horror show and that was that. This was his life now. He was getting by. He wanted to go back to school, get an apprenticeship, but he was illegal.'

Rachel thought of the post-mortem report, the historic injuries. She knew fuck all about Nigeria but imagined war, rival factions, chaos. Sound reasons to get out, run and hide.

'Were either of them religious?' Rachel said. 'For the funerals?'

Shirelle swallowed. 'Christian,' she said, blinking quickly, 'both of them'

'Shirelle Young, that's your full name?'

'Yes.'

'And your date of birth?' Rachel said.

'Why?'

'I need all your details. There's a chance

238

you may need to give a witness statement, be prepared to come to court.'

'No way,' she said abruptly, 'I'm not a witness. I don't know anything about it.'

'You've been very helpful, you've given us their identity, you knew them and even if you've not been in touch recently I'm sure you want us to catch who did this,' Rachel said. 'Date of birth?'

Shirelle still hesitated. Finally, 'May third, 1992.' Making her twenty.

As she stepped out into the fresh air, Rachel considered what she'd learned. There were plenty of questions in her head. Not least how someone on Jobseeker's Allowance paid for designer furniture, a new kitchen and a state-of-the-art TV.

Rachel, in the car outside Hawkins House, called in the ID information on their latest victims. She also requested someone check out the pizza delivery and establish whether the courier from Gino's could confirm seeing Shirelle Young on Friday and what time that had been.

Rachel didn't have to wait long before Shirelle came out of the tower, wearing fancy neon trainers and with a small rucksack on her back. A minicab drew into the side of the road and the girl climbed in. Rachel followed as the cab drove out on to Shuttling Way and headed left away from Oldham town centre.

They crossed the ring road and drove into Werneth. Rachel slowed down and allowed a people carrier to overtake her, putting it between her and the taxi so as not to arouse suspicion.

When the taxi stopped outside a house on Crescent Drive, Rachel drove past, noting the number, and parked further down the road outside a barber's.

The taxi didn't leave and five minutes later Shirelle came out of the house and got back into the car, which took her home. Shirelle went into Hawkins House again and twenty minutes later she came out and went on foot to the other tower block.

Another fifteen minutes and she reappeared and then headed off into the estate. Rachel couldn't follow her unless she was on foot.

18

Rachel Bailey looked very pleased with herself, Gill thought. Fair dos. The DC had got them names for the dead couple and identified an associate.

'She's got the place kitted out like *Ideal Home*,' Rachel was saying. 'She swore blind that Victor and Lydia didn't do drugs, but

240

the word on the street is just the opposite.' She glanced at Mitch, who nodded his agreement.

'I'm sure she was making house calls after she'd picked the stuff up in Werneth and I'm not talking Avon.' Rachel's eyes were dancing, exhilarated by the progress they'd made.'

Kevin yawned noisily, arching back in his chair and stretching his arms up and out.

'Keeping you up, Kevin? Late night?' Gill said.

'Bit late,' Kevin grinned, 'couple of pints after here then—'

'Not boring you then?'

'No, boss.' Oblivious.

'Hate to bore you. What with this being a murder inquiry and everything. Keeping you up late an' all.'

'It's fine, boss,' said Kevin.

'Is it? Fine?' She saw his face alter. Light dawning. Dimly but there. 'Let me tell you, what is far from fine is you sitting here in my syndicate yawning with a mouth like the Mersey Tunnel. That is not fine, that is rude and disrespectful. You want to yawn or fart or belch or scratch your arse, you do it in your own time. Clear?'

'Yes, boss.'

'Now where were we. Oh, murder.'

'The address in Werneth is for Stanley Keane,' said Pete.

'Williams's muscle man?' Gill said.

'That's right. Previous convictions for assault, GBH, dangerous driving, handling stolen goods and possession with intent.'

'Mr Nice Guy,' Gill said.

Pete swung his laptop around so they could see Keane's charge sheet. The picture showed him to be a bulky man with a bushy beard.

'Looks to match,' Gill said. 'I think we have reasonable grounds for a search of Keane's house and the same for Shirelle Young's place ASAP.'

'Her alibi for Friday is solid,' Rachel said. 'Doesn't necessarily cover the whole of the time frame for the double murder but comes slap bang in the middle of when we estimate it was kicking off, going by when the fire took hold. And when I told her they'd been shot, well, I don't think she'd any idea.'

Gill looked round the rest of the team. 'What else do we have? Greg Tandy?'

'Still no trace,' Mitch said.

'Has he got a passport?' Gill said.

'Nothing current,' Kevin said.

'He could have fled using a false one,' Rachel said.

Gill's phone rang and she dragged it out. *Dave.* She killed it. 'OK, let's deal with the Richard Kavanagh charges first. Kevin with Rachel and Mitch in with Lee, hold their hands, walk them through the case, point out the crater-sized holes in their accounts

242

and see if they have anything to add. Then charge them. Happy?'

They were.

Except it wasn't that simple. Noel Perry, on being brought into the interview room with his lawyer, saw Lee and performed in true knuckle-dragging style. 'I'm not talking to him.'

The solicitor tried to intervene but Noel wasn't having it. 'I'm not talking to some fucking ape in a suit.'

'Mr Perry,' Mitch said, 'abusive language is not acceptable.'

'So fucking sue me, I ain't talking to any niggers.'

Gill was watching the unsavoury display, on playback. Lee and Mitch beside her.

'You OK?' Gill said.

Lee smiled. 'Nothing I haven't heard before. You want to put Pete in?'

'No way! No lowlife tosser sits in my station and uses that sort of language against one of my officers then gets to call the shots. On the other hand you do not have to take that sort of abuse. Your shout. You go back in, if you're happy to, and if he won't play ball then move straight to charge.' She had paused the video. It showed Noel Perry, eyes blazing, lips pulled back showing his teeth, the tendons in his neck taut like ropes. *Every mother's dream.*

'A pleasure,' said Lee.

Neil Perry had a sneaky, sly look to him from the start. Cat got the cream. Even the way he sat was cocky, legs wide apart like his balls were the size of grapefruits whereas Rachel knew that steroids made them shrivel. His were probably pea-sized. Like his brain.

'Mr Perry,' Rachel said, 'I want to talk to you some more about the death of Richard Kavanagh. Yesterday you told me you were in Langley on Wednesday evening but we have several eyewitnesses who saw you in Manorclough. Can you explain that to me?'

There was a light in his eyes, not intelligence, not even low cunning but some kind of twisted humour.

'Must be seeing things. Tapped, probably mental.' He gave a sickly grin. He'd not brushed his teeth and they were yellow, gummy around the edges.

'You were also questioned about the presence of gunshot residue on your clothing. Residue which indicated you had fired a gun. How did that residue get on your clothes?'

'No idea,' he yawned.

Rachel stifled the reflex to yawn herself. She spoke more quickly. 'You were unable to account for petrol traces found on your clothing and footwear. Perhaps you could tell me how that got there?'

'It's a mystery,' he said and smiled again. Almost like he was high. But he'd not be able to get drugs in the police station, it was more secure that way than prison, where the drug trade thrived. Half the saddos in jail were addicts and if they couldn't get stuff smuggled in they'd try making mind-altering substances from cleaning fluids or anything else. She remembered the twins' father had died from a lethal batch of prison hooch.

'Mr Perry, have you anything to add?' she said, wasting her breath but it was important for the record to extend the invitation.

He shook his head.

'Please wait a moment.' She got to her feet.

'You married?' he said, grinning.

Rachel glared at him. Tosser.

'You got a ring on. That's just for show, innit? You're a muff muncher, i'nt you?'

She wanted to slap his fat, smug face. As she reached the door, he said, 'All right then, I did it, I shot him. And I set him on fire. I confess.' The grin widened, showing his gums, and a bead of blood burst on the sore by his mouth.

Fuck me! Perry's lawyer looked as shocked as Rachel was but the turnaround accounted for why Perry had been smiling like a loon.

'We would like to get a new statement from Mr Perry in the light of this admission-of guilt,' Rachel said to the solicitor.

'Go for it,' Neil Perry said.

Rachel announced that they would begin

again in half an hour. Which would just give her time for a fag, a very large coffee and a chance to talk to Godzilla and find out what the other twin was doing.

Elise suggested taking flowers too but flowers didn't seem right to Janet. They could send some for the funeral if that's what Vivien and Ken wanted, the card would be enough for now. She said this to Elise, who answered, 'Just a card?'

'You could include a note, something personal about Olivia, your memories, what a good friend she was.'

Elise's face compressed and she turned away. They were in a café. Janet couldn't get Elise to have anything to eat but she had drunk a milkshake and Janet had a coffee. She'd had far too much coffee in the last forty-eight hours, could feel her nerves singing with false energy. Hard to resist though. There was a television on in the corner, the sound muted, thank God, as the news began with Olivia as the top story. Pictures of Olivia were everywhere. Time and again Janet's stomach turned over, still not desensitized to the image of the girl who'd been part of their lives in such a shocking context, still not ready to accept the reality of her death.

'You don't have to do it all today,' Janet said. 'We could drop a card round now and then you can send something more when you've had time to think about it.'

'OK,' Elise said quietly.

She chose a card without a message, rejecting all the condolence cards with pictures of doves and crosses and phrases that she said were tacky. The card had a white background, embossed with shells, almost abstract. Janet had a pen in her bag.

'What shall I put?'

'Keep it simple,' Janet said, 'maybe that you're thinking of them?'

Elise wrote nothing for long enough and Janet was beginning to get impatient. 'How about we send it from all of us?' Janet said.

Elise shook her head. She finally put pen to paper. 'It's not right.' She showed Janet.

I am so very sorry. Olivia was the best, most brilliant, loving and caring friend I ever had. I will miss her so much. And I am thinking of you all.

'It's fine, it's lovely. Come on.'

There were several cars on the road outside the house. More family, Janet assumed, come together in support. Janet pulled in across the driveway entrance.

'Don't knock, just post it,' Janet said. 'They'll have all sorts going on right now.'

Elise nodded. She got out of the car, leaving the door ajar, and ran up to the porch. At that moment the front door opened, Ken appeared, showing some visitors out. A couple, the man looked like Ken. His

247

brother perhaps?

Elise stood to one side. The pair left.

'Elise,' Ken said. He was white, drained.

'I just brought this.' Janet could hear Elise. Then she heard Vivien call from inside. 'Ken?' Then louder, 'Ken? Is that Elise?'

Vivien came to the door. Janet got out of the car, ready to explain they were passing, when Vivien said to Elise, 'How dare you!'

Elise recoiled as if she'd been slapped. 'How dare you come to my house when you gave her ... you. After what you've done.'

Ken was talking, trying to restrain his wife. 'Vivien, don't. Just leave her, let's go in.' But Vivien was frantic with distress. 'She wouldn't have been there if–'

'Elise.' Janet reached her, took her arm.

'I'm sorry,' Elise, her face bright red, said to Vivien.

'You stupid little fool,' Vivien cried.

'That's enough,' Janet said, 'it wasn't Elise's fault. It was nobody's fault.'

'Rubbish! If it hadn't been for your bloody daughter, Olivia would still be here!'

Other people, alerted by the noise, appeared behind Vivien and Ken in the hall. Ken took Vivien's shoulder, she thrust his hand away angrily.

Janet was trembling with adrenaline, anger bubbling inside but, determined to defuse rather than inflate the situation, she spoke slowly, emphatically. 'What happened was an

248

awful, awful tragedy. It was an accident. It could've been Elise who died, or anyone else at the party. The girls were there together, they thought the world of each other. You know that.'

Vivien shook her head violently, not wanting to hear what Janet was saying. 'I've lost my child. You have no idea what I'm going through.'

The tiny body, unnaturally still, blue lips, their first baby, Joshua. That raw terror, the endless black grief. Janet said nothing. This wasn't a competition. She just needed Vivien to stop persecuting Elise. To see how wrong she was. 'No one forced Olivia to go there, to take what she did. That's the awful thing about an accidental death, there is no one to blame.'

Ken said, 'I'm sorry,' but Vivien did not relent. 'Go away,' she said, looking from Janet to Elise. 'Get in your car and piss off and don't come here again. You're not welcome.'

Elise burst into tears and ran back to the car.

'Vivien,' Ken remonstrated.

Janet, stung, turned and walked away.

'Oh, sweetheart,' said Janet, 'she's mad with grief. She doesn't know what she's saying. She's just lashing out. Come on, I'll take you home.'

'Can we go to Gran's?'

'Gran's?'

'Please. I want to go there. You could go back to work.'

'I'm going nowhere,' Janet said.

'I want you to.' She turned her tear-stained face to her mother. 'I want things to be normal again. There's nothing you can do now anyway, is there?'

'I can be around.'

'I know but you don't have to be around all the time. You'll be home tonight.'

'I don't know,' Janet said.

But Elise seemed set on it and Janet felt like a spare part after half an hour sitting with her mother and daughter. Finally she stood up, said maybe she would call into work, just for an hour or so, if Elise still felt OK about it.

'I do,' Elise said, 'I want you to.'

Dorothy arranged to take Elise home once Ade and Taisie were back.

'I am sorry,' Janet said as she was going. She kissed Elise's head. 'For all of it. Listen, it will get better. It might not seem like it now but it won't always feel like this.'

Janet rang and left a message for Ade, telling him that Vivien had lost it, that Elise had sent her back to work and that she'd be home later. 'Be gentle with her,' she added, still aching for her daughter.

19

Gill said two words when she saw Janet in the office: 'Go home.'

'I'm fine,' Janet said.

'You're on leave, go on.' Gill tipped her hand towards the door. 'You should be with Elise.'

'It was Elise who sent me here, and I'll be back there like a shot if she so much as whistles, but there's no point in me sitting there twiddling my thumbs when she's happier with her gran.'

'How is she?' Gill said.

'Gutted, totally.' Janet felt the pressure rise in her chest. 'Vivien, Olivia's mother, had a go at her. But this is what Elise wants.'

'She's made a statement?' Gill asked.

'Yes, this morning.'

Gill looked at her, apparently coming to a decision. 'We could do with you. We've a double murder now as well, two bodies from the warehouse fire, young couple from Nigeria shot.'

'Good God! Just give me something to do,' Janet said, 'please. Where are we up to with Kavanagh, with the Perry twins?'

'Mea culpa,' Gill said.

'Really! They confessed?'

'Singing in harmony and all consistent with the forensics,' the boss said. 'We're about to get full statements, if you're up to another round with the delightful Noel?'

Janet smiled.

'Before you go down, get yourself up to speed.' Gill nodded to the incident room where the latest reports were collated and displayed on the whiteboards.

When Janet went in, the indexers were typing away, inputting material on the HOLMES system, a web of information covering every last detail of the lines of inquiry. Invaluable for finding connections. Other staff, the readers, were analysing what came in.

Janet was familiarizing herself with the day's developments, reading about Rachel's encounter with Shirelle Young, when she felt a sting of recognition. She went to find Gill. 'Where's Rachel?'

'In with Neil Perry, why?'

'Shirelle Young, the description, that's exactly how Elise described the dealer supplying drugs to the party.'

Gill's face was intent. 'Right, you leave that with me. We still don't know exactly what Shirelle can tell us about the murders but she had a previous close relationship with the male victim in the double shooting and she has apparently lied to us on a number of points. We're about to execute a warrant for her place. You can't go anywhere near her.'

Janet was burning to find out more but had to distance herself. Anything related to Shirelle Young she must treat as though it had a great big *No Entry* sign slapped over it. That was the only way to ensure that further down the line there wouldn't be any repercussions. 'You don't need to worry,' Janet said, holding her hands up, 'I don't intend to.'

'Better than monkey man, anyway,' Noel Perry said once they were settled.

Janet ignored the comment, focused on getting down to business.

'Mr Perry, earlier today you confessed to the murder of Richard Kavanagh. What we wish to do now is get a full statement from you about the events of that night, Wednesday night. Can you tell me what happened?'

'We went to the chapel,' he said.

'You and–?' She couldn't put words into his mouth.

'Our Neil. We went there and we shot him and then we set fire to him.' His tone was gloating.

They needed more detail and Janet set about gathering it. 'What time did you go to the Old Chapel?'

'Half seven,' he said.

'And how did you get in?'

'There's a gap in the fence and then you go down these steps, to the cellar door.'

'Did you know Mr Kavanagh would be there?' Janet said.

'Yeah. We've seen him, we was watching him.'

'Why was that?'

''Cos we wanted to do him,' he said.

Janet felt a chill at the casual nature of his words. 'Do him?' she said.

'Kill him.'

'Why was that?'

'Old wino, i'nt he. Vermin. Needed getting rid of.'

Janet thought of the websites the twins had visited, the comments they posted, the twisted crap they espoused. Hate was what it boiled down to, hate and rage.

She took a breath, said calmly, 'When you entered the building, could you see Mr Kavanagh?'

'Yeah. He was dossing down.'

'What did you do?'

'Told him we were gonna kill him,' he smiled.

'What did Mr Kavanagh do?'

'He stood up, started gabbing.'

'Then what?'

'I shot him,' he gave a quick laugh, 'and then I give the gun to Neil, and he shot him.'

'You shot him where?'

'In the chest, aim for the heart, head shot's

too risky,' he said.

'Then what happened?' Janet said.

'We chucked some petrol on him and round about and then we lit it.'

'Who lit it?'

'Neil.'

'What with?'

'Matches.' He was grinning.

'Then?' Janet said.

'We went up the shops, the precinct, could see from there, near enough.' He made an explosive sound, gestured with his hands. 'Didn't take long to get going.'

'Had you had any contact with Mr Kavanagh before this?'

'No,' he sneered.

'Where did you get the gun?'

His face stilled. 'No comment,' he said.

'Where is the gun now?'

'No comment.' A complete change of attitude.

'Does the name Greg Tandy mean anything to you?' Janet said.

'Never heard of him.'

'Even though we showed you film taken of you outside Bobbins on Tuesday, when your brother went in to meet with Mr Tandy? Do you remember now?'

'No comment.'

'We have reason to suspect you acquired a firearm from Greg Tandy on Tuesday, is that true?'

'No comment.'

'Where did you get the petrol?'

He scratched his side. 'Petrol station.'

'When?'

'Coupla weeks back,' he said.

'What did you carry it in?'

'Petrol can,' he sneered.

'Which petrol station?' Janet said.

'Shell, on the ring road.'

'What were you wearing on Wednesday evening?'

'Hoodie, jeans, trainers.'

Janet produced the evidence bags. 'Are these the items?' She read the evidence log numbers for the tape.

'Yeah, them's mine.'

Everything fitted She saw no reason to prolong the interview.

'Thank you,' she said. 'You will now be formally charged and remanded in custody. You will appear before the magistrates' court in the morning. Is there anything you wish to add?'

He gave a slow smile, his gums showing. 'One down.' He raised his hand. Made a pistol shape, pointed it at Janet, mimed shooting and made an explosive noise. 'A million to go.'

While Lee and Kevin went to execute the warrant at Shirelle's, Rachel paired up with Mitch for Stanley Keane's. They took a couple of uniformed officers with them.

Stanley Keane's house was a new-build on an open-plan development. Tiny houses, big cars, 4x4s in several of the driveways, out-size satellite dishes on each house.

The uniforms went round to guard the back and stop anyone trying to exit.

Mitch knocked on the door and they waited for a response. When none came, he banged again, more loudly.

Rachel saw movement out of the side of her eye, a woman next door peering out of the window, probably alerted by the police cars parked outside, blocking Keane's driveway and his car.

Sudden commotion from the back sent them both racing around the side of the house to the rear. Stanley Keane had apparently opened the back door, seen the welcome party and bolted back inside with the uniforms trying unsuccessfully to gain entry.

Rachel rolled her eyes at Mitch and at that very moment realized the front of the property was now unprotected. *Shit!*

She ran back round, vaulting over the little garden wall and scouring the street. There he was. Running. Perhaps two hundred yards ahead, just before the road bent to the right, an impression of bulk, dark clothing. Rachel gave chase, willing herself on, the houses passing in a blur, her footsteps loud on the paving stones, breath coming fast. He was soon out of sight. Reaching the T-junction, breathless and sweaty, she looked right and left, alert to any movement, but there was nothing save for the two or three cars travelling along it. She listened, tried to discern anything beyond the thud of her heart and the swoosh of blood in her ears. There was no sign of the man. *Fuck!*

Back at the house, her windpipe tight from the run and the sweat now cold on her back, she found Mitch and the two others had forced an entry. Harder these days when everything was made from PVC and double glazing.

'Check down here,' Mitch said to the uniforms, 'we'll take upstairs.'

The stairs led up to a short landing, where the door straight ahead was most likely the bathroom. Rachel waited to one side while Mitch swung it open. Empty. Two steps took them up on to the main landing with three doors, back, middle and front. All closed. Mitch gestured to Rachel that he'd take the front ones. Keane lived alone as far as their intel went, an assumption that was reinforced when Mitch gave her the thumbs-up from his end of the corridor.

Rachel opened the door of the back bedroom on to a small space that smelled strongly of cigarette smoke. The single bed was rumpled, the ashtray on the floor at its side half full. Clothes, men's clothes, were draped over the chair by the window to her right. An old-fashioned wooden wardrobe on the wall opposite was the only other furniture. Rachel walked round the bed to reach it. She was almost there when she heard the rustle of movement behind her, felt the change in the air as a man darted out from behind the bedroom door and ran.

Rachel yelled, 'Stop! Police, stop,' and flew after him, aware of Mitch in her wake.

He raced downstairs and had reached the front door when Rachel, halfway down, jumped the remaining distance. She felt the giddy sensation of flying and then the solid impact of the man as she landed on his back, smashing him into the door, banging her knees and shoulder.

'Bloody hell!' said one of the uniforms.

'Lara Croft, innit,' the other one added.

Rachel ignored the jarring pains and yanked the man around. Slick black hair, red cheeks, startled eyes. The bloke from the CCTV at Bobbins, the one meeting Neil Perry. Greg Tandy. Missing for days. He was twitching, poised to bolt. Rachel shoved him round again. 'Hands behind your back. Now. Do it.' She snapped the cuffs on, her hands shaking from the adrenaline.

After losing Stanley Keane, Rachel took great satisfaction in arresting Tandy on suspicion of firearms offences. And sending him to the police station with the uniforms.

Rachel and Mitch searched the house. They found a substantial quantity of illegal drugs, glassine bags containing white powder, various forms of cannabis and an array of brightly coloured pills.

'Pick and mix,' said Rachel.

In the back bedroom, on top of the wardrobe, they found something else even more interesting.

Rachel rang the boss. 'We're at Stanley Keane's,' she said. 'Guess who's been sleeping over?'

'Goldilocks?'

'Greg Tandy,' said Rachel, 'we just picked him up. Greg Tandy and a bag full of guns.'

Godzilla called Rachel in as soon as she got back. Janet was already there.

'The gun we want, it's not with the cache of arms, so it's still missing,' the boss said.

Rachel had a thought. 'It could be at Tandy's own place.'

'We'll look, I'll apply for a warrant,' the boss said. 'Janet, can you step out a minute?'

Janet nodded, no argument.

Once she'd left, Her Maj said, 'Searches at Shirelle Young's turned up Class A and Class Bs as well as some unclassified, Paradise and meow meow or some version of. From what you told me earlier I think we can show that she was dealing. Same as the drugs you recovered from Stanley Keane's house.'

'He was supplying Shirelle,' Rachel said, just like she'd guessed. 'Shirelle gets the goods from Keane's and goes off on her rounds. Maybe Victor and Lydia were one of her stops.'

'Never mix business and pleasure,' Gill said.

'And all that stuff about not seeing Victor since January, that's bollocks. She's just trying to cover her tracks. Though she's in the clear for the murders.' Rachel thought for a moment. 'Greg Tandy knows the Perry brothers, he sells them the gun, he also knows Stanley Keane – well enough to be staying there.' She considered the connections.

'Why did Tandy leave home?' Godzilla said. 'And when? Suspicious to do so when he's out on licence, as is hoiking a case of firearms about. Find out.'

If Neil Perry reminded Rachel of a malevolent teddy bear, Greg Tandy made her think of a ventriloquist's dummy. The large round eyes under the monobrow, the dark slicked-back hair, round cheeks splotched with colour, too many teeth in his mouth. He stank of fags, and he'd buggered up his lungs with it because he wheezed and whistled with each breath. Prison, one of the few public institutions where you could still smoke.

'Mr Tandy, you have been arrested on sus-

261

picion of supplying a firearm and for possession of a firearm as a prohibited person.' She read him the caution and then said, 'Before we begin, do you understand the charge?'

'Yes,' he said.

'On Tuesday the eighth of May you met Neil Perry at Bobbins public house, can you confirm that?'

'No comment,' he said.

'You know Mr Perry?'

'No comment.'

So that was how it was going to be.

'Did you supply Neil Perry with a handgun?'

'No comment.'

And so it went. He offered no comment to all Rachel's questions. It didn't matter whether she asked him about his move from the marital home, or the weapons, or his movements over the last few days. In between the repetitive replies was the hiss and squeak of his breath.

Rachel wondered how Mrs Tandy put up with the sound. Sean snored when he'd had a skinful, but a sharp elbow was enough to get him to roll over and pack it in. But this chronic noise, it'd drive you barmy. Mind you, Mrs Tandy had had the bed to herself for the past few years. Maybe she kicked him out for disturbing her sleep.

Rachel kept going. 'I am now showing Mr Tandy a CCTV recording, exhibit number

JS18. This is you on the tape, is that correct?'

'No comment.'

'And here you leave the bar with Mr Perry and go into the men's toilets. Can you tell me why?'

'No comment.' All that he said. On and on, with his clownish face and his toothy mouth and the rattling breath.

20

'I'll not keep you long,' Gill told the team together, 'but I want to make sure you've all got your eyes on the ball. One slip, one cock-up and we risk losing all the hours you put in, all the work you've done. Perrys have been charged for the Kavanagh murder, they're up in court in the morning, we ask for them to be remanded in custody and then we arrest them on new charges for Victor and Lydia and begin interviews.'

'The only thing we don't have from the confessions is the gun,' Janet said.

'Protecting their source on that,' the boss said. 'What about motive for the double murder, any thoughts?'

'If Victor and Lydia were dealing,' said Pete, 'maybe they were taking liberties, hands in the till and Williams wanted to teach them a lesson.'

'Bit extreme,' Gill said, 'a rap over the knuckles would be enough. You think he put out a contract on the couple? We haven't found any intelligence that links the Perry brothers to Williams.'

'What about switching it round?' said Lee. 'A robbery, the twins decide to help themselves but Victor and Lydia resist. Bang. Bang.'

'They were sitting down, weren't they?' Rachel said. 'Not like there'd been a struggle, or either of them made a run for it.'

'If someone is pointing a gun, you're not going to run, that's an invitation to open fire,' Kevin said.

'True,' Gill nodded to Kevin, 'but also true there was no sign of a fight.'

'They could have been sleeping,' said Mitch.

'The Perrys are known racists. Kavanagh was a hate crime, this could be too,' Lee said.

'So ... what? Noddy and Big Ears are on some clean-up-the streets mission?' Gill said.

'One down, a million to go,' said Janet, repeating Noel Perry's sound bite.

Bragging or more than that?

'Or they're just dickheads,' Rachel said, getting a laugh.

Gill's phone buzzed. She glanced at the display, *Dave*, left it. 'We have no formal proof of identity for Victor and Lydia?' she asked, looking at Mitch.

'No, but surnames used at the food bank are the same as those given when Lydia attended the walk-in clinic: Lydia Oluwaseyi and Victor Tosin.'

'Refer to them as "known as" to be on the safe side,' Gill said. 'We don't want some smart-arse defence lawyer down the line claiming that Lydia Oluwaseyi was actually Lydia Oluwa, and so the charges were inaccurate.'

Rachel nodded and Janet made a note in her book.

'We are looking for Shirelle Young.' Gill glanced over at Lee.

'Not been back to the flat,' he said.

'Not with us crawling all over it,' said Rachel.

'Done a runner?' Kevin said.

'It's possible,' Gill said. 'Local neighbourhood patrols will continue to be on the lookout. What have we got from house-to-house in the vicinity of the warehouse?'

'Dead loss,' Kevin said, 'no one saw anything.'

'Or they're not willing to admit it,' Rachel said.

'The fire investigation officer tells me a fifth bullet has been recovered among the debris at the warehouse.' Gill glanced at her watch. 'Anything else? OK. Coffee run?'

Lee volunteered, raising his hand.

'Double americano,' Gill requested. She picked up her files and went to the office. Stretched to relieve some of the tension in her neck and shoulders. She checked her phone: missed call, no message. She was relieved Dave hadn't left some rambling diatribe she'd have to listen to.

Gill thought of the phone call she had made earlier to Richard Kavanagh's wife, now widow, who had not seen her husband for thirteen years but nevertheless was appalled and saddened by the manner of his death and the purported reason.

'We have charged both men,' Gill had told Judith Kavanagh, 'and we have every expectation that they will be convicted as they have confessed to the crime.'

'Why did they do it?' Judith had said. 'Was it a fight?'

More like an execution, Gill thought. The murder of Richard Kavanagh had not been carried out in the heat of a furious bust-up but as a calculated, cold-blooded killing of someone the men hated, simply because of his lifestyle.

'Did they get into an argument?' Judith went on. 'Richard never argued. He used to walk away. He never even raised his voice. How many men can you say that about?' She was talking too much; Gill recognized the behaviour – not ready for an answer to

266

her question.

'Mrs Kavanagh, I'm sorry to have to tell you that this is what we call a hate crime: when someone is targeted simply because of who they are, their identity, their membership of a group which the attacker hates.'

'You mean like racists?'

'Yes, exactly, but we also use this term for any group who can be singled out in this way, gay people or travellers for example,' Gill said.

'So what ... because Richard was homeless?' she said slowly.

'Yes.'

'I keep thinking about the fire–'

'I can tell you that Richard was shot twice in the chest. He would have died very quickly from those injuries. He would not have been conscious when the fire was lit.' Gill knew Rachel and Janet would have told her as much when they visited but it bore repeating – as often as was necessary.

Gill listened to the other woman breathe, heard her composing herself. 'Thank you for letting me know,' Mrs Kavanagh said eventually.

Now Gill wondered how on earth they might find the relatives of the young immigrants. Checks had confirmed no record of them entering the country legally, as asylum-seekers for example. With no dates of birth, no documents, it would be a long search.

The Nigerian community in the UK might help get word out. Had they been sending money to their families? Immigrants often did, it could be a lifesaver for people back home. Or were Lydia and Victor orphans, or estranged from their families? Whoever they were, whatever they had done with their short lives, no one on earth deserved to die like that, shot then burned. No one deserved to die at the hand of another. Gill couldn't do much to stop it happening but she would do her utmost to make those responsible pay.

She allowed herself a flush of pleasure at the thought of being able to solve all three murders and the prospect of taking Topsy and Turvy out of circulation for good.

Rachel's phone went. She didn't recognize the number. 'DC Rachel Bailey,' she answered.

'It's Liam Kelly, from the shop.'

'Yes.' *The newsagent.*

'We've just found Shirelle in the alley outside, beaten up,' he said 'You were asking about her. I've called an ambulance.'

'I'm on my way.'

Rachel went to the boss. 'Shirelle Young, beaten up at the shops. I'll go see.'

'Keep me posted,' the boss said.

'Yes.' Rachel was already wondering if the beating related to the murders or the drug-dealing or if it was personal. Remembering the slightly built girl, her nerves as they had talked at the flat, the way she repeatedly looked to the door. Expecting trouble.

Shirelle was still there, on a stretcher in the back of the ambulance that had manoeuvred down the alley and stopped outside the back entrance of the newsagent's.

Rachel identified herself to a uniformed officer and then spoke to the paramedics. 'How is she?'

'Battered. Respiration and circulation's satisfactory. Concussed.'

'Can I?' Rachel nodded to the ambulance.

'We're going now.'

'Two ticks,' Rachel said.

She stepped up into the van. The girl's face was a mess, swollen, one eye pulped, cuts across her cheek and a torn lip. Her white leather jacket scuffed and spotted with blood.

There'd be no talking to her until she was back in the land of the living.

Rachel recognized some of the group waiting in the alley, Liam Kelly and Mels from the newsagent's and Connor Tandy. Connor presumably had no idea his father had been picked up and was mixed up in the murder inquiry. And Rachel knew she mustn't give anything away, or the search at the Tandys' in the morning and the further questions for mother and son could go tits up. No sign of

269

the chip-shop woman, though judging by the smell in the air they were still serving. Liam Kelly introduced her to Mrs Muhammad from Soapy Joe's, whom Janet had spoken to, and her daughter Rabia, and in turn Rabia named her friend, Amina.

'Can you all move back.' Rachel assisted the uniformed officer to secure the area. It was hard to see if there was anything of interest in the dim light from the lamp post at the end of the passageway; people had probably already trampled over any evidence but it was still important to try to recover what they could.

'Come down to our shop,' Mrs Muhammad said, 'there's more room in there than yours,' she gestured to Liam Kelly.

Mrs Muhammad led the way, skirting the cobbles where Shirelle had been lying, and going into the back of the launderette. She switched the alarm off and put the strip lights on.

'How did you find her?' Rachel asked Liam Kelly.

'It was Mrs Muhammad,' he said.

'Rabia told me,' the Asian woman said.

'She was just lying there,' the teenager explained, 'when we were coming back through the alley.'

'You were smoking,' her mother interrupted, 'you think I'm daft? I wasn't born yesterday.'

'Did she say anything?' Rachel asked them.

'No, she was unconscious,' Rabia said.

'Was she breathing though?' Amina said dramatically, clutching Rabia's arm.

'Course she was, you div, or they'd have used the oxygen.'

'Did you see anyone else?' Rachel asked the girls. 'Hear anyone? A car driving off?' Had she been attacked where she was found or dumped in the alley afterwards?

They shook their heads.

'Do you all know Shirelle?' Rachel asked.

Everyone nodded.

'She's a local,' Mels said.

And a drug pusher, Rachel thought. Did they all know that too?

'Are you aware of anyone who wished her harm?'

No one spoke.

'Any boyfriend, partner?'

Mels shook her head. 'She used to come in with Victor,' she said. 'Not for a while though.'

There was a moment's quiet – news of the double murder had been released late that afternoon. Another shock for the community.

'Maybe she shot them, Victor and that,' Amina said, a thrill dancing in her eyes, like it wasn't real, unaffected by seeing the mess that someone had made of Shirelle's face.

'Don't be thick,' Rabia nudged her friend.

'Do you know anything about that?'

Rachel said to Amina.

'No.'

'Who'd want to hurt Shirelle?' Rachel said, looking around.

'The EBA,' Rabia said. 'They're stirring things up. People say we need to defend ourselves. This is our estate as well.'

'That sort of talk just makes things worse,' Mrs Muhammad said. 'One lot of hotheads after another.'

'No, Ma,' Rabia said, 'we need protection. You know what they say, take the town back for the British.'

'You're British,' her mother said.

'Try telling them that!' Rabia said.

'The police are here to protect you,' Rachel said.

'Oh, great. Like you did in the riots?' The girl's tone was sarcastic

Eleven years ago, Rachel thought, Rabia would have been a little kid but she'd probably grown up hearing all about it.

'You think it was a racist attack?' Rachel said.

'She's mixed race, worst of both worlds,' Amina chipped in.

Liam Kelly shrugged.

It was all speculation, bound to happen but she'd got nothing she could take back to the inquiry.

'Anyone think of anything else, hear anything, call me,' Rachel said.

'Have you any more news about Rick – Richard?' Liam Kelly said.

'We've charged two men with his murder.'

'The Perrys?' Connor said

Rachel inclined her head slightly but did not commit herself verbally. 'It'll be made public in the morning.'

After leaving them, Rachel rang in and reported the serious assault of a person of interest, then called the hospital and left her details so they could contact her once Shirelle was fit to be interviewed.

Sean had left her a voicemail message: *We're at the pub if you fancy a drink on the way home.*

She did. A drink with her husband at the end of a long, long day.

Rachel walked round from the pub car park and in the main entrance to the Ladies where she gave her hair a quick brush-through and applied some lip gloss. She'd do. Sean probably wouldn't notice. He thought she was gorgeous, told her so at regular intervals.

She went through to the bar and spotted him playing darts with a couple of the lads. She signalled to him to see if he wanted a drink. He shook his head, raised a full pint. Rachel bought herself a large red wine, had a sip then set it on a table near the lads and went out to the beer garden for a fag.

And found her mother.

273

'What the f– are you doing here?' Rachel said.

Sharon, wearing some sort of tiger-striped fake-fur jacket, was leaning back against the wall, fag in hand, and a drink on the table in front of her. She cut her eyes at Rachel.

'Sean was coming for a drink, he invited me along.'

You invited yourself, more like.

Rachel didn't know what to say, couldn't bring herself to say what she really felt: *Fuck off and leave me alone. When I said I'd meet you, I didn't mean every other bloody night.*

Instead she remembered telling her mother to wait for an invitation. Rachel needed the distance. Twenty years Sharon had been on the lam, she couldn't just pick up the reins like it had never happened.

'He ring you up, did he?' Rachel couldn't leave it. She struck her lighter, a tug of wind snuffed out the flame.

'I rang him, as it happens, see how you all were. He said he was coming here.'

'I've no cash,' Rachel said, 'if that's what you're angling for.'

'How dare you,' Sharon said, her face alive with outrage.

'Just a few free drinks, was it?'

'You little bitch.'

'Listen, you ... you can't just waltz back in,' Rachel said.

'You think you're better than me,' Sharon

said, 'you think because you've got a job as a copper and a fancy flat and a few bob you can look down on me.'

'It's nothing to do with–'

Sharon interrupted, 'How could you do it? Your own brother, flesh and blood. That gain you a step up the ladder, did it?'

What the fuck? 'Who told you?' Rachel said.

'That doesn't matter, what matters–'

'Who told you?' Rachel shouted. Sharon was not meant to know. She was a virtual stranger, this woman, and Rachel was certainly not ready to share something so personal, so important, with her. And Sharon hadn't seen Alison, so...

'Sean,' Sharon said, 'he thought I already knew. I should've known. My own daughter dobbing in my own son. Grassing up her little brother.'

Rachel's cheeks were burning, her chest felt tight. Her hand was shaking as she pointed two fingers, ciggie between them, at Sharon. 'He killed someone,' Rachel said.

'He was looking after you, by all accounts,' she retorted.

'By taking a life? By making it look like I put him up to it? I'd have been in there with him if Sean hadn't found I'd an alibi.' The taxi driver who had taken a very drunken Rachel home while Dominic was kicking seven shades of shit out of her ex-lover Nick Savage.

'This fellow, he'd tried to have you killed, Sean says, this lawyer bloke.'

'That doesn't make it right,' Rachel said.

'Grassing on your family's not right, neither. Not in my book.'

'It's got fuck all to do with you.'

'I'm still your mother,' Sharon said.

'When it suits. Not for twenty years, you weren't. You can't be meddling like this.'

'Meddling! You're a selfish little shit, Rachel, you always were. And this, this really takes the biscuit.' She threw her tab end down, snatched up her drink and went inside, heels smacking on the flagstones.

Rachel stared, head raised; blinking back tears. She wasn't supposed to be here, not like this, not with these people. She'd spent years building a life as different as possible. She'd escaped Langley, escaped her family, and made her own way. But they'd all come crawling after her, zombies who wouldn't stay buried, determined to drag her back to the fold. Her mother, Dominic, Sean, they wouldn't let her go. Bloodsuckers. She didn't want to be that Rachel Bailey, their Rachel Bailey. That wasn't her any more.

It was hard to breathe, as though there was no air. She looked at the sky above. Only clouds there, sickly orange clouds and nothing else.

21

Gill was at her desk, trying to keep abreast of the multiple strands of the three murder inquiries and make sure her files were up to date, when her phone rang. The ringtone was loud in the empty office, the only background noise the whirr of the computer fan.

'Gill Murray,' she answered.

'Mrs Murray, this is Secure XX, we've a call alert through from your security system. Would you like us to check it out?'

Shit! Gill was still embarrassed by the encounter with the local bobbies and would rather not have anyone else coming up to the house until she'd established what was going on. Probably a fox, anyway, setting off the alarm at the gate. She'd closed the gate after Dave's recent antics and activated that zone. Sammy was at Orla's tonight so it couldn't be him.

'I'm leaving for home now,' she said, 'it's probably a false alarm. I left the outer zone on today, it can be a bit temperamental. I'll get back to you if I have any concerns. I'm sorry for the bother.'

She switched everything off and made her way down and out to the car park. Her mind was on Greg Tandy. He had committed previous offences in possession and supply of firearms but had not, in the course of his stellar criminal career, ever been found guilty of shooting someone. He was an arms dealer, not a hitman, so what had this been? Had he joined the twins on a killing spree? Or had he been doing a favour for Williams? And why? It was risky enough to be in possession of firearms but murder was a whole other league.

She drove on autopilot. Home, on the edge of the moors, was only a few minutes' drive at this time of night when the roads were deserted. She slowed when her headlights picked out a dark shadow on the ground ahead. A ball? The ball moved, scuttling to the ditch at the side of the road. Hedgehog. They had them in the garden quite often. Sammy used to put dog food out for them. He wanted to keep one as a pet but she'd explained it was a wild animal, needed to roam and wouldn't be happy cooped up. They'd got a gerbil instead, which kept Sammy entertained for all of two weeks until the novelty faded and Gill was left nagging him to feed and water the creature and clean it out.

Gill reached the top of the hill and glanced, as she always did, in her rear-view mirror at the lights of the town in the valley below. She took a turning between the stone walls and stopped at the end of the little lane. Ahead her gate was pushed back, wide open. No fox could've undone the latch. She looked at the house to her left. The alarm box was flashing. The only lights inside the property were the ones set to come on with the timer.

She considered what to do. She would investigate a little further but leave her car ready for a quick escape in case she found intruders. She had a police baton in the car and a heavy-duty torch. She took them with her. She walked up to the gate, aware that if anyone was there they would've heard the engine. She shone the torch along the drive-way that led down the right-hand side of the house to the double garage at the end.

And saw Dave's car.

She let out a breath, felt her shoulders slump with relief. She rang the police station and told them all was well, just the gate not properly secured.

She drove in, and parked alongside Dave's car. Where was he? He didn't have a key. She thought he might be sleeping it off in the back seat of the car but when she looked there was no sign.

She shook her head, exasperated by his messing about. He could be in the summer-house, keeping warm. She needed to disable the burglar alarm first before playing bloody hide and seek in the garden.

After unlocking the door and entering the code on the panel, Sammy's birthday backwards, she listened for a moment to make completely sure that the house was empty. It sounded and felt exactly like it usually did when she was on her own. Besides, if anyone had got into the property it would've triggered other zones on the alarm but only the gate LED had been flashing on the controls.

Gill went back outside, called Dave's name. Nothing. She swung the torch around, the cone of light travelling over the grass at the far side of the garden, picking out the white pips of the cherries below the tree. The birds had taken all the fruit. No sign of him out here.

The security lights snapped on as she crossed the patio and stepped on to the lawn. The light illuminated the lawn and shrubs but didn't quite reach as far as the summerhouse. The garden was large, it went round the house on all four sides. It was something they'd asked for when they had the plans drawn up. The front of the house faced across the narrow road to the moors. The summerhouse at the rear caught the afternoon sun. It wasn't used much these days, usually by Sammy, who would have mates round and set up camp out there, but even that had changed in recent months with the arrival on the scene of Orla. They had electricity out there but there was no glow of light from the mullioned windows.

She pointed the beam ahead of her and walked over the grass, damp with dew and spongy from the recent rain, to the summer-house. One of the windows was broken; fragments of glass, uneven triangles, ringed the frame. She felt her heart pick up pace.

She shone the light and peered in, saw the camping chairs, folded leaning against the wall, the clutter of bats and sticks and racquets next to them and then Dave, prone on the sun-lounger, his face white in the gloom.

The door wasn't quite closed and Gill caught the stink of vomit, high and sharp, as she pushed it open and stepped inside, saw by torchlight that his lips and chin were speckled with sick, there was a pool of it by his right cheek and a patch on that shoulder.

He was too still.

Fear zipped through her, heart thundering in her chest, blood pounding in her ears, half-formed thoughts, risk of choking, asphyxiation, major cause of accidental death.

'Dave!' she shouted at him. 'Dave!'

No response.

In the dark she heard the harsh cries of the magpie from the guttering. Those calls he'd made, the ones she'd ignored earlier in the day, would this be happening now if she'd answered? Would it have made any difference?

She crouched closer, ignoring the smell, slapped his other cheek, repeating his name. Her mind raced ahead, tripping up over what she might have to do, clear the airways, start chest compressions.

A second slap and he groaned.

'Dave!'

His upper body jerked, he made a gargling sound and bucked, flung up an arm, his hand slamming into her nose and cheekbone, sending a sickening pain through her face.

She fell back, giddy with relief, blinked away tears and got to her feet. He was breathing, harsh rasping sounds, eyes closed. 'Dave,' she said.

He hadn't a clue what he was doing. Pillock, stupid pillock. Trembling with adrenaline, she pulled her phone from her pocket and took a photograph of him in all his glory. Proof, should she need it.

She saw then that there was blood on his other arm, the left one, lots of blood.

'Dave, wake up!'

His eyelids fluttered opened, he struggled to focus. 'Sit up, get up,' she said.

He moaned as if complaining.

'Sit up, now.'

With effort he hoisted himself up on his right elbow. Gill grabbed his feet and swung them round.

He closed his eyes again. His jacket was

282

slashed, the left sleeve, he must have cut it reaching through the shattered pane to release the latch.

Gill pulled at the sleeve, raised it a few inches, did the same with his shirt sleeve. She saw the cut, a gash on the lower edge of his arm, three inches long. Deep, gaping and glistening with blood.

'You need stitches,' she said. She might have been able to clean it up and dress it but what if it became infected, if he got blood poisoning? Besides, it might not heal properly without professional medical care.

'Dave?'

He murmured, she had no idea if he could understand her.

'Take this off.' She tugged at his jacket, she wasn't going to take him anywhere covered in vomit. 'Come on.' It was like trying to undress a sleeping fifteen-stone toddler but eventually she wrested the jacket from him and left it on the floor.

Dave swayed gently on the lounger, opening his eyes sporadically.

'You stupid dickhead,' she said, 'what do you think you're playing at?' Her voice wobbled. 'Stay there.'

In the house she collected a damp flannel and towel, a clean cloth and some water.

She wiped his face and neck then made him drink some water. She wrapped the cloth around the cut and pinned it in place. Then she brought her car as close to the lawn as she could and chivvied Dave until he got to his feet. She made him walk to the car.

He was unsteady and she knew if he keeled over she had no chance of shifting him, but thankfully he got to the car and she steered him into the passenger seat.

At the hospital she could feel the fury and frustration scalding inside her as they waited for him to be seen and stitched up.

The staff were practical, distant, unsmiling as they asked their questions and cleaned and sewed the wound and gave him the tetanus jab and Gill knew there was a sub-text: here was a man who couldn't hold his drink, who was only in A&E because of his drinking, who had brought injury on him-self. A pisshead. It was clear from the smell of him and the sight of him with his bleary, bloodshot eyes and from his behaviour, the clumsy gait, the long pause before he replied to any questions, marshalling the words in the right order, the vacant smile he switched on at seemingly random moments to show what a good guy he was. Like the police, a great many of the people they dealt with in A&E were off their heads.

Back home in the depth of the night, she showed him to the sofa. He'd stopped nod-ding off but was quiet, avoiding eye contact. She imagined the tide of shame was rising, washing over him in ever larger waves. She made him tea, brought him paracetamols.

He thanked her, his voice whispery.

'You could have drowned in your own vomit,' she said, 'or bled to death, another inch and it would have been an artery. Look.' She swiped at her phone, pulling up the picture. 'Look. Proud of that?'

His mouth tightened and he looked away.

'It stops now,' she said. 'You're obviously incapable of dealing with it yourself so in the–'

'I'll ring round tomorrow,' he said, 'find a clinic.'

'You do that.'

He gave a nod and she went upstairs.

She ached everywhere, the shock and upset had lodged in her spine and her limbs making it impossible to relax, to rest. She lay awake, her mind circling around Dave and the grief he'd brought to her door, around the case and the muddle of it all, and in the end she gave up on sleep. She showered and dressed and watched the sun rise over the hills and heard the birds greet the new day, hoping it would be a damn sight better than the one that had gone before.

Day 6

Tuesday 15 May

22

'Did you sleep here?' Janet found Gill already at her desk when she got into work early.

'No, I didn't,' Gill said, her tone clipped, brusque. Janet looked at her; she had dark circles under her eyes. Janet knew Gill could manage on five hours a night but it didn't look like she'd even had that.

'Did you want something?' Gill said without looking up.

Janet felt awkward. 'No,' she said. *Pardon me for breathing.* She retreated to the outer room, hung up her coat and logged on to the system but she found it hard to concentrate, wondering why Gill had been so short with her.

Gill could be sharp, critical, but only when someone had done something wrong or not done something important and needed a kick up the arse. She was fair, she didn't lose her temper without good reason and she wasn't ever manipulative or sulky. If something got up her nose she tackled it head on. Janet shuffled in her seat, tried to focus on the statements she was reviewing and shut out the voice in her head, quibbling about

Gill cold-shouldering her.

Lee came in and waved hello, then Kevin.

Had she misheard? Had Gill just been so preoccupied with work that she'd made the remarks without being aware how curt she sounded? Or was it to do with Olivia's death? Had something happened that Gill couldn't tell her about?

This is bloody ridiculous. She got up and went to Gill's door. Knocked and went in without waiting for permission. 'What's going on?' she said.

'What?' Gill scowled, took her specs off.

'Something's up. I'd rather know what it was than sit out there trying to guess.'

Gill stared at her, looking annoyed, a glint in her gaze. Janet held her ground.

'It's nothing,' Gill said, 'just–' Then her mouth twitched and Janet was stunned to see her eyes fill with tears.

'Come on,' Janet said. The ladies' toilet was the place of sanctuary, somewhere away from prying eyes and the demands of phones and e-mails. Gill followed her there, perched against the sinks, arms folded.

Janet leaned on the wall. 'I understand, if it's about Olivia, if you can't tell me–'

Gill shook her head, screwed up her mouth, and squeezed her eyes shut. Then she looked across at Janet. 'It's Dave,' she said.

Janet felt a stab of relief. Not her then. Not Elise. 'Now what's he done?'

290

Gill tried to speak, faltered. 'He ... erm ... stupid bugger's on the piss, big time. All the time.'

'Oh, no.'

'Found him covered in his own sick last night, out in our summerhouse,' Gill said.

'Oh, Gill.'

'Idiot.'

'But he's all right?' Janet said.

'After a fashion. He'd cut his arm breaking in,' she shook her head, 'ten stitches.'

'Was Sammy–'

'No, he was out.'

'What are you doing here? You should be–'

'Pot, kettle?' Gill tipped her head on one side. 'Where else would I be? Not sitting at his bedside wiping his sweaty brow. I hate him,' she said, 'I bloody hate him.'

'I don't blame you,' Janet said.

The door swung open and Rachel came in, paused as she saw Janet and Gill. Janet made eyes at her, tipped her head. *On your way*. Rachel withdrew.

'You mustn't tell anyone. Not Rachel, no one. Promise?' Gill said.

'I won't.'

'Lee and Kevin have already seen him drunk as a skunk on the office floor.'

'Here? When?' Janet said.

'Saturday.'

Janet remembered the smell in the office, how she'd thought someone was drinking on the job.

'He thinks he's invincible. Captain Thunderpants. Like there's no problem, no consequences. I tried to tell him – the job, there's a limit to what people will accept. I went to see him Sunday evening. Told him to sort himself out, to get into rehab, join AA, anything. I thought maybe I'd got through. Obviously not,' she said, shaking her head.

'Where is he now?'

'At home. He's finally agreed to a stint in rehab. Well – it was that or see a photo of him, pissed and covered in his own chunder posted online.'

Janet looked sceptical.

'OK,' Gill said, 'no, I wouldn't but I did take one and showed him so he couldn't do that whole denial thing.' She screwed her hands into fists, groaned. 'I'm sorry, kid, you've enough shit to deal with–'

Janet cut her off. 'Doesn't work like that.' All the times Gill had held her hand, passed the tissues, watched her back. After Joshua died was the first time but many others since then and she'd done the same for Gill, when Dave walked out forcing Gill to leave the job she loved best to be closer to home, when Sammy moved in with his dad, when Chris finished with Gill.

'How is Elise?' Gill said.

'She's devastated. And she's fifteen so of course she can't believe it ever gets any better, gets easier. She has to find out for herself, experience it. It hurts – watching.'

'Families,' Gill said.

'What would we do without them?' Janet said.

'She'll be all right, she's a bright girl and she's got you and Adrian.'

'Ade blames me,' Janet said.

'What?'

'We had a humdinger last night, except the girls were in bed so it was all whispered.'

'Blames you how?' Gill said.

'Because I said we should let them go to the party, because I said we should trust them, because Elise told him that she didn't want to buy anything illegal in case she did get caught and then I might lose my job.'

Gill raised her eyebrows. 'If that were true then half of the Manchester Met force would be stood down by now.'

'What else could I have done? I did trust her. And now what? Do we think of her as a liar and a sneak for the rest of her life?'

'No,' Gill said.

'I know.'

Gill sighed, turned to the mirror, raked her fingers through her hair and took a deep breath. 'Right, mate, once more into the fray?'

As one of the investigating officers, Rachel took on the task of attending the magistrates' court with the Perrys, where the charges against them were noted and the case sent to Crown Court. Rachel requested that the men be remanded in police custody. She then re-arrested and cautioned them on suspicion of murder in the case of Victor Tosin and Lydia Oluwaseyi. Noel Perry looked outraged when she did so though he offered no comment but Neil grinned and nodded as if he'd been expecting it, as if it was some sort of badge of merit to be accused of further offences.

Her mother's voice kept echoing in her head, a nasty little earworm, maggot more like. *You're a selfish little shit, Rachel, you always were. My own daughter dobbing in my own son. Grassing up her little brother.* Didn't the silly cow understand that Rachel would've done anything rather than see Dom lose his freedom, his chance at something resembling a decent life. Anything except collude in covering up a murder, anything except lose her job, which was her life more or less.

While the twins waited for transport back to the police station, Rachel returned and joined the briefing, wondering what the drama had been earlier with Her Maj, trying to catch Janet's eye and signal her curiosity. But Janet was keeping her head down, so in the end Rachel did too. Focused on the new developments they had to tackle.

In the viewing room, Gill was able to see

both interview rooms on the separate monitors and hear the conversations. The similarity between the twins was overwhelming, she could discern absolutely no difference in facial features, gestures or intonation. The only way she could differentiate between the two men was because the tattoo on Noel Perry's neck was on the left-hand side while the same design was on Neil Perry's right side, some sort of monsters.

Lee had stayed with her to watch. Janet's interview began first, Rachel just coming into view on the other screen as Janet said, 'Mr Perry, you have been arrested on suspicion of the murder of persons known as Lydia Oluwaseyi and Victor Tosin, on Friday the eleventh of May. You are formally under caution and anything you do say may be given in evidence. You have the right...'

Gill sipped at her coffee.

'Tandy,' Lee said, 'he was at the English Bulldog Army meeting at the George Inn. The same night the twins were there, Sunday the sixth.'

'They met then?' Gill said. 'Exchanged numbers?'

Janet had finished the caution and preamble. 'Is there anything you wish to say?'

Noel Perry looked dull, impassive, then his expression broke. Hard to tell whether it was a grimace or a smile when he said, 'I did it, I killed them.'

Gill froze. Lee stared at the monitor, open-mouthed.

'Let me be clear,' Janet was saying, 'you're admitting responsibility for the deaths of the two victims, known as Lydia Oluwaseyi and Victor Tosin found in the warehouse on Shuttling Way after the fire which was started on Friday the eleventh of May?'

'Yeah.' He braced his hands on his knees, legs apart.

'Fuck me,' murmured Gill, 'that was easy. Lee, take a message. Tell Janet to carry on, we want a full statement, A to Z. We want to know exactly how the deaths were carried out and how he set the fire. His movements before and after. And motive.'

'I'd hazard a guess,' Lee said dryly as he left.

On the other screen, Rachel was going through the charge and Gill notched, the volume up. Neil Perry answered the first question, 'No comment.' And the second. 'No comment.' Gill leaned closer, intrigued now at an emerging difference between the brothers.

Janet began by letting Noel speak uninterrupted. She would then revisit each point of his story and tease out the detail.

'I went there on Friday, and it was like with the dosser. I shot 'em and then torched the place. That's it.' He shrugged.

Could it have been any balder? 'What time on Friday was it?'

'Dunno,' he said.

'Afternoon, evening?'

'Dunno,' he said.

'Was it dark?' Janet said.

'Yeah.'

Janet felt a prick of doubt. One-word answers were never a good sign.

'How did you get into the warehouse?'

'Off of the bridge, by the canal, there's a broken bit in the panelling there, you can get through then to the building. In one of the doors.'

'The door wasn't locked?'

'Padlock's long gone.' More voluble now.

'Had you been there before?' Janet said.

He hesitated. *Why?* 'Yes.'

'Why was that?' Janet said.

'To get some stuff.'

'You mean drugs?'

'Yeah.'

'Who did you get the drugs from?'

'The nignogs.'

'Are you referring to the victims, Lydia Oluwaseyi and Victor Tosin?'

'Yeah,' he said.

'On Friday you went in the warehouse door, then what?' Janet said.

'Shot 'em, like I said.' He rolled his shoulders back, twisted his head to and fro as though he was tired of the situation.

'Whereabouts were they?' Janet said.

'Just inside. That was their squat.'

'Whereabouts in the space?' she persisted.

'Just there,' he said.

'Standing, walking, sitting?'

He seemed unsure. 'Standing.'

Janet didn't miss a step. 'Who did you shoot first?'

'The bloke.'

'Victor. Where was he?'

'In the place, I told you.'

'Was he sitting or standing when you shot him?'

'Standing,' he said.

'Where did you hit him?' she said.

'In the chest.' He banged, a fist on his own breastbone.

'How many times?'

'Once.'

'Then what?'

'I did her.'

'Lydia, where was she?'

He started to shrug then gave another sickly grin. 'Trying to get away.'

'You shot her how many times?'

'Don't remember,' he said.

'Try and remember,' Janet said.

'Once, in the back.'

'What happened next?'

'I poured the petrol on them, lit it up.'

Janet nodded though her mind was racing, trying to work out how what she was hearing fitted with the facts. Or didn't. 'And after that?'

'Went home.' He shuffled in his seat, rubbed his hand on his forearm where the fancy lettering spelled out the infamous quotes from Hitler's bible.

'Did anyone see you arrive home?' Janet said.

'Mum was out.'

'What about Neil?'

'Dunno,' he said.

'He wasn't involved?' Janet said.

'No comment.'

'Where's the gun now?'

He fell silent.

'Don't you know?' she said.

A shrug.

'Was it the same gun that you used to kill Richard Kavanagh?'

'Yes,' he said.

'Where did you get the gun?'

He shook his head.

'You need to speak,' Janet said.

'No comment.'

'What about the petrol, where did you get that?'

'Same as before,' he said, 'the Shell place.'

'So let me be clear, when you shot Victor he was standing how far away from you?'

'Few feet.'

'How many?' Janet said.

'No idea. Didn't measure it.'

'Was he facing you?'

'Yeah.'

'Did he say anything?'

'He was praying,' he sneered. 'Lord save me!' Noel Perry widened his eyes and shook his hands in some ghastly parody.

'Did you go to the warehouse intending to harm the victims?' Janet said.

'Yeah.' Amusement in his eyes.

'Why was that?'

'Immigrants. Coons. Shouldn't be here. Parasites spreading AIDS. Taking British jobs, houses.'

'You were happy to buy drugs from them?' Janet said.

'Business.'

'The drugs in your home, did you buy those from Victor and Lydia?'

'Yes,' he said.

'You didn't steal them?' Janet said.

'No.'

'When did you buy them?'

He paused. His face hardened. 'Can't remember.'

He scratched his arm, shifted in his seat. It was all off kilter. What he'd said did not mesh with the forensics.

'How could you see?' Janet said.

'What?'

'The windows in the warehouse are boarded up, there are no lights. How could you see, to shoot them?'

He was silent for several beats then said, almost with relief, 'There was candles.'

'Did you touch the bodies after you had shot them?'

'No way!'

'Where did you pour the petrol?' Janet said.

'On them and all around.'

'And they were both lying on the floor?'

'Yes.'

'How far apart?'

'Dunno.' He shifted in his seat again, threw his head back in a show of boredom.

'Approximately?' Janet said.

'Fifteen, twenty feet.'

'When did you buy the petrol?' she said.

'Can't remember.'

'Whereabouts did you shoot Victor, where on the body?'

'I've told you. For fuck's sake–' He turned to his solicitor. 'I'm not saying any more. I did it. Game over.'

'He's lying,' Godzilla said to Rachel and Janet and Lee. 'The details don't stack up with what we know.' She summarized the problems with Noel Perry's confession, counting them off on her fingers. 'One, we've no accurate time of day given for the shootings. Two, the description of the actual killings is wildly inaccurate. He doesn't refer to the victims sitting, he can't even get the number of shots fired right. Three, his claim to have started the blaze with petrol is contradicted by the hard evidence. If we contrast this with the joint accounts of the Richard Kavanagh murder, which were consistent, coherent, detailed and supported by forensics, I think we are looking at a false confession.'

Janet agreed. 'Minimal detail, the less you say, the easier to keep on top of the lies. The only bit that seemed coherent was the account of previous visits and how he gained access.'

'So I think we can accept that he was familiar with the warehouse,' the boss said. 'And he admits going there to buy drugs but his brother is no comment. From what we've seen so far these two don't even fart without the other joining in, so I don't buy Noel Perry suddenly going solo, and committing a double murder. And I don't think Neil has any idea that his brother has confessed.'

'With Kavanagh,' Rachel said, 'they both suddenly owned up, didn't they, couldn't get a cigarette paper between the stories, but this time only Noel does.' It was a weird one all right.

'With Kavanagh they had time to discuss it before we picked them up,' Janet said, '"if it's getting close to charge we'll own up," that sort of thing. But they were already in custody when the warehouse victims were discovered so they'd not have any chance to talk about it.'

'Even if they were responsible,' Rachel added sarcastically.

'Why a false confession, Lee?' Her Maj said.

'There are different types, different categories, but in this context I'm thinking attention-seeking. More stripes on his sleeve,' he said.

'Or is he protecting someone?' This from the boss.

'Greg Tandy?' Rachel said. 'Or Marcus Williams if it is drug-related?'

'So we don't charge Noel Perry?' Janet said.

'Wasting police time,' Rachel joked.

The boss's phone went and she rolled her eyes. She pulled it out, then held up a finger, red claw at the tip, signalling she had to take it.

'Harry, what you got?' she said.

Her face sharpened as she listened, then she thanked the caller.

'What?' Rachel said, alert to the shift in tension in the room.

'Curiouser and curiouser,' the boss said, her eyes bright. 'Tests on items recovered from the Keane house, in a holdall in Greg Tandy's room, namely a pair of leather gloves, bear significant amounts of gunshot residue and traces of barbecue lighter fuel.'

'So the twins kill Kavanagh but Tandy does the double murder?' said Rachel, excited that they might have their killer.

'I don't know if he did but I think we can safely say the Perry twins did not,' Her Maj said. 'Unless some startling new evidence crawls out of the woodwork and starts clog-dancing by the end of the day, we ship them off to prison. Janet, arrest Tandy and interview him on suspicion of the murders; Rachel, talk to his family and oversee the search.'

'Boss,' Rachel said, 'what about the hospital?'

'What?' Godzilla barked, a weird look on her face. Something flashed across Janet's face too.

'Shirelle,' Rachel said, 'if she comes round and I'm at the Tandys'...'

'You're not the only rat in the alley, Rachel. If you are still tied up we send someone else. Teamwork. Hard to grasp, I know, but keep trying,' Her Maj said in a snotty tone of voice. God knows what Rachel had done now, parted her hair the wrong way, but she was glad the meeting was almost over. Eager to get out there and get on with it.

23

Gloria Tandy was not best pleased that her husband was 'assisting the police with their inquiries'.

'What? For fuck's sake!' she swore. 'What inquiries?' She had greeted Rachel and her colleagues who would do the search with the same ill grace as before.

Rachel evaded the question. 'You've not seen him then, not missed him?'

Gloria stared at her and finally said, 'He moved out, Friday.'

'You failed to mention that,' Rachel said.

'Yeah, well.'

'Why did he leave?'

'We weren't getting on,' Gloria said.

Really? Or did he need to go to ground after the killings at the warehouse? Mind you, the fact that Tandy hadn't informed his nearest and dearest that he was down the nick just might support Gloria's account of things.

'What time did he leave?'

Gloria kept swinging her foot, a rhythm of restless irritation. 'Two o'clock, around about then.'

She glanced at the quartet of officers who

had accompanied Rachel. 'What's them lot doing?'

'This is a warrant to search your property.' Rachel showed her the paper. 'Is anyone else at home?'

'Connor's in bed.'

'If you could wake him and you'll both have to wait down here with me.'

Gloria gave a bitter snort then called up the stairs. 'Connor? Connor, get up. The police are here, they want to check the house. What for?' She turned to Rachel. 'You have to give a reason.'

Rachel nodded at the warrant, 'A search for firearms and proscribed drugs.'

'Drugs?' she said. 'He doesn't touch drugs.' No mention of weapons.

Connor came downstairs. When he saw them all in the living room he threw back his head and raised his arms, then let them drop heavily in a gesture of despair.

'Anyone else in the house?' Rachel checked.

Gloria gave a shake of her head. Rachel gestured for the team to go upstairs and begin looking.

'Your husband attended a meeting at the George Inn on Sunday the sixth of May?'

'Don't know,' Gloria said.

'Free country, innit?' Connor said.

'Do you know if your husband had any dealings with Noel and Neil Perry?'

'He's been locked up since 2007.'

'Since he came out,' Rachel said.

'He never,' said Connor, 'they're nutters, them.'

'Connor, shut it,' his mother said. 'He never told me anything,' she said to Rachel. 'I wouldn't want to know anyway.'

'Did your husband, to your knowledge, bring any weapons into the house?'

'You want to ask me any questions like that, you'd best caution me and get a brief.'

'He hasn't done nothing,' Connor said defensively, 'it's harassment, innit?'

'Connor,' Gloria warned.

Connor kicked at the kitchen table. 'It's all shit.'

'Shut the fuck up,' Gloria bawled, 'you are doing my head in. It's bad enough having this lot crawling all over the place without your bloody chuntering.'

Connor glowered at his mother.

The minutes ticked by and finally the police came downstairs empty-handed.

'Would you like to wait upstairs while they search down here?' Rachel said.

'In the kitchen,' Gloria said. 'I want to see what they're doing. They leave it like a pig-sty if you don't watch.'

The trio moved into the kitchen while the searchers began systematically checking the living room. Gloria Tandy's phone went and she began a conversation with someone about a christening, going through the living room to wait by the front door as she did so.

Connor moved over and got a can of Coke from the fridge. He popped it open and drank, watching Rachel the whole time. Finally he said, 'If I tell you something, you won't say who told you?'

'I can't promise that,' Rachel said. 'Depends what it is.'

He rubbed his nose, thought for a moment. 'You was asking about the warehouse, well, the Perry boys, they was there Friday.'

Rachel's spine stiffened. 'You sure?'

'I saw them coming away over the bridge,' he said.

'What time?'

'About nine.'

'You're sure they'd been at the warehouse?'

'Well, they'd come up the hill from there. I seen them from my window.' He shook his drink as if testing how much was left.

'Why didn't you say anything before?' Rachel said.

'Didn't want to mess with them. They're off their heads.'

'They've been charged already,' Rachel tried to reassure him, 'they won't be out for a long time.'

'It could still go wrong, innit. Not even go to trial for months. Anything could happen. I ain't no witness.'

'Connor–'

'What you on about?' Gloria was back, phone in hand.

'Nothing,' he said quickly.

Why was he telling her now, Rachel wondered? Because the twins were in custody and he felt safer? It had been on the news: two men who have been charged with the murder of Richard Kavanagh continue to be questioned on further serious charges.

Or was it because Connor suspected his dad's involvement and he wanted to throw the police off track? She knew Connor wouldn't say anything else with his mother back in earshot. So instead Rachel tried Gloria. 'Your husband know Victor and Lydia?'

'Who? Did he heck?'

'Done in here,' the man leading the search team said and Rachel and the Tandys shuffled into the living room while the police examined the kitchen and the back yard.

They found nothing.

Rachel had done the babysitting and was able to leave but whether the new information she had got was gold dust or dirt, she'd no idea. If Connor Tandy really had seen the twins coming from the warehouse on Friday at nine, did that actually help matters given it seemed evident that the twins were not responsible for the double murder? Or did it just muddy the water even more?

Janet had looked at Rachel's interview with Greg Tandy. The guy was *no comment* all, the way. He was an odd-looking man, doll-like, his round eyes and high eyebrows gave him a surprised look. But his repeated answer was dull and flat, stripped of any intonation.

Janet wondered if she would do any better now evidence was stacking up against him.

Greg Tandy hadn't shaved; his jaw was dusted with black dots like pepper where his stubble was growing in. His disposable suit added to the impression Janet had of him looking like a toy, or a puppet, Andy Pandy, Thunderbirds.

'Mr Tandy, there are two separate matters I wish to talk to you about today,' Janet said. 'I'd like to begin by informing you that a search of the house in Crescent Drive where you were staying revealed a cache of fire-arms, as seen in this picture. I'm now showing Mr Tandy a photograph, exhibit number MG4. Can you explain to me what you were doing with these weapons?'

'No comment.'

'Can you tell me how you acquired them?'

'No comment.'

He had long teeth, uneven and protruding so his lips never fully closed. And he'd a smoker's cough.

'Have you supplied a weapon to anyone since your release from prison?' she said.

'No comment.'

'You understand possession of a firearm is an offence punishable by law?'

'Yes,' he said. He coughed, cleared his throat, a sound like a car revving and trying to catch.

'Did you supply Neil Perry with a weapon on Tuesday May the eighth?' she said.

'No comment.'

'A search is currently being carried out at your home in Manton Road. Can you tell me if there are more firearms there?' Janet said.

'No,' but he looked sick. Because they'd find something there or because his family would be affected?

'Mr Tandy, is there anything you wish to tell me in relation to the firearms found in your possession?'

'No comment.'

Janet nodded. Turned over the page of her notes, skimmed over them, then sat back. 'Have you fired a gun recently?'

'No,' he said.

'Are you certain about that?' Janet said.

'Yes.'

'You haven't fired a weapon since your release from prison?' Leading him along the path, closer to the trap.

'No,' he said, with some impatience.

'I am now showing Mr Tandy exhibit number MG10. A photograph. Do you recognize

311

this bag?'

He stared at the picture, whistling in his throat. Something, consternation rippling through his expression? 'No comment,' he said.

'This bag was found on top of the wardrobe where you were staying. You own a bag like this?'

'No comment.'

'This is exhibit number MG16. You recognize these gloves?'

'No comment.'

'They were found, along with a balaclava and a boiler suit, in the bag. Are they your gloves?' she said

'No comment.'

'We believe they are. We expect DNA testing to corroborate that.'

He gave a hacking cough.

Janet continued, walking him up to the gaping big hole in his account. 'You have just told me that you have not fired a gun recently, yet the gloves recovered from your belongings contain significantly high levels of gunshot residue. How do you account for that?'

He snorted, eyes hot, the patches of colour on his cheeks darkened. 'It's a bloody fit-up,' he said, 'you can't do that.'

'I can assure you that none of the evidence recovered has been tampered with and we have watertight continuity for everything here,' she said.

He shook his head, rattled off a cough. 'It's a fucking fit-up.' He turned to his solicitor, 'I want that on the record.'

Janet didn't give him time to compose himself. 'We also found significant traces of kerosene, that's like paraffin. Highly flammable, sometimes used as a fire accelerant.'

He caught on quickly. 'No way, no fucking way. I had nothing to do with that, with them shootings. No way.'

'You refer to the murders of Lydia Oluwaseyi and Victor Tosin.'

'Any murders. You can't put that on me. I didn't even know them,' he said.

'Perhaps you can explain then how your gloves came to be drenched in lighter fuel and thick with gunshot residue?'

There was a moment when he faltered, almost imperceptible, but Janet saw it in the minute changes in the muscles around his mouth, and the flash in his eyes, the hiatus in his breathing. He'd realized something, worked something out or remembered something. The moment passed in an instant and he resumed his defence.

'No comment,' he said, his lips twitching, reminding Janet of a horse baring its teeth.

'Can you tell me where you were on Friday between the hours of seven and nine pm?'

'No comment.' Face closing down, he looked beyond Janet and into the middle distance. A stare of measured indifference, the mask was back in place. She knew he wouldn't tell her anything else but she was intrigued by his violent reaction to the evidence on his gloves.

24

Rachel reported to hospital reception and asked for Shirelle Young. She needed the ward number.

'Are you a relative?' the clerk said.

'Police.' Rachel showed her warrant card.

Finally the clerk found Shirelle listed and directed Rachel up to the second floor, to the ward at the end of the corridor. When Rachel got there the ward was locked, a laminated notice stated that visiting hours were *2–4 and 6–8. No visitors at any other time*. Someone had underlined *No visitors* and *any other time* with several strokes of a marker pen.

Rachel rang the buzzer and waited. No one answered. She peered through the glass in the door; the ward looked deserted but she saw someone at the far end cross from one bay to another.

Rachel pressed the buzzer again, kept it pressed as she counted to twenty. A disembodied voice answered, 'Yes?' Making it sound like a slap.

'Police, here to see Shirelle Young.'

'Visiting hours are two till four and–'

'Police,' Rachel repeated, 'here to speak to a victim of serious crime.'

'God, sorry. Thought you said please.' A giggle. 'Come in.' The tone sounded and Rachel pushed through the door.

It was a big ward, with the nurses' station halfway down. As she drew closer Rachel could hear someone calling, 'Nurse, nurse!'

There was an air of abandonment to the place. Rachel hoped she'd die at home, or outside, anywhere but somewhere like this. She hated hospitals, the smells and the mess.

The nurses' station was deserted. Shirelle's name was written up on the board behind but, unlike the others, there was no bed number assigned to it.

Exasperated, Rachel poked her head into the nearest bay. Saw only sick people, dozing, drips in their arms. None of them Shirelle.

She walked further down the corridor. The tremulous voice kept on calling, 'Nurse? Nurse?' and someone struggled with a hacking cough. Rachel heard a peal of laughter. In an anteroom, two nurses, one tiny, the other like a beanpole, were heaping laundry into bags. 'Shirelle Young,' Rachel said, flashing her ID to stop any argument. 'Admitted last night.'

'Should be on the board,' the titchy one said.

'No,' Rachel said, 'not her bed number.'

There was a pause. Titch frowned, the other one shrugged.

'I could go round every bed,' Rachel said sharply, 'if you've lost her.'

That riled the smaller nurse, who got all huffy and said, 'Take a seat, we'll check for you.'

The seats were a little further along, tucked in an alcove out of sight. Rachel sat, impatient, glanced at the notice banning mobile phones and checked hers. No messages. No one ever paid any attention to the signs. She wondered why they still bothered.

'Nurse! Nurse! I need the commode!'

Oh, for fuck's sake.

As far as Rachel could tell, there were only those two nurses, and whoever it was had buzzed her in, covering the ward. That couldn't be right, could it?

Then the lanky one was back. 'She's gone,' she said. She was trying to look relaxed about it but Rachel could see worry in her eyes.

'Discharged?' Rachel said.

'Not officially. I think she's just left.'

Rachel's pulse jumped. 'Where was the bed?'

'Near the door.' The nurse pointed to the entrance to the ward.

'When was she last seen?' Rachel said.

'She got her meds ten minutes ago.'

'Oh, for fuck's sake. Call security. She's a potential witness as well as a victim, she could be at risk. She mustn't leave the hospital. You can describe her?'

'Yes, sure,' the nurse said defensively.

'Then do it.'

The woman blinked and Rachel ran. She took the stairs, judging it would be quicker than the lift. The stairwell was empty apart from a bloke in scrubs running up. At the bottom Rachel looked about. The place wasn't too busy out of visiting hours but there were still patients heading into consultations and clinics and others being moved between departments by porters.

Rachel waited, focusing to catch any movement that seemed too swift, out of synch with the slow flow of people. There was only one way in and out, the main entrance. Rachel ran to the automatic doors, skirting past the woman pushing an old bloke in a wheelchair. From the top of the ramp she had a good view of the grounds, across the lawned slopes to the car parks and bus stops below, either side of the road.

She scrutinized people systematically, eyes roving over faces, body shapes and clothing, looking for a match. Her gaze snagged on a figure leaning on a low wall, half turned away from her about eighty yards from where she stood. The white jacket, her size, the shape of her head, the dark hair all fitted. Rachel was halfway there when Shirelle looked round, sensing her approach, and began to move, running in an uneven gait down towards the road.

Not this time, matey. Losing Keane yesterday had been bad enough. Rachel pelted down the slope, gaining on the girl. Ahead Shirelle stumbled and Rachel would've got to her but for a family group, five adults with two buggies, who chose that moment to cross the road and block the pavement.

Swerving around them, Rachel cut into the traffic. A taxi braked hard, blaring its horn, the driver mouthing outrage when Rachel's hand glanced off the bonnet. She felt sweat break across her neck and back, the thunder of her heart in her head. Rachel regained the pavement, Shirelle veered right and back up the grass slope towards the hospital outbuildings, perhaps looking for cover. Rachel followed, chest aching, legs straining, heat in her face.

Shirelle was slowing. Rachel could hear her panting as she closed the distance between them. When she was near enough, Rachel lunged, grabbed Shirelle in a flying tackle that sent them both on to the grass with a thump. Shirelle screamed. The impact forced the air from Rachel's lungs, jolting her elbows, reawakening the tenderness where Neil Perry had throttled her and the bruises from Tandy's arrest.

'What you doing?' A scandalized voice, an Asian bloke. 'Get off her, leave her alone.'

Other people drifted their way, adding their own comments. 'Twice her size, she is.'

'Probably pissed.'

'Let her alone.'

Rachel could smell the grass and earth and some faint perfume on Shirelle's hair and a whiff of antiseptic.

'Nasty bitch.'

'Cat fight, is it?'

'Get security guards,' some man yelled.

'What have you done to her?' a woman said, face like a whippet. 'That's brutality, that is.'

'I'm calling the police,' the good Samaritan yelled at Rachel, phone at the ready. 'Get off her now.'

For fuck's sake. Rachel rolled off Shirelle and planted one hand between her shoulder blades to keep her prone.

'I am the police,' Rachel said.

'Yeah, right, and I'm the Queen of Sheba.' The guy looked around, inviting the clot of onlookers to share his derision. The Whippet was using her phone camera.

'If you want a witness,' she said loudly to Shirelle, 'it's all on here, darling.'

Oh, frigging perfect, Rachel thought, be all over YouTube.

319

Rachel reached for her warrant card and swung it around with her free hand. 'Satisfied?'

Some of the crowd melted away but most stayed for the sideshow while Rachel dragged Shirelle to her feet and said, 'I am arresting you on suspicion of the possession of banned substances with intent to supply. You do not have to say anything but it may harm your defence if you do not mention, when questioned, something which you later rely on in court. Anything you do say may be given in evidence against you.'

The Asian guy stood his ground, face still like a smacked arse, mouth pursed, shaking his head as if deeply disappointed in Rachel and how she'd conducted herself.

Shirelle looked worse in the clear light of day, her face more swollen. Stitches ran across the deeper cuts over her eyelid and cheek and lip. She had lost teeth too, gaps at the front. Livid bruises on her forearms and hands. Rachel imagined the blows, smashing the girl against the hard ground. Boots or fists or bats?

Nevertheless Shirelle had been examined by the police doctor and found fit for interview. A duty solicitor was present. Rachel stated the grounds under which Shirelle had been arrested, and cautioned her.

'You know we searched your flat,' Rachel

said. 'We found a number of items banned under the Misuse of Drugs Act.'

Shirelle gave a small sigh.

'Can you tell me why you had these drugs in your possession?'

'No.' Her voice painfully hoarse.

'What were you doing at Stanley Keane's? Getting stocked up?'

'No,' Shirelle said quickly.

'Is he responsible for your injuries?'

'No.'

'We can help, you know. You don't have to deal with it on your own. And we can keep you safe, if that's what you're worried about. Keane works with Marcus Williams, doesn't he? The Williamses of this world, they sit up there, king of the shit heap, raking in the money, calling the shots, but it's people like you always pay the price. I don't think that's fair.'

The girl was unmoved.

Rachel said, 'I want to talk to you again about Victor and Lydia. We know they were dealing, I think you were supplying them. Is that the case?'

'No,' she said.

'You're not in work – is that true?'

'That's right.'

'Claiming Jobseeker's?' Rachel said.

'So?'

'Can you explain to me how you've furn-ished your flat and paid for a new kitchen on sixty quid a week?'

Shirelle gave a little snort, said nothing.

'From the proceeds of drug-dealing perhaps?'

'No way.'

'We have a witness saw Noel and Neil Perry near the warehouse on the Friday evening. Did the Perrys visit the squat?'

'Maybe.' *Which meant yes.*

'Did you see them there recently?' Shirelle hesitated. She must realize, Rachel thought, that she'd be incriminating herself to some extent if she admitted regular visits to Victor and Lydia, even if she stopped short of saying they were buying drugs from her.

'We've got enough to do you for supply,' Rachel said, putting a bit of pressure on. 'Well, did you see them?'

The girl didn't reply.

'Come on, Shirelle. He was a friend, wasn't he? Victor. Or are you protecting someone. Was this beating to keep you quiet?'

'No. Thursday, I seen them,' she said.

'The Perrys. What time?'

'About four, I was leaving the squat.'

'Not Friday?' Rachel said.

Shirelle shook her head slowly to the right then left. 'You see Victor on Friday?'

'Yes.'

'What time?'

A pause. 'Same,' she said.

'But not the twins?'

'No.'

Rachel thought of the stash that the Perry brothers had, more than personal use. 'Were they dealing, the Perrys?'

'No,' she said.

'Heavy users?'

'Dunno. Ain't exactly mates.'

'They're racist tossers but they're happy enough to deal with Victor?' Rachel said.

'Hypocrites, in't they.'

'And on Saturday you were up on Middleton Road, with a bagful of party poppers. You heard the girl died?'

Shirelle closed her good eye.

'Not your week, is it?' Rachel said.

'It was legal.'

'That might have been, the rest isn't. Class As, Shirelle, you can get life for that. You going to do that for Williams? Reckon he'll thank you for it? Even if it's accepted you played a lesser role, you're looking at seven years. What's keeping you here? Family? We heard you're on your own. Think about it: new name, new flat, new chance. This all goes away.'

'I i'nt a grass.'

Rachel had an image of Sharon, the night before, the disgust on her face, disgust at Rachel. The rotten ache of it inside her.

'They could have killed you,' Rachel said. 'You don't matter, you're disposable.'

Shirelle didn't speak.

'It's one of the lines of our investigation, whether associates of Williams were behind the murders, Victor's murder.'

Shirelle's expression hardened. 'They weren't, no way.'

'You liked Victor, you went out with him, and I thought you'd at least want to see whoever killed him pay for it. Perhaps Victor double-crossed Williams, perhaps he was cutting the product?'

'No,' she repeated, 'he never. It wasn't any of them.' Shirelle was adamant.

'You know who, then?'

'No.'

Rachel held her gaze, tried to see beyond the cuts and the bloodshot eye.

'That's the truth,' she said, 'I swear.'

'What do you know about Greg Tandy?' Rachel asked.

'Who?' But there was a false note to the question.

'He was staying at Keane's. Connor's dad. You know Connor?'

'I know Connor,' she said, 'I don't know his dad.'

Rachel wasn't sure she believed her. Aware that when any probing came close to Williams or his grubby little empire, Shirelle watched her step.

'What was he like, Victor?' With no family, no records, any information on the man was patchy to say the least. They probably knew more about Richard Kavanagh. Didn't even have any photographs.

'He was a big kid.' She paused, but the temptation to talk about him must have won her over. 'Like when we were together, he was still friendly with Lydia and I said, "I don't share," but he just fooled about, like it was a joke. He never grew up.' For the first time, behind the words blunted by her injuries, Rachel heard grief in what Shirelle was saying.

Most of them don't grow up, Rachel thought. Would Sean? Had he? This, the marriage, pushing Rachel to meet her mother, was that grown-up behaviour? He still found farting and cock jokes totally hilarious.

'Is there anything else you wish to add?' Rachel was ready to wind things up, they had enough to charge her with possession with intent to supply.

'The Paradise,' Shirelle said, 'it's been OK.' A sliver of remorse.

'I know,' Rachel said, 'and then it wasn't.'

25

The café, self-service, was cheap and cheerful, not too greasy, ideal for a quick lunch.

'What are you getting?' Rachel said.

Janet looked at her watch, they hadn't long but she needed something hot and filling. 'Macaroni cheese.' Rachel ordered the pasta and a steak and mushroom pie. They took their meals to an empty table in the corner.

'So, what's wrong with Her Majesty?' Rachel said.

Janet shook her head. 'None of your business.'

Rachel gave a heavy sigh.

Janet didn't care, there was no way she was going to betray Gill's confidence. Friendship was rooted in trust. Sometimes she wasn't sure whether Rachel understood that.

'How's Elise?'

Janet told Rachel the same she'd told Gill earlier, including the fact that Ade blamed Janet and Olivia's mother had turned on Elise.

'You want to tell her what's what,' Rachel said. 'If it was Olivia egging Elise on, Olivia lying about the party, then...'

'There's a time and a place,' Janet said.

'She's mad with shock.'

'But for Elise–'

'I've explained it to Elise, she sort of gets it. She just feels bloody awful. It certainly hasn't helped.'

'What about Taisie?' Rachel said.

'She's completely confused. She's meant to be the awkward one. Elise never puts a foot wrong. And Taisie really liked Olivia so she's in bits. Of course she's still at the "why-would-anyone-want-to-take-drugs" age so she can't understand it.'

Taisie had sought Janet out the previous evening, in tears. She sat on Janet's knee, something she hadn't done for years, as she asked her questions. Why did they buy the drugs? Was it like heroin? Why did only Olivia die?

Then Elise had woken her in the night, saying her heart was beating too fast and she daren't go to sleep because she might dream about Olivia. Janet had felt her own body pick up on the panic in her daughter, echoing the same physical sensation.

She had coaxed her daughter back to bed after a milky drink and a talk. Told her to breathe very slowly and deliberately, that it was harder for anxiety to overwhelm you if your breathing was steady and regular. That what you did with your body could help soothe your mind, your emotions. But today Janet herself found it hard to breathe deeply.

Her guts were in knots.

She ate some food, hoping it would help settle the jittery feeling she'd had ever since Saturday's phone call from Elise. What if she was losing it again? Twice she'd been mentally ill, the spectacular breakdown in her teens that had come from nowhere, then the depression and anxiety that followed Joshua's death. Both times Ade had been a rock, helping her cope, waiting for her to heal, believing she would recover, that they had a future. That wouldn't happen if she cracked up now, and what effect would it have on the girls?

'Oy, Dolly Daydream,' Rachel broke into her thoughts, 'did you hear me?'

'What?'

'Forget it,' Rachel said.

'No, go on, what?'

'I was just saying it could have been worse. She won't have a criminal record–'

'Somebody died,' Janet said, 'I call that worse.'

'But if she'd been prosecuted for supplying, had to go through the courts–'

'She'll have to go to the coroner's inquest.' That would be an ordeal in itself. Janet had attended inquests as a police officer, for sudden deaths that the police determined to be accidental or suicide.

'All I'm saying–'

'Leave it, please. I know you're only looking for a bright side but honestly it doesn't help,' she said sharply.

Rachel looked taken aback. She'd get over it. Janet was in no mood to start tip-toeing around, worrying about Rachel. Rachel could look after herself.

Janet stared at her plate and felt her appetite drain away. She'd eaten half of it. That would have to do.

'You coming?' she said to Rachel, who had polished off her meal.

'Well, I'm not staying here, am I?' Rachel snapped, her bolshie side showing again.

Dave had found a place in a rehab clinic. He could use some of his private health insurance to pay for it, and didn't have to wait. Gill had arranged to drive him there because she didn't quite trust him to go.

She asked Janet to keep an eye on things at work and if anyone asked to just tell them she had a hospital appointment. Noel and Neil Perry were awaiting transfer to prison. The vans did their rounds at the beginning and end of the day, delivering suspects to court, bringing defendants back to prison after their time in the dock. If further investigation led the police back to either of the Perrys in relation to Victor and Lydia, the police could apply to the prison to have them produced for interview. Gill thought there was little chance of this happening.

They hadn't been involved in the double murder, she was sure of it.

The chief superintendent was happy to give them a twelve-hour extension to continue questioning Greg Tandy, given that the evidence now pointed to his possible involvement in those killings.

'Or I could ask Lee,' Gill said to Janet, 'in case Elise wants–'

'It'll be fine but if I am needed I'll hand things over to Lee. You won't be all that long, will you, anyway?'

'You're right.' Gill shuddered, wishing it could all be over.

She picked him up from his mother's. His mother answered the door and didn't seem to know what to say. Gill had no idea whether Dave had spoken to her in any detail about it all. Anyway his mother settled for, 'It's very good of you. He just needs a bit of breathing space.' It must have been a nightmare for her, her middle-aged son suddenly going into a 40 per cent proof meltdown in her spare room, after years of independence.

Dave came downstairs carrying a suitcase, said hello with no warmth, flat and resigned. He gave his mother a brief hug then took his case outside. Gill followed, popped the boot. Once he'd stowed it away, he got in beside her.

The first part of the journey was in

silence, the atmosphere strained.

'My car,' he said, as she reached the motorway heading south.

'Don't worry, I put it in the garage. It can stay there for now.'

'Emma...'

The whore.

'I'd rather she didn't know I was–' He nodded in their direction of travel.

'Wouldn't dream of it,' Gill said. She'd no idea where things were up to with Dave and the whore. Had presumed that with his drinking and general fuckwittery he had queered his pitch and burned his bridges and hence the move back to his mother's. Did Dave really imagine there might be life in that relationship? If he was hiding his treatment from the woman then it really didn't sound like a match made in heaven. In sickness and in health. And what was all the bollocks about starting again with Gill? She didn't care any more. They could fuck off into the sunset together if that's what they wanted.

Gill pulled out into the fast lane, over-taking a trio of Morrison's lorries. Tired of the silence, she switched on the radio, caught the news. 'Manchester Metropolitan Police have announced there will be no criminal proceedings following the death of fifteen-year-old Olivia Canning at a party in Old-ham on Saturday. Olivia is believed to have died from complications after taking the legal high known as Paradise. A spokesman for the police said, "We continue to caution the public against the use of any drug that is untested and can, as in this case, be potentially fatal. Policing the trade in so-called legal highs remains a minefield as small changes to the composition of the drug when a substance is banned means producers are able to avoid prosecution and continue to sell to the public. It's a game of catch-up," said Sergeant Phillip Whitaker, "we'll never be able to identify and proscribe the drugs as fast as the chemists invent new ones."'

'Janet's daughter Elise was with that girl,' Gill said.

Dave grunted, stared ahead out of the window.

She made no further attempts at small talk. Part of her longed to confront him, to stop the car and drag him out and berate him for his thoughtless, selfish behaviour. But she bit her tongue. Letting rip wouldn't help beyond getting rid of some of the tension wound up inside her. He was sick, raddled with alcohol. Bawling him out would probably serve to confirm whatever shitty thoughts he had running around his brain. Best to keep quiet, and later she would thump her pillows or break something or weep. Alone, with no one to worry about.

He needed support, in her head she understood that. At least he'd get it where he was going, she hoped. Taking him there was the most she could muster.

Another twenty minutes and they arrived. Gill pressed an intercom at the gates and gave his name before the barrier lifted. She parked and turned off the engine. He sighed then said, 'Thanks,' still with that level, unemotional tone. She watched as he dragged his case across the paving to the doors marked Reception. A tall man, broad-shouldered, the hair on his crown beginning to thin.

When he had disappeared inside, swallowed up by the automatic doors, she turned the engine on and reversed out of the parking space. Relief that he was gone, off her hands, washed over her, mingling with a deep sadness that it had come to this.

'Janet,' her mother sounded weird, 'Elise has gone.'

'Gone? What do you mean she's gone?'

'She was going home, but Taisie's just rung up asking for her. She should be there by now.'

'When did she leave?' Janet said, her guts tightening.

'An hour ago,' Dorothy said.

Christ. It took fifteen, twenty minutes tops to walk the distance between the houses. 'I could have collected her,' Janet said, 'or Ade. Why did you just let her go?' She regretted saying it as soon as the words were out of her mouth. Chucking blame at Dorothy was no solution.

There was a brief silence before Dorothy replied, the hurt clear in her voice. 'She said she wanted to walk. I'm sorry.'

'Look, Mum, it's probably just–' All the usual explanations ... she's called at Olivia's, she's with friends, she's got something after school ... no longer applied. 'I'll go look for her. I'll ring Ade. You stay there in case she comes back.'

Janet told Lee she had to go, asked him to cover until Gill returned. She rang Ade, heard his phone go to voicemail as she clattered down the stairs. She wondered about leaving a message explaining to him what had happened but hated the thought of the alarm it might cause. Instead she just asked him to call her as soon as he'd picked up her message. When she tried Elise's phone she got the automated response 'unable to take your call', suggesting the handset was either dead or off.

Janet drove as quickly as she dared. She decided to check in with Taisie first and then trace the route back to Dorothy's. There were a handful of shops between the two, might Elise have stopped off at one of them?

Taisie was in tears, her face pinched with worry. Janet's heart flipped over at the sight of her.

'Hey,' Janet pulled her close, 'come here.' No point in telling her not to cry. Of course she should cry if she felt like it. 'I'm going to go look.'

'Can I come?' Taisie begged.

'No, I need you here so you can let me know if she gets back. Keep trying her phone, yes, every ten minutes, you ring me if you hear anything – and ring round her friends, any you've got numbers for.'

Taisie sniffed, nodded. 'OK.' Taisie rarely cried, most often in anger, when she was frustrated with the world.

'Good girl.'

'Mum?' Taisie became agitated again as Janet reached the front door, a high note in her question.

She needed reassurance, Janet saw. Olivia dead, now her big sister missing, the world must suddenly seem such a treacherous place. Janet didn't usually lie to her girls, she felt it was part of her role as a parent to answer their questions about life with un-flinching honesty. Now she took a breath, put her hands on Taisie's head, a benedic-tion, kissing her forehead. 'It's going to be all right,' she said, 'she'll be fine.'

She prayed the lie would not come back and destroy them all.

Janet drove along the road to her mother's and back twice, the knots in her stomach twisting tighter with each pass. At the back of her mind a question thrummed. She did her best to ignore it. It was like a drill boring into masonry, or a woodpecker hammering on a tree over and over. *What if she's done something stupid?* It happened, Janet knew, too often, more usually to boys than girls but still... In the course of the job she'd attended some heartbreaking scenes. Pushing the images away, she turned into the side street close to the run of shops and parked.

She selected a photo of Elise on her phone, ignored the lump in her throat, and asked in each place, a hairdresser's, hardware store, bakery, newsagent's and Indian takeaway, if anyone had seen her daughter. All she got were negative replies and pitying looks.

Janet went back to her car. Half an hour had passed with no word. An hour and a half since Elise had left her grandma's. Maybe Janet should report her missing. Fifteen, vulnerable given recent events, a witness to a sudden death. She felt a spike of fear. Might Elise have attracted the wrong sort of attention, could someone have seen them going to the police station yesterday? That's stupid, she told herself, you're being paranoid. But what if she ignored these fears and in doing so exposed Elise to danger?

She drove back towards home, unsure what to do next, sick with worry. A band of pain tight around her head. When her mobile rang she braked quickly and pulled in, earning a blast of the horn and a raised middle finger from the driver following.

'Ade?'

'You found her?'

'How did you know?' Janet said.

'I've had Taisie on. Well?'

'No sign, I've been up and down the road. I've tried the shops.'

'Well, where the fuck is she?'

'Don't shout at me, Ade, that isn't helping.'

'Have you tried the common?' he said.

The common, some reclaimed land that had once been a tip, ran south of the main road about a block away. Janet hadn't been there for years and she'd no idea if Elise had. The rough ground had been landscaped and grassed over, saplings planted. She remembered a pool in the centre.

'I'll go there now.'

Janet parked at the end of the cul-de-sac. Carved tree trunks, an owl and a fox, guarded the entrance. Signs warned about dog fouling, fire lighting and camping.

The saplings were more mature now, in leaf too, and there was little sign of the area's previous use save for occasional bits of rubble, concrete blocks, half-bricks, lumps of cinder which must've worked their way to the surface in among the grass hillocks.

The light was dappled on the path and Janet walked quickly. She remembered rightly that the main route followed close to the outskirts of the grounds with several smaller paths leading from it to the centre, like the spokes of a wheel. Occasionally there were benches made of fake wood which were flame and vandal resistant. She met a man with a spaniel and showed him Elise's photo. He shook his head, 'Sorry.'

Once she had made a full circle she took the next path into the middle. As she drew closer she could see the tall rushes that edged the pond, obscuring a clear view across. The water was an opaque grey-green, sickly looking, grease on the surface. Ducks and ducklings paddled in the shallows.

Janet went left, her eyes burning, fists and jaw clenched. Would she be here now, her daughter lost, if Vivien hadn't been so cruel?

She rounded the curve of the shore and her legs went weak. Elise was there, on a bench, perfectly still, her face in profile, gazing at the water.

Janet fought the temptation to cry out, to run, and made her way to the bench.

Elise glanced up at her. She looked exhausted, pale, her eyes rimmed with shadows. She scowled at the light.

'We were worried about you.' Janet sat down.

'Sorry,' Elise said.

There was silence, broken only by the occasional squabbling of the ducks and the alarm call of a blackbird somewhere in the trees.

Janet's head was full of recriminations: why weren't you answering your phone, Elise, how could you just disappear, have you any idea what that might do to us? But she kept her counsel. Elise had already had one deranged mother badmouthing her.

Janet steadied her breathing, waiting for her body to recognize that the immediate trauma was over, to shift into a lower gear. She texted Ade. *All OK back soon. Tell T and D.*

'We used to come here last summer,' Elise said; 'after school sometimes.'

I didn't know. Did Ade? Was that how he knew to look here? Something else I missed because of work?

Janet watched the water, the dimples made by insects, the patterns cast by the bulrushes. Her daughter was here, safe. She could hear her, each breath, see the way she absentmindedly threaded her fingers together. But Vivien ... who would never again share a moment sitting side by side with Olivia, whose life would never be complete... Janet looked up. The sky was blank, a suffocating white.

'Oh, Mum,' said Elise, still staring out across the water.

'I know,' Janet said, 'I know.'

26

Rachel had the police scanner on, force of habit as she was driving back to Manorclough. The boss wanted more on Greg Tandy. The fact that his house was close to the warehouse, just over the canal, meant sightings of him in the vicinity could be completely innocent. Rachel would talk to his neighbours, see if she could plot his comings and goings.

When a burst of static came over the airwaves followed by a call-out to patrols in Manorclough with reports of shots fired in Manton Road, she felt the shock jolt through her. *Tandy's street!*

Rachel took the next left, flooring the accelerator as soon as she was round the corner. This road had ramps but she didn't slow down as the car bucked and banged over them. Protocol for incidents involving firearms was to isolate the area and wait for the armed response unit. But she was so close. There might be something she could do to help.

She flew along Shuttling Way and then turned on to Derby Fold Lane, past the ruined warehouse and over the bridge then sharp left into Manton Road.

As she jumped out she could hear sirens not far away and she saw several people gathered outside the house, among them Connor Tandy and his mother Gloria. The air smelled of cordite. The front downstairs window was smashed, glass glittered on the pavement, the front door was wrecked with bullet holes. The lights were on in the house, the curtains, closed but shredded, billowing out of the broken window, the TV still burbling away.

Rachel pushed through the crowd to reach Gloria and Connor. They looked terrified, standing shivering. Gloria had a cigarette in one hand; when she raised it, her hand shook uncontrollably.

'What happened?' Rachel asked.

'They shot at us!' Connor's words were jerky.

'Who, did you see anyone?'

He shook his head, his mother copying him. 'I was upstairs,' Gloria said, 'getting changed. Connor was—' she choked, 'he was in there.' Tears glinted in her eyes as she nodded to the front room.

'You're not hurt?' Rachel looked at the boy's face, his hands. The cut on his cheek from when he'd fallen off his bike was almost healed.

'No.' He shook his head, frowning, and pressed his hands to his ears. That many shots a few feet away from him, he'd be half deafened. It was a miracle he hadn't been hit. Had the gunman aimed to kill or just frighten and silence those inside?

'You can't go back in,' said Rachel.

'But our stuff?' Gloria said

'We need to recover the bullets, they might help us work out who did this. Can you think of anyone who would?'

Surely, if the woman knew, she'd tell Rachel now, having come so close to losing her boy.

'I don't know,' she said and seemed genuinely bewildered. 'Who the fuck would do this? What's he ever done,' she pointed her fag at Connor, 'or me?'

Or did the culprits think Greg Tandy was still in residence?

'We're going to get you moved,' Rachel said.

'What?' Gloria scowled.

'You can't stay here.'

The squad cars arrived and Rachel had a word with the officers and agreed on where to erect the cordon. 'Take statements from all the onlookers,' she told them. 'Did anyone hear or see anything? Was there a car, or motorbike, any words shouted, anyone behaving oddly. Yes?'

The officers agreed.

Rachel rang Gill but got Janet instead. 'Someone's been shooting up Greg Tandy's, no casualties but we need a safe house for Mrs Tandy and Connor. Can you find out what's available and get back to me?'

'Of course.'

Rachel took the Tandys to sit in the back of her vehicle while she waited for an address.

Janet finally got back to her with the location of a house in Bolton. Someone would meet them there with basic provisions: tea, milk, bread and margarine. 'What size are they, clothes wise?' Janet said.

Rachel relayed the question.

'Twelve,' Gloria said, 'why?'

'We need to take your clothes,' Rachel said, 'get you new ones.'

'Why?' Connor asked.

'In case there's evidence on them, you were in the middle of a crime scene. It's standard procedure. What size shoes?'

'Six,' Gloria said.

'Connor? Clothes?' Rachel said.

'Don't know,' he shrugged.

'Men's – small,' his mum said.

'Feet?'

'Sevens,' he said.

Rachel passed on the information to Janet.

'How long will we be there?' Connor asked.

'Don't know.'

'What about work?' This from Gloria.

'You can't go,' Rachel said. 'Not until we've assessed the risk.' *Which is pretty fucking high given what just happened.*

The witness protection service was, of course, hush-hush. Cops like Rachel knew next to nothing about how it worked, beyond being able to access safe houses in an emergency for vulnerable or intimidated witnesses and victims.

Mother and son were subdued as Rachel drove the twenty miles to their destination. The wind was getting up and bringing rain with it, heavy squalls that spattered the windscreen and drummed on the car roof. Rachel checked in the rear-view mirror regularly but no vehicles stayed on their tail long enough to concern her.

She stopped as instructed on the roadside outside the house at the end of a row of Georgian terraces and was met by a woman who was driving a small van. The woman checked Rachel's identity but did not share her own, handed her the key to the house, told her there was an intercom and panic alarms throughout and handed her two large laundry bags with clothing and shoes and a bag of groceries.

Like some spooks movie. But Rachel didn't mind if this was the way to safeguard Connor and Gloria.

Most of the houses nearby had been converted into offices with brass nameplates by the door. Presumably it was easier to be anonymous here when people were only around during office hours.

The safety measures were apparent: no glass in the front door, bolts and locks on that, double-glazed frosted-glass windows with wrought-iron screens too, tastefully, done but they would significantly increase the security. Intercom at the door provided a means to check out by both audio and video link who was calling, and there were bright-red panic buttons in every room. The door to the upstairs was locked and had a no-entry notice on. But the ground floor provided two bedrooms, a dining kitchen, lounge and shower room. There was no back door.

The furnishings were practical, minimal. Industrial-style carpet, flecked so as to mask marks. Formica table and four dining chairs; a modest TV. Plain green curtains. No paintings or cushions, no touches to make it anything other than a place of transit. Rachel thought of a budget hotel crossed with a clinic or a dentist's. Bland pretending to be homely and failing.

'I'm starving,' said Connor.

'There's bread and milk.' Rachel held up the bag.

The kitchen smelled stale though the pedal bin and fridge were empty. The fridge was switched off so she turned it on. Gloria examined the central heating controls and set that going. 'It's freezing,' she said.

'You'll be cold from the shock, too,' Rachel said. 'There's a toaster,' she showed Connor.

'Don't just want toast,' he complained.

'I saw a chippie down the way. I'll go, give you a chance to try the intercom when I get back.'

'Sound!' He grinned like it was a game.

'Change your clothes and shoes first, put everything you are wearing now in these.' She gave each of them evidence sacks and passed them the bags of new gear.

'I'm not going out like this,' Connor moaned when he re-emerged. 'What are these – Primark?' He stuck out a foot in a blue and black trainer.

'Beggars can't be choosers,' Rachel said.

Gloria didn't want anything to eat, but Connor asked for chicken and chips, or sausage, chips and gravy. And Coke. Rachel wondered if she could claim it on expenses.

She let herself out, put the evidence bags in the car and walked along past the lawyers' and accountants' offices, shielding her cigarette from the wind and rain to light it.

She wondered if there was a link between the attack on Shirelle and this one. All three targets – Shirelle, Gloria and Connor – were on the fringes of the case, close to potential main players. Shirelle knew the murder victims and worked with Keane, who might be a suspect. Connor also knew the dead couple, well enough to tell Rachel that Shirelle had dated Victor. And Gloria was married to a man who was now a candidate for the killing of the two young people. A man with access to weapons and with accelerant on his gloves.

When she got back to the safe house she pressed the intercom.

'Who is it?' Connor's voice crackled.

'It's me, you daft git, let me in.'

'Not if you're calling me names,' he said.

'I'll eat your chips then, shall I?'

He buzzed her in.

While Connor ate in front of the telly, Gloria sat in the kitchen, smoking and drinking tea. Her earlier shock and exhaustion gave way to a burst of anger when she said to Rachel, 'This is him, isn't it? Greg, it's because of him?'

'Why do you think that?'

'What else can it be?' she hissed.

'We're trying to establish what Mr Tandy has been doing. If you can help–'

'I don't know.' She shook her head sharply. 'All I know is he was shooting his fucking mouth off after that tramp got killed and I told him I didn't want to hear it. He could go. So he did. No argument. We hadn't been getting on since he came out,

347

not for a long while before that.'

'What was he saying about the tramp?'

'How it was a good thing, people like that scrounging off the rest of us, scum of the earth. He'd like to shake the hand of whoever did it. He was pissed,' she added. 'Not like it was a Muslim, is it?'

'Kavanagh?' Rachel said.

'Yeah. Not a terrorist, a Paki. I could understand that. Coming over here and blowing stuff up. Forced marriages. Grooming our kids. And they're dirty.'

Rachel didn't know where to start with that little lot. Didn't even try. 'So you argued?'

'I'd had enough. He'd only been home a week and I knew he was up to something. I don't want Connor going the same way.'

Rachel remembered Connor's earlier comments, *They all look the same to me, niggers.* A chip off the old block.

'Connor wanted to go with him. They don't get it at that age. You try and keep them steady but–'

'You wouldn't let him?'

'No. To God knows where, and with the probation after Greg once they find out he's not at home. Anyway...' She ground out her cigarette and as if on automatic took the ashtray and emptied it into the bin. 'I said I wasn't having it so then I'm in the doghouse with Connor, and Greg goes and makes it ten times worse by saying that he didn't need a kid hanging round his neck, whining all day. And now this – whatever he's done.'

Rachel didn't give her anything. Better not to say.

'That's it,' Gloria said. 'If he's brought this down on us, he can forget it. I'll divorce him.'

'What about Marcus Williams or Stanley Keane?' Rachel said. 'Did Greg say anything about them? Could they have been behind the attack?'

'No, he never said anything about anybody,' Gloria insisted.

Rachel went over the precautions with them one more time before she left. 'You are not under house arrest, you are here for your own protection. You can go out, though I'd advise you to stay here as much as possible. Do not go anywhere you may be recognized. That means staying away from home, work, family, friends, school. Yes?'

'Cool,' Connor smiled.

Gloria rolled her eyes. 'How long for?'

'I don't know. We need to identify the threat. If you do speak to anyone on the phone do not reveal your whereabouts.'

Rachel sat outside in her car and rang in. Godzilla answered.

'Rachel. Everyone all right?'

'Yes, boss, settled in for the night.'

'Good. We've recovered several bullets

from the scene.'

'Any witnesses?' Rachel said.

'None. All too busy tucked up watching the soaps.'

'I've got the clothes to log in,' Rachel said. 'Boss, I didn't get to talk to the neighbours about Tandy's recent movements.'

'Briefing tomorrow, we'll look at that then.'

Another inch, Rachel thought, a different angle of entry and they would have had another fatality on their hands, a scrappy, mouthy fourteen-year-old, shot watching TV.

27

Rachel had been brooding about Sean blabbing to her mother for twenty-four hours. It all came to a head as soon as she got in. He started wittering on about tomorrow's football and where to watch it, like nothing was wrong. Even Sean must have noticed the god-awful atmosphere last night and her mother's sudden departure from the pub.

'How could you tell Sharon about Dom, about me turning him in?' Rachel said. 'That was private.'

'But she's your mam,' Sean said, 'Dom's too.'

'In name only. You had no right!'

'Rachel, please, calm down.'

'Don't tell me to calm down.'

'I thought she knew, knew he was in prison, I thought you'd have told her.'

'That I fucking put him there? And now she's playing the bloody martyr, the saint. *Blood is thicker than water. You look out for your own.* Fucking hypocrite.'

'Look, I'm sorry,' he said, 'but at least it's out in the open.'

He really did not get it. He thought shoving people back together again meant they'd all play happy families. He did not see the Baileys were more your *Jeremy Kyle*-style family. Fractured and fucking hopeless. She should never have married him. The thought was like a knife, swift, lancing through her. Oh God. She felt awful, disloyal, and cruel. Don't be daft, she told herself, give it time.

'You know what she's like,' she was saying, 'a bloody disaster.'

'She's not all bad,' he said.

'I can't be doing with her, Sean, every time I turn round she's here, wanting things, talking–' She didn't know how to make him see it.

'She's missed a lot,' he said.

'And whose fault is that?'

'But it's water under the bridge, isn't it? Think of the future.'

She didn't want to. 'I need to take it more slowly,' she said, 'small doses, you know?'

'OK.' He sounded reluctant.

'So don't encourage her. If she comes round, tell her we're busy or we're going out.'

He looked pained. For all his street smarts Sean was rubbish at lying, at playing games.

'Though we probably won't see her for a bit, the way we left things. Least not till she's running short,' Rachel said.

Sean nodded, pulled her close, kissed her. Rachel felt uncomfortable, too hot, and twitchy. She drew away. 'Think I'll have a run,' she said.

'Now?'

'Wind down.'

'What's wrong with the sofa, Thai chicken curry?'

'Sean–'

'All right,' he said, 'do what you got to do.'

He was so grateful to have her there he'd bend over backwards rather than say anything to challenge her. But instead of being thankful, that made her feel worse. She made an excuse: 'Bitch of a day.'

'Go,' he said, 'I'll be here when you get back.'

'Yeah,' she said, 'course you will.'

'Sammy, I need to talk to you,' Gill said. 'Turn that off.'

'I cleared up the other day,' he objected.

'It's not that.'

He looked at her, picking up on her serious tone, paused his game.

Gill crossed and sat in the armchair. She felt anxiety fluttering behind her breastbone. 'It's about your dad,' she said. 'He's gone into rehab.'

'Where?' Sammy said.

'A place in Cheshire. Like a hotel.'

'Without a minibar.'

She smiled, 'Exactly.'

'How long will he be there?' Sammy asked.

'I don't know, as long as he needs.'

'OK.'

She rubbed at the cloth, the piping around the edge of the chair arm. They had picked the design together, her and Dave, argued about the colour scheme. She won. And later he admitted it worked, both comfortable and stylish at the same time. They had christened the couch the night it was delivered. Days when they couldn't keep their hands off each other. Sammy sound asleep upstairs. They'd been so bright back then, nothing seemed too hard. Gill working all hours solving murders, Dave gaining promotion. Both ambitious. Both still on the way up, proud of each other. Good prospects. Good money. Enough to build this place, enough for good food and clothes and cars. And Sammy. The blessing of Sammy.

All that and now this.

She made a fist, tapped it on the chair a

couple of times. 'Your dad, he's been – well, you know he's been having problems for a while.'

'Yeah,' a hint of sarcasm there. She was stating the bleeding obvious. She kicked herself. 'Well, he came here drunk last night, broke into the summerhouse, blacked out. And now he's getting help, professional help.'

Sammy's mouth twisted, he shook his head in disgust. Seeing this, his loss of respect for his dad, hurt more than anything.

'It's hard for us to understand,' she said, 'but it's a disease, an illness. It's not about you or me or anyone else. He still loves you, Sammy, whatever else. You know that?'

'I suppose.'

'He does. And so do I.' She gave him a hug. 'We're going to be all right.'

'I know,' he said.

'How's Orla?' She changed the subject.

'Good, yeah.'

'We should go out some time,' she said, 'the three of us, a meal.'

'Right,' he said, 'before Christmas or after?' Sarky. Sarky was OK.

'I do have days off,' she chided him. 'I'll tell you when and you can ask her.'

'OK.'

'She's not vegan or anything?'

'No,' he said.

'OK, that's a date to be arranged.'

She expected him to return to his game

354

but he switched it off and disappeared up-stairs.

Gill closed her eyes, took a breath and let it out slowly. She looked outside where the cherry tree stood in shadow, the rain falling steadily against the windows. She closed the curtains.

It's going to be all right, she told herself. Who knows what might have happened if she hadn't found Dave when she did, if she hadn't forced him to see what was so blind-ingly obvious, if she hadn't finally got through to him. And now he was off her back, out of circulation and, she dearly hoped, was going to make a good recovery. She'd need to get the glass fixed in the summerhouse, clear out the mess in there. But not now. Not tonight. Tonight she meant to eat something decent and get a good sleep and try to feel halfway normal again. For her and her boy.

It was all going to be all right.

Day 7

Wednesday 16 May

28

'What the fuck is going on out there? See this?' Gill held up a copy of the *Sun*. *DEATH TOWN* screamed the headline. 'We've got three murders, a high-profile drug death, and now people are running around beating up and shooting at potential witnesses. We know the same weapon was used in all three killings but we do not have that weapon.' She took a breath. 'What we do have is a man in custody, in possession of incriminating evidence. The clock's ticking and we need more on him. Anyone?'

Rachel spoke up. 'For the timeline, Tandy left the family home on Friday. He'd heard about the Kavanagh murder, reckoned it was good news. His missus had had enough. They argued. No contact between him and the family since, according to her.'

'The lab has found his DNA on the gloves.'

'Brilliant!' Rachel said.

'Hold your horses – there's also another profile,' Gill said.

'On the system?' Janet asked.

'No,' Gill said. It weakened their case. Tandy's defence could always claim that someone else, identity unknown, wore the gloves, fired the gun and used the accelerant.

'It's not Stanley Keane, he is on the DNA database?' Janet again.

'Yes he is and it's not him,' Kevin said.

'Where is Keane?' Gill said.

'No sign.' This from Mitch.

'Time we paid Marcus Williams a visit, maybe Keane is staying there,' Gill said.

'Are you thinking Keane might have shot Lydia and Victor?' said Janet.

'The items recovered, the gloves, were at his address, we can link him to Shirelle and the drug business, he's a known associate of Williams but ... the DNA doesn't fit.' Gill felt boxed in; the evidence they acquired kept weakening the case rather than supporting their suspicions. 'Sticking with Tandy,' she went on, 'if he is our killer, what's the likely sequence of events? Starting with his release.'

'We know he went to the George Inn for the EBA meeting and that the Perry twins were there,' said Janet.

'And he met with Neil Perry at Bobbins on Tuesday,' said Rachel, 'possibly to supply the weapon. He gets chucked out by his missus on Friday when he's cheering about the first shooting. He takes his gear, the firearms, clothes, the gloves and stuff, to Keane's.'

'At some point he gets the gun back from the Perrys,' Janet said, 'he acquires a can of barbecue lighter fuel and he goes to the warehouse, shoots the victims, sets the fire. Returns to Keane's.'

'What then?' said Gill. 'Where is the gun now? And where did he get the lighter fuel? It's a plausible narrative as far as it goes but at the moment it's a fairy story. We need much more.' The lack of CCTV in the area was another obstacle, no record of who was going to and from the warehouse or on the approach roads.

'We have no motive–' Janet said.

'Unless Tandy wanted to make a name for himself with the Bulldogs. Bit of ethnic cleansing,' said Mitch.

'Or there's some drugs war simmering, something we've not uncovered,' said Lee.

'However,' Gill held up her hands, 'motive is the least of our concerns. Janet and Rachel, you carry on checking for any sightings of Tandy with the neighbours and then at Keane's. Mitch and Lee, pay a visit to Williams, we get a search warrant.'

Her phone rang. 'DCI Murray.'

'Alan here, from ballistics.'

'Go on,' she said.

'Bullets recovered from the Manton Road address, we've run a comparison and they match those used in all three murder cases.'

Gill felt dizzy. 'All of them?'

'Yes, one weapon, six bullets, all fired from the same gun. The one you're looking for,' he said, emphasizing the point.

'Thanks, Alan. The missing gun,' she told the team, 'it was used in last night's attack at Tandy's house.'

'Could that be Keane?' said Rachel. 'Sending a warning to Tandy to keep his gob shut?'

'It could be bloody Batman for all we know,' Gill said, 'but it tells us that if Tandy did the warehouse murders, he got rid of the gun between Friday night and Monday when we brought him in. We may never get that gun.' In organized crime, weapons were passed from hand to hand, hired, sold, borrowed, hidden, looked after. The same weapon used by different people in the commission of diverse offences, as appeared to be the case now.

'Maybe Tandy just went apeshit, lost the plot,' Rachel said. 'He's out and back home but it's the same shitty little life. His wife is on at him, she actually tells him to do one. So what's it all for? He pulls a Terminator, picks on someone to hurt, someone who won't stand a chance. Justifies it to himself 'cos he's a racist dickhead.'

'Why copy the Kavanagh killing?' Gill said.

'He'd been bigging it up,' Rachel said. 'That's why Gloria chucked him out – well, partly. He gets the idea then.'

'How did he know to go after the victims?' Janet asked. 'Victor and Lydia? He's not a user.'

'No,' Gill agreed, 'nothing on his medical.'

'Stuff in the house, though,' Kevin said, 'Keane's house.'

'But not in the room Tandy was occupying.' This from Lee.

'His missus said he never touched drugs,' said Rachel.

'What if the twins told him about them? Could it be a challenge? We'll do the wino, you do the black kids,' Rachel said, 'we can tell you where they'll be.'

Gill sighed. 'Greg Tandy is a career criminal, a gun man. I can't see him entering some pact with a pair of lowlife scumbags like the Perry twins.'

'If it was Tandy, he'd know to get rid of evidence,' Rachel said, 'so why hang on to the gloves then?'

'Could Keane have been involved and then fitted Tandy up?' Gill said.

No one answered.

'Enough,' Gill said. 'Bring me something solid, quick as you like.'

They got bugger all from Tandy's neighbours, apart from a lot of nosy questions about where the wife and boy had gone and rumours that Greg had shot at his own family. Given he was in custody at the time, that didn't hold water. As for anyone seeing him any time on the Friday evening going to or from the warehouse, they drew a big fat blank.

Over in Werneth, where Stanley Keane lived, there were no fences at the front of the properties so it would be easy for the residents to see people coming and going. The neighbours to the left of Keane were out, no cars in the drive, no one home. At the other side, Janet and Rachel were greeted by a young woman in a yellow onesie, her eyes furred with fake lashes and her fingernails individually designed.

She'd not really paid attention to next door until all the police showed up. Stan Keane was a nice man, friendly enough. No, she didn't know him well. Hadn't seen him for a few days.

Janet showed her a photograph of Greg Tandy. 'What about this man?'

'The one you arrested Monday. Saw him then. You were there.' She nodded at Rachel.

'That's right.'

'Before that, can you remember when you first saw him?' Janet said.

The woman narrowed her eyes. 'Today is Wednesday?'

'Yes.'

She sucked her teeth, dazzling white, Janet noticed, set off by vivid-pink lipstick. 'Friday. 'Cos I was heading out. Girls' night.' She seemed pleased that she could remember.

'What time was this?'

'Half seven,' she said.

'And where was this man?' said Janet.

'He was going out too, just ahead of me.'

Heading for the warehouse, wondered Janet? 'Was he carrying anything?'

'Not that I remember.'

'Did you see him after that?'

'Well, I didn't surface until the Saturday afternoon. Serious hangover, well trollied,' she laughed. 'Saw him coming in. He'd a bag then,' she smiled, 'probably been to the gym. No way was I going to make it, I tell you. I usually go Saturday.'

'A gym bag?' Janet's heart gave a kick in her chest.

'Well, holdall.'

'What colour?'

'Blue.' The girl laughed. 'The things you remember!'

'And after that?'

'Didn't see him until the police came.' She lowered her voice, leaned closer. 'What's he done?' Janet caught a whiff of fake tan.

'That's what we're trying to find out,' Janet said. 'Thanks for your help.'

'The bag he had his gloves in,' Rachel said as they crossed the road.

'Sounds the same.'

'But she reckons it was the Saturday and he didn't have the bag on the Friday.'

'That would have been too perfect,' Janet said.

'Maybe he left the bag somewhere on the

Friday after the murders and went to fetch it on the Saturday.'

'Why? Where?'

'His house? Though I don't know that Gloria would have let him over the threshold.'

At the house opposite Stanley Keane's, a Polish man answered. He explained his nationality when he spelled out his name, which consisted mainly of consonants. His English was excellent and barely accented. He too had noticed Tandy, the new resident, but found it harder to recall dates and times. He worked twelve-hour shifts in a call centre and when he was home he was usually in bed or half asleep.

He thought some more and then said, 'I did see him going into Wetherspoon's. That would have been about eight o'clock, on my way home from the bus.'

'Which day?'

'Thursday or Friday.'

'It would be a great help if you could remember which,' Janet said.

'Sorry,' he apologized. 'I'd done twenty days in a row. Saturday was a day off so I know it wasn't Saturday but before that.'

'If you remember,' Janet said, 'please get in touch.' She gave him her card.

The man knew Stanley Keane by sight but they had never spoken. He'd last seen him on Sunday evening, putting the bins out.

The manager at Wetherspoon's didn't recall Greg Tandy but the girl who was chalking up meals on the blackboard did. 'Friday,' she said, 'it's the only night I work here. He reminded me of Jimmy Carr, the comedian, but an older version. You know, the black hair and the big eyes. He sat over there, by the slot machines, on his own at first.'

'Someone joined him?' Janet said.

'Yes, about half nine. Bigger bloke, beard and biker's jacket, comes in here sometimes.'

Stanley Keane.

'How long did they stay?'

'Till closing,' she said.

Janet felt her heart sink. The girl seemed to be on the ball and if her sighting was accurate then there was no way Greg Tandy could have been ten miles away shooting Victor and Lydia.

29

Rachel and Janet followed Gill into the meeting room.

'The Wetherspoon's sighting gives Tandy an alibi but Keane could have done it,' said Rachel. 'Keane didn't get to the pub till later and the gloves were at his house.'

'He fitted Tandy up for the murder?' Gill said. 'Wouldn't Tandy shop him? The man's only just been released. And why would Keane want to kill the Nigerians?'

'Why would anyone?' Janet said.

'It doesn't work,' Gill shook her head, 'because if Keane was behind it we'd have his DNA on those gloves and we've not. And we've nothing at his house that points to him bar the gloves.'

'We could find out if he bought lighter fuel?' Rachel suggested.

'Doesn't get us very far,' Gill said. 'You can buy it anywhere: petrol stations, super-markets, DIY stores. People have it at home, everyone's got a barbecue.'

'I've not,' Rachel said.

'Sean will soon see to that, I bet you,' Janet said.

'What is it with men and barbecues?'

'Throwback,' said Gill, 'they like to imagine they've just caught the animal, killed it and dressed it. Proud hunters all. Bringing home the bacon.'

'When it's actually a value party pack of quarter pounders or sausages from the farm shop,' Janet said.

Rachel pulled a face.

'A shop, attached to a farm,' Janet spelled out.

'I know! Behave.'

'We questioned Tandy about his movements on the Friday night,' Gill said. 'He told us nothing. Now we find he has an alibi? Strong?' She looked at Janet.

'An independent witness.'

'So why didn't he give us it?' Gill said.

'He's frightened? Protecting someone?' said Rachel.

Gill sighed. They had seemed to be getting closer but first they'd eliminated Noel Perry and now Tandy was in the clear. It felt like they were back at square one. 'Charge Tandy with the firearms offences and ship him back to prison.'

The search at Marcus Williams's house revealed nothing. No Keane, no gun, no drugs.

'Teflon as per usual,' said Mitch as Kevin handed out the sandwich orders. Not only did Williams keep well away from the merchandise and the illicit activities of his network, he also drove within the speed limit, paid his council tax on time and had obviously found a way to launder his money.

'Think about it from Marcus Williams's point of view,' said Gill. 'Suppose he wants to get rid of Victor and Lydia, motive unknown for now. How might that play out?'

'Well, Williams won't be anywhere near,' said Mitch.

'So he finds someone to do the deed,' Lee said.

'Stanley Keane,' Rachel said, taking the

baguette Kevin passed her. 'Keane gets the gun off Tandy–'

'Who must have got it back from the Perry brothers after the Kavanagh shooting,' Gill said, 'some time between Wednesday and Friday evening.'

'Keane borrows or steals the gloves too,' said Janet. 'He gets lighter fuel and goes to the warehouse, shoots Victor and Lydia, torches the place. Then joins Greg Tandy for a couple of pints in his local.'

'An attempt at an alibi?' Gill said.

'Keane gets rid of the gun,' said Janet, 'why keep the gloves? Why not dump them?'

'Unless he's trying to frame Tandy,' Mitch said.

'Boss,' Pete had answered his phone and now interrupted. 'We've found something on CCTV for Monday night. Shirelle Young and Stanley Keane.'

'I want it here, now,' Gill said.

The CCTV, in grainy black and white, was from the cameras at the green man crossing near the shopping parade. Shirelle, in her white jacket, could be seen walking briskly. Then she stops in her tracks. Gill peered, holding her breath. A man approaches, grabs her wrists and kicks her legs from under her. He picks her up and at that moment his bearded face is clearly visible, livid with anger.

'Stanley Keane,' said Mitch.

'What's he so mad about?' Gill said.

'She led us to his house earlier, we found Tandy, we found the drugs,' Rachel said.

'This is five past eight,' Janet said.

'And Shirelle was found fifteen minutes later,' said Rachel.

'So,' Gill said, 'he beats up Shirelle and then he targets the Tandy house. He'd know we are holding Tandy so either that is a warning to Tandy to keep quiet or a warning to the family.'

'It could've been a lot more than a warning,' Rachel said. 'The curtains were closed, they could both have been in the line of fire.'

'Reckless,' Lee agreed.

'Someone must be sheltering him, someone must know where he is. Lee, Mitch, dig out family, old connections. We can assume he is still armed,' Gill said. 'I'll discuss it with the chief superintendent. Much of what we have is circumstantial but erring on the side of caution, as far as public safety is concerned, I think we should be plastering his pretty little face all over the shop.'

'What's she like, the wife, Gloria?' Janet said. 'Reckon she knows any more than she's saying? She examined her teeth in the washroom mirror, checking there were no stray bits of food stuck in them.

Rachel shrugged. 'Don't know. I think

she's had enough of him – the way she tells it. Glad to be shot. Ha ha!'

'Funny,' Janet said.

'Well, she probably does better on her own. Tandy comes home and all hell's let loose. Tossers, the lot of 'em.' Rachel sounded angry.

'You all right?'

'Fine,' Rachel said crossly, 'pig in shit.' She did that, hackles up like a dog at the slightest excuse. Particularly when she thought people were criticizing her or asking about personal stuff.

'Bite my head off,' Janet said.

'I wasn't. God, you're so touchy.'

Janet gave her a look.

'I. Was. Not.'

'You sound like our Taisie.'

Rachel brushed her hair, didn't speak.

'Sean all right then?' Janet said.

'Will you leave it? Sean is fine. I am fine. My mad frigging mother is fine. We are all fucking dandy. Why do you have to be so nebby, sticking your nose in all the time?'

Janet was stung, her chest tightened. Normally she'd have tried to defuse the situation, joke about it or back off, but she'd run out of patience.

'You need to grow up,' she said coldly, 'and get a fucking grip. I'll be upstairs.'

But halfway there her phone went. *Mum calling.*

'Hello?' she said.

'I know you must be busy,' Dorothy said, 'but you did say to ring...'

'Yes?'

'Well, Elise is in a right state. Up in her room, crying her eyes out. I asked her if she'd like me to get you.'

'OK,' Janet said, 'tell her I'm on my way.'

She went quickly to the office and signed out. Told Lee she had to get home, personal business, and asked him to let Rachel know she'd have to go and talk to the Tandys on her own. Janet would check in with her later if she could.

Elise was still crying when Janet got home, lying on her bed, face red, nose and lips puffy from it all.

Dorothy made herself scarce and Janet sat down next to Elise. 'Hey.' She ran her hand over Elise's head. 'What's to do?'

'Holly messaged me. There's going to be a service for Olivia, like a celebration of her life, and people are doing things, cards and poems and music and stuff,' she gulped, 'and I can't go.'

'Says who?'

'Vivien. She said I'm not welcome. She said that to them, Mum. Olivia was my best friend, for ever, I loved her so much and I'm not even allowed–' She couldn't continue, she was sobbing so hard.

Janet sighed and stroked her back. 'That's not fair,' she said, 'it's mean and it's hurtful but that's because Vivien is hurt and she's looking for someone to blame and she's picked on you. But listen to me, she's wrong. This was not your fault, you are just being made into the scapegoat.'

'Holly said some of them, they don't think it's fair and if I can't go then they won't either. Like a boycott,' Elise said.

Janet sighed. 'I don't think that's the answer. It's good to know that they would do that to support you, that they understand, but then the service would become about you and who's there and who's not and who's right and wrong and all the ins and outs of Olivia's death and that wouldn't be right, would it?'

'No,' Elise agreed.

'We'll just have to have our own private thing. I'm sure Taisie would like to do something, she's really upset too, and your dad and I would.'

'What like?' Elise blew her nose.

'Well, we can make cards, read poems, and take flowers to the cemetery once they've had the funeral. We could plant a tree.'

Elise pulled a face at the last suggestion.

'You think about it,' Janet said, 'think what you'd like to do.'

'OK.'

'Have you had anything to eat today?'

She shook her head.

'You need to have something. Soup?'

Elise shrugged.

'Soup it is then, chicken or tomato?'

'Tomato.'

It was vindictive of Vivien, Janet thought, demonizing Elise; perhaps in the future she would come round and see that it was unjust. The ostracism pained Janet but she took heart from the fact that some of the girls' friends were mature enough to support Elise and want to include her.

30

Rachel pressed the entry phone at the safe house and was buzzed in. Connor was in the living room, the TV was on, loud, an action film going by the soundtrack but Rachel couldn't put a name to it.

'Where's your mum?' Rachel said.

'Shopping.'

'Shopping where?'

'That Aldi you told her about.' He seemed twitchy, scratching at his arms and his neck, his eyes glittering. Was he high?

'Can you turn that down a bit,' she said, 'or off?'

'Why?'

'I want to talk to you.'

He nudged the volume down a notch.

She rolled her eyes. He gave a heavy sigh and snapped it off.

'Thank you.'

'What's happening with me dad?'

'I can't discuss that with you,' she said.

'Why not?' He stood and paced over to the window. 'He's my dad.'

'I know. Connor, I wanted to ask you about a man called Stanley Keane. You know him?'

'No,' he scowled.

'You sure?'

'Yes, I said, didn't I?'

'Has anyone been to the house to see your dad since he came home?'

He groaned, hit at his head with the heels of his hands. 'Why won't you just get it? My dad, he's done nothing. You've got to let him go.'

'Once we're satisfied–' she began but he jumped in. 'No! No!' he shouted, stabbing his finger at her. He *was* off his face, wired up on something, she was sure. She could see the sweat darken his hairline.

'You think he did those niggers, he never. He never.' He swung away from her. The sweatshirt they'd supplied was too big for him, covering half of his hands and down to his knees.

'We'll see. Please, Connor, sit down.'

'No! We won't see,' he mimicked her.

'You've got to let him go. You haven't got the gun, have you?'

'What do you know about the gun?' she said.

He sniffed, scratched the back of his head. He was stepping side to side, unable to keep still.

'Connor? Did you see someone last night shooting at your house? You can tell me.'

He ignored her and said, 'He wasn't around on Friday night, he'd gone. Did he tell you that? It wasn't him.' He hadn't gone far though – to Keane's – but he was ensconced in the boozer when the murders happened, which left Stanley Keane as their key candidate.

'We have to go by the evidence,' Rachel said. None of which quite matched anyone. Yet.

'You haven't got the gun, have you?' he said again.

'Not yet,' she said. 'Connor, I can't talk about it, but your dad is still in custody and he'll be there as long as we require him to be. And I'll tell you this for nothing, he's going back inside. He's broken the terms of his licence.'

'No!' he yelled. 'Fucking bitch.' He moved his hand quickly, behind his back, and then he had the gun. The barrel pointing straight at her. Maybe three feet between them. He couldn't miss.

'Put that down,' she said, her mouth dry, sweat slicking her skin, buzzing in her ears. The gun wavered; firearms were heavy, Rachel knew. She also knew she had to keep him talking, had to engage him if she stood a hope in hell of getting out of there. 'This isn't going to help anyone,' she said, 'not your dad or you.'

'You tell them to let him go.' His eyes shone.

'It doesn't work like that, Connor.'

She was so hot, burning up, and her stomach clenched hard as rock. 'No one will do anything while you're holding a gun.'

He walked up to her and touched the weapon to the base of her throat. She felt the hard cold steel. Smelled oil and a hint of gun smoke, and his sweat pungent and acrid. 'Sit down,' he said, moving the gun away a little. She did, trying not to betray the fear thick in her blood.

He took a step back, then another, the gun levelled at her but his hold on it unsteady. The drugs, whatever he was on, affecting his motor skills, or maybe it was the excitement.

'We can sort something out,' she said, her voice catching. She coughed to clear it. 'Maybe you want to see your dad, but not like this. Think about it. I'm a police officer.'

'A pig, yeah,' he said, 'two niggers and a pig. That'll show him.'

'Who?'

Her phone rang, a shocking blare of sound. He jabbed the gun at her. 'Leave it.'

'It'll be work,' she said. 'If I don't answer, they'll be round here in minutes.'

He looked doubtful. The ringtone repeated.

'It's a safety thing, me on my own. They call, we answer. No answer – rapid response.' She moved to get her phone but he said, 'No,' moved closer.

'I'll tell them I'm fine,' she said, 'clocking off, yeah. Done here. Then they'll leave it. Your call, Connor, they won't hang on for ever.'

'You say anything...' he threatened.

'With a gun to my head? I'm not fuckin' stupid.'

He gave a sharp nod and she pulled the handset from her pocket, her heart hurting in her chest; her pulse galloping. Glanced at the display, hit the green key and said, 'Hi, Janet, everything's OK here.'

Connor was poised, eyes locked on her gun too.

Janet began to speak but Rachel kept on, 'I'm going to clock off after this, nearly done, shocking migraine so I'll go straight home.'

'Migraine?' said Janet. 'Since when have–'

'Like your Taisie, eh? Head's banging fit to burst.' *Please please, fuckin' get it.* 'Mrs Tandy's out shopping so we'll have a word with her in the morning.'

Connor began to make winding motions with his free hand.

'What's wrong?' Janet said, very quietly.

Connor moved forward, the gun swinging in his hand, his face darkening.

'Got to go,' Rachel said.

She made a show of ending the call but immediately after pressing the button she activated the voice recorder and set the handset on the seat beside her.

So what's the plan? she wanted to ask him. *You stupid little shitbag. What? You kill me too? Or hold me hostage and escape in a helicopter to a boat waiting to whisk you and your dad away to a far-flung country with no extradition agreement, like some shit-stupid video game.*

'Can I ask you something?' she said.

'What?'

'Why did you kill them? Victor and Lydia?'

'To show him.' His mouth worked for a moment then he went on. 'He wouldn't take me with him – said I was just a kid, a nancy mummy's boy. To get in touch when I'd grown a pair.' His eyes were hot with rage. 'He'd been well impressed with the wino. But I done two, black bastards. Coons.' Hatred livened his face.

'I heard you knew them, used to hang out. Friendly,' she said.

'So what?' he said. 'He's blood, my dad, he's family.'

And he doesn't give a fuck.

'What about your mum? She looked after you all the time he was away.'

'She chucked him out,' he yelled, spittle flying from his lips. 'She started it,' he complained, an outraged child.

'Where did you get the gun? Did you nick it from your dad?'

Connor laughed, making the gun swing wildly, and Rachel flinched.

'No, off of Victor. The Perrys, they sold it to Victor for some gear. They wanted rid, after doing the alkie, I reckon. Victor was showing it off. I asked to hold it. Bare luck, wasn't it?' He shook his head, grinning. 'I had a knife – that could have got messy. Victor had the gun. How good is that?' Delight danced across his face.

'And the accelerant?'

A sudden blast of sound sent electric shocks through Rachel's arms. The buzzer from the entry phone. They both glanced up at the screen. Janet.

'You fucking tricked me, you bitch!' he screamed.

'No,' Rachel said, scrambling up, 'no, wait–'

The gunshot cracked loud as a mortar. Rachel was flung back, swung round, searing pain in her upper arm, and the stink of gunpowder in her throat. She fell, landing on her back, smacking her head on the floor. Her ears were ringing, roaring, and she could just make out the noise of the buzzer sounding again and again.

'Fuck!' She heard him swear.

There was a throbbing in her left side, a deep ache travelled down her arm and through her back. A safe house, shot to death in a safe house. Fucking ironic, no?

She would not let him do this to her. Not some fucked-up little tosser from Manorclough adding her to his hit list, to impress his racist twat of a father. No way, mate.

Rachel felt the floor shake as he came closer, sensed him bending over her. Felt him nudge her with his foot. A move that sent pain slicing through her and brought vomit in her throat. She played dead, tried to still her breathing and cracked open an eyelid the smallest possible fraction.

She would have one chance.

'Fuck,' he said again.

Rachel lunged. One hand, her good hand, a vice around his ankle. Her right foot flying up, knee bent, to kick at his wrist. She heard the muffled snap as she connected with the bones, his howl and her own yelp as the agony washed through her afresh, the world spinning and darkness looming. The crash as the gun hit the sliding frosted-glass door to the kitchen, shattering it like crystal rain.

He bent to free himself from her grasp and once he was low enough she let go of his leg and grabbed his arm, using his own

He glared at her, defiant. She felt nauseous, tried to swallow but her mouth was parched. Her hand tickled, she glanced down and saw the blood running along the creases in her palm. Love line. Life line.

'Go on,' she said, keeping her voice as firm as she could.

'Or what? You going to shoot me?' he taunted her.

'If I have to.'

He didn't move.

'It's over,' she said. Her head was spinning. If she collapsed ... if he got the gun... 'Walk,' she said.

He gave her another bitter look. She could see the rage, the tension, bunching the muscles of his face. Then he went ahead along the hallway to the front door.

'There are officers outside,' Rachel said, her voice still echoing in her head, her hearing distorted from the blast. 'Some will be armed.' He wouldn't know she was bluffing, had no idea what was happening in the street. Yes, the cavalry might be on their way but the response wouldn't be instantaneous. 'No sudden movements. When we get outside you put your hands on your head, d'you understand?'

He didn't answer.

'Do you understand?' she repeated.

'Yes.'

She held the gun on him as he pulled back

the bolts, the ones she had secured when she arrived, then he undid the latch.

He pulled back the door and the brightness of the light hurt her eyes. 'Hands on head,' she said.

Janet looked at them, surprise on her face at seeing Connor held at gunpoint. She balked when she saw the blood on Rachel.

'Connor Tandy,' Rachel said as they walked him to the car, the howl of sirens growing closer. 'I am arresting you on suspicion of the murder of Victor Tosin and Lydia Oluwaseyi. You do not have to say anything but it may harm your defence if you do not mention when questioned–' she caught her breath, the pain in her arm was changing, a numb tingling like pins and needles replacing the sharp streaks of acute pain, 'something which you later rely on in court. Anything you do say may be given in evidence.'

Janet opened the rear side door. Rachel still held the gun. 'Got any ties?' she said to Janet. They needed to cuff him.

'In the boot, I'll get you a bag for that too.' Janet nodded at the gun. Her face was chalk white, Rachel could see the fear that edged her eyes though to anyone else Janet would appear perfectly calm.

'Wait there,' Rachel said to Connor, pushing the door closed. She felt her vision pitch and swim, tried to blink it away and concentrate.

Janet opened the car boot, Rachel moved so she could see her. 'What the fuck was that?' she hissed at Janet. She looked down at her blouse, the bloodstain growing. 'Jesus, Janet?'

'I didn't know he was armed, you never said–'

'I couldn't say, he was pointing a gun at me.'

'Are you all right?' Janet said.

'Apart from being shot, you mean?'

Janet's face grew narrower, pinched. '"Migraine," you said. Migraine means come and get me, migraine means I want to go home, I want a lift home now. "Like Taisie," you said.'

'If you'd used your imagination–' Rachel said.

'I came, didn't I? I'm here. Look, I'm really sorry–'

A noise made Rachel spin round. Connor was climbing out of the car.

'Oi,' she said, 'get your hands on your–'

He dived at her, the light glinting on a wide arced blade that he swung at Rachel, cutting through her sleeve, her right arm. And he legged it.

Janet shouted, 'Throw the gun into the car!' Then to Connor, 'Stop! Stop now!'

He was halfway down the street.

Rachel ran.

Unable to move her left arm like a piston

as she normally would, she found herself lurching to the side and almost stumbling into the walls and railings that fronted the Regency properties. She saw Connor dive into an alleyway. She could hear Janet behind her, the ring of her heels on the pavement and her voice shouting details of their location for the back-up.

The alley joined a wider passageway that ran behind the houses. Connor turned left. Seeing him increase the distance between them, Rachel willed herself on. Her head was thudding, the air in her lungs burned as though she was breathing fire, her eyesight kept blurring.

Wheelie bins, blue, brown and black, were dotted along the path in twos and threes. A cat skittered out of the way, as Connor belted along. Sirens were upon them.

Rachel looked ahead to the end where the alley met the road and saw vertical lines. She blinked and realized it was a gate. The alley was gated as a safety measure. Connor was trapped.

He hurled himself at the wrought iron and tried to get a purchase, to climb, but slithered down again and again.

Rachel was closer. Ten yards, five. A stitch crippling in her side. When she stopped running, just feet from him, he turned, the knife shiny and speckled red where it had sliced into her arm.

'Drop the knife,' she gasped.

He was panting, sweat on his skin, his face reddened with exertion.

Rachel saw Janet beyond the gates, she must've gone round the other way. The sirens were too loud for Connor to hear her approach.

'Drop the knife,' Rachel said.

'You want it? Come and get it.'

Rachel's breath caught, she felt the world tilt. She bent slightly, putting her right hand, the one she could still feel though sticky with blood from the cut, on her right knee for support.

Janet reached the far side of the gate. 'Connor,' she shouted behind him. He twisted round and she squirted his eyes with CS gas.

Connor screamed and dropped the knife, raised his hands and rubbed at his eyes.

'Put your hands through the gate,' Janet yelled.

'My eyes,' he squealed, 'I can't see! My fucking eyes.'

'Hands. Now. Put your hands through the gate,' Janet repeated.

He did as she said, tears streaming down his face, coughing and swinging his head as if he could dislodge the blindness caused by the chemical.

Janet snapped the plastic cuffs on, effectively tying him to the bars.

Rachel saw the vans pull up on the roadside near Janet. The men piling out. The sirens cut out with one last 'whoop' and she heard shouting, glimpsed Mrs Tandy dropping her shopping bags, yelling, and one of the men restraining her.

Rachel moved to lean against the wall, head spinning in time to the blue flashing lights, filling with bubbles, so dizzy, and her knees dissolving. Everything falling away.

31

Janet waited for Rachel in A&E. If she never had to see the inside of a hospital again it'd be too soon. They should have given her a uniform by now, or a mop and bucket. First there'd been her own near-death experience, belly sliced open requiring multiple surgeries, then once she was up and running, her mother had collapsed at home, thankfully having enough time and wit to call Janet for help. After the emergency appendectomy Dorothy had needed a hysterectomy. Then there had been Olivia. And now Rachel.

Janet clung to the fact that Rachel had been upright and able to go after Connor. Surely it couldn't have been anything major if she could run like that? But what if the bullet had nicked a lung, or some minor debris had worked its way round to her heart or brain?

Janet got to her feet, walked over and stared unseeing at a noticeboard. Elise hadn't hesitated when Janet heard Rachel needed her. 'Go, Mum,' she'd said, 'go.'

But a thousand worries flew through Janet's head: *I should be here with you. Family first. I might be putting myself in harm's way.*

'I'll be fine,' Elise said, sitting up straighter, 'go on.' Elise understood the friendship, how much it meant, how deep it went. Something Janet's mother had never been able to fathom. Because Janet and Rachel were so very different. Rachel with her devil-may-care approach, her appalling choice in men (though maybe Sean was a turning point), her indifference to kids, her dysfunctional family; then Janet – daughter of teachers, hard-working, reliable, solid, settled. Until the Andy business. The one definitive thing she and Rachel had in common was the job, love of the job, commitment, compassion. You had to have that to survive in the syndicate.

Janet could not imagine work without Rachel, though in time if Rachel passed her sergeant's exam the process of moving up and away would start.

So Janet had gone to Rachel. Ade would hate it, she could hear him now. 'You're a middle-aged woman, Janet, for Christ's sake.

The older you get, the less sense you seem to have. Did you think about anyone else? About your daughters?'

Gill wouldn't be best pleased either. Janet's stomach turned over at the thought of facing her.

She had called Gill from outside the safe house, reporting the sound of gunfire and the call from Rachel.

'I'll organize an armed response unit and a hostage negotiator,' Gill said. 'Do we know who is in there?'

'Not sure,' Janet had said, 'once I get–'

'No, Janet. You withdraw now to a safe distance. Stay well back. You don't go anywhere near–'

Janet clenched her teeth. 'Sorry? Gill, you're breaking up. Can you repeat that? Gill... I can't hear you, Gill?' Then she had switched the phone off.

There was movement at the end of the waiting room and Rachel was there. Left arm and shoulder dressed and bandaged in a sort of sling, right forearm dressed. Blanket over her. Camisole soaked in blood.

A wave of relief coursed through Janet and she walked quickly over, smiling, a lump in her throat. 'You,' she said, hugging her, careful not to squeeze.

She felt Rachel stiffen. Never one for displays of affection. Then Rachel relaxed a fraction, pressed Janet's shoulder briefly before she drew away.

'What did they say?' Janet asked.

'Bullet nicked the bone in the top of my arm but went straight through. May or may not need surgery, depends on how it heals. Knife wound's superficial, keep it clean, blah blah. No driving, no heavy lifting.' She sighed. 'That little gobshite.' She gave a rueful smile. 'I can get a cab.'

'Don't talk daft,' Janet said. 'Besides the boss wants to see us. Her exact words were, "If Rachel Bailey is not laid out in a mortuary somewhere, I want her here – pronto."'

Rachel pulled a face, looked down at her stained clothes and said, 'Maybe we could call at mine on the way; clean up a bit?'

'Where the fuck do I start?' Godzilla said, eyes blazing, red nails flashing like she'd claw at them any moment. Rachel, sitting in the chair at Her Maj's insistence. 'You, Fairy Lightfoot, sit down before you fall.' Janet perched next to her, half sitting on the storage cupboards; the boss, on the other side of her desk, on her feet, on the move.

She had listened while Rachel played the voice recording of the conversation in the safe house, Connor's confession. Not made under caution but still – bloody good groundwork for formal interviews.

Then Godzilla had wanted to know what happened afterwards. Taking turns, Janet and Rachel had described Connor's flight, their pursuit, his recapture, giving the bare bones of the story, keeping it simple, sticking to the facts.

'Do I start with the fact that you,' she dipped her head at Janet, 'ignored my express instructions and went riding off like a bloody knight on a white charger?'

'The phone—' Janet began.

'Don't lie,' Godzilla pointed a finger at her, 'do not lie to me.'

Rachel swallowed. Janet never got a bollocking like this; well, hardly ever. Because Janet did as she was told, agreed with the boss's strategy. Janet thought things through. She didn't go off half-cocked.

'Has it occurred to you,' the boss went on, 'that without your little intervention we might be facing a very different outcome. That if left to the experts, those officers expressly trained in hostage situations and armed response, we might have secured an arrest without an officer being shot and stabbed?'

'We got a confession,' Rachel said, 'we—'

'Am I talking to you?' Godzilla roared. 'Be quiet.'

Rachel's cheeks burned. *Bitch*. She could feel the wound in her right forearm, the supposedly superficial one, throbbing in spite of the painkillers they'd given her.

'The armed response unit didn't reach the

scene until at least ten minutes after I did,'
Janet said, sounding furious. 'He could've
shot and killed Rachel by then. He could
have got out and run amok.'

'We'll never know, will we?' The boss
wheeled round and then back, placed her
palms together. 'And perhaps if you hadn't
piled in like a fucking rhinoceros he
wouldn't have freaked and shot her anyway.
Did you think of that?'

Janet said nothing.

'Protocol is there for a reason, because it
works.'

'Yes, boss,' Janet said, a cold fury in her
reply.

'As for you,' Godzilla glared at Rachel,
'you're injured, first you are shot and then
you are knifed and then you go barrelling
after an armed man. Have you got a fucking
death wish? Had you got your body vest on?
No. Taser? No. Baton? No.'

Anger flickering through her, Rachel said,
'I just wanted to stop him.'

'Just? There is no "just" about it. You didn't
think, Rachel.'

'I got him,' she said, 'we got him.'

'You could have been seriously hurt. More
seriously. You and Janet both. I could have
been going round to your husband...'

Rachel blinked, still surprised that she had
a husband.

'...to Janet's family. If I wanted to run a

training exercise in how not to deal with a violent offender, I could use this, you know.' She walked across the width of her office and back. 'You should know better,' she said to Janet. 'I thought you did. And you,' her eyes bored into Rachel's, 'give me strength. When are you going to learn? I don't want to be burying you with your bloody badge on the coffin and the police pipe band playing, but every time there's a situation like this you turn into some suicidal nutjob.'

Godzilla took a breath then spoke slowly. 'If someone is running around with a knife, someone who has already shown a predilection for violence, you do not pursue them. You run the other way. You alert people to the danger. You minimize the risk. Mi-ni-mize. Three syllables. Do I need to carve it on your forehead?'

There was a long pause. Rachel broke the silence. 'Connor Tandy?'

'You're going nowhere near him, lady. Too much history. Too involved. Get someone to transcribe that confession,' she pointed at Rachel's phone, 'and sod off home. Janet, you prep for the interview. His mother will act as an appropriate adult. Solicitor is ready, with him now. But at his medical he declared he's taken amphetamines so we can't interview him until he's clean. Doc reckons another couple of hours. Now go,' she said.

'You reckon Greg Tandy knew it was Connor?' Rachel asked Janet.

Janet thought back to the interviews. The fleeting reaction to the physical evidence, that moment when he'd faltered. 'I'm not sure, I think at first he thought he was being framed, thought it was a fit-up. But maybe he worked it out. Figured out who had access to his gloves. He was carrying the bag when the neighbour saw him on the Saturday but not on the Friday.'

'Been to fetch it on the Saturday?' Rachel said. 'He left the family home on the Friday after the argument.'

'You walk out,' Janet said, 'you don't necessarily take everything with you.'

'He'd take the guns, keep them close. Maybe some clothes.' Rachel coughed and winced.

'Should you be here?'

'Don't you start,' Rachel said. 'So you'll ask Connor about the gloves and the accelerant?'

Janet nodded. 'We have the twins and Greg Tandy meeting at the Bulldog Army malarkey on Sunday. Maybe they've heard he's the go-to man for firearms. They get his number, rendezvous at Bobbins on the Tuesday and buy the gun.'

'Not hired,' Rachel said. 'If they'd hired it, they'd have given Tandy it back but according to Connor they sold it to Victor in exchange for some gear.'

'Which we found in their bedroom,' Janet said. 'So, the twins kill Richard Kavanagh and burn the Old Chapel. They go to the warehouse, sell the gun and get the drugs.'

'On the Thursday!' Rachel said. 'Shirelle saw them leaving that day when she was on her way with new merchandise. She takes the money Victor and Lydia have made, stocks them up and calls at Keane's on the Friday to give him the takings and get more drugs. Once the murder is made public, Greg Tandy's cheering about it and his missus chucks him out but he won't take Connor, in fact he slags him off and the stupid lad decides he'll prove himself by committing a double murder.'

'It fits,' Janet said, 'it all works.'

'Don't mess it up,' Rachel said.

What the...? Janet stared at her. 'Me, mess it up? I'm not the one you want to worry about. Did you listen to a word–'

'Just saying,' Rachel retorted, 'we're nearly there. If you–'

'Zip it,' Janet said.

'I only meant we're so close–'

'The hole's deep enough. Stop digging.' Unlike his father, Connor Tandy was prepared to answer questions. If only his mother would let him get a word in edgeways. She'd interrupted twice already, running him down, and Janet had to ask her to be quiet and let him talk.

'You had your knife,' Janet prompted him.

'Yes. And we had some fuel for the barbie out the back. I took that and an old wine bottle and a bit of cloth. My lighter.'

'Anything else?' Janet said.

He thought. 'A bag to carry it all and some gloves. In case of fingerprints.'

Janet nodded, non-judgemental, as if they were discussing the weather or bus time-tables. She placed a photograph of Greg Tandy's holdall on the desk and the gloves in their protective bag.

'I am now showing Connor exhibit MG10 and exhibit MG16. Are these the gloves and the bag?'

'Yes,' he said.

'Your dad's?' Mrs Tandy said. 'You stupid little idiot. What the fuck did you use his for?'

'Mrs Tandy,' Janet said sharply, 'please. Just let Connor speak. Go on.'

'I went down there when it was getting dark.'

'To the warehouse?'

'Yes. They were just chilling.'

'Victor and Lydia. Had they taken any drugs?' Janet said.

'Yes, and I had some weed ... I was working out what to do, who to do first...' His voice trembled slightly, the first emotion he had betrayed. '...then Victor, he says, "Check this out." And he's got a gun. I says, "Where'd you get it?" and he says, "The Perry boys," and if he sells it on how much will he get? Or maybe he'll keep it for protection, right? In case of trouble. Lydia, she wants him to sell it though. They're arguing but not shouting and I says, "Can I see it?" And he says sure. And I take it and I shoot him, two pops and she's screaming, trying to get up, and I do her, three, 'cos the first one misses.'

'Oh God, Connor.' His mother covered her eyes.

'Then I get the bottle ready and light it and chuck it by them and it works. Starts the fire.'

'What were you, what in God's ... Jesus, Connor.' Mrs Tandy sputtered to a halt.

'What then?' Janet said.

'I went home,' he said.

'The bag and the gloves?'

'Put them back under the stairs.'

'And do you know what happened to them?' Janet said.

'My dad must have taken them.'

'He did.' Gloria shook her head. 'He came round and got his stuff on the Saturday.'

'You didn't see him?' Janet said to Connor.

He gave a shrug. 'I was in bed.'

'And the gun?' Janet said.

'Kept it in my room.'

'We searched your house,' she said.

'Yeah, I had it on me. You weren't going to

strip-search us,' he said. A light in his eyes, some cheek, pleasure in tricking the police.

'And yesterday when shots were fired into your house...'

'I did that. You had me dad but you didn't have the gun, so if the gun was used you'd know it wasn't him that done it.'

'I don't believe this,' Gloria Tandy said, 'I don't bleeding believe it. What did you think would happen?'

'They'd let him go,' he retorted.

'He'd broken his terms,' she yelled, 'let alone he'd a bagful of shooters.'

'But that's not murder,' he said, 'he wouldn't go down for murder.'

'Hang on a minute,' Janet intervened.

'But you will, you stupid fucker!' Gloria Tandy shouted.

'Mrs Tandy, if you interrupt again I'm going to request that we find an alternative appropriate adult. Do you understand?'

Gloria Tandy crimped her mouth shut, tears standing in her eyes. She was heartbroken, Janet could tell, beneath the swearing and shouting she was devastated that she was losing her son.

Janet spoke to Connor. 'Earlier today you shot and injured a serving police officer. Why did you do that?'

'She lied to me, she was messing with me.'

'And you admit to killing Victor Tosin and Lydia Oluwaseyi?'

401

'Yes.'

'And can you tell me why you did that?'

'To show him, my dad, to show him and everyone. He wouldn't let me go with him, said I was still a little kid, no guts, no balls, probably a fucking pansy. Get back in touch again when my balls had dropped. And he hated them, coons, Pakis, immigrants. I'm not scared,' Connor said. 'I proved it.'

By killing two young people in cold blood? Two kids who fled God knows what horrors at home to eke out a living squatting in the unforgiving cold of a damp and desolate northern warehouse. Clinging to survival. Janet's eyes burned. She blinked and took a breath, then thanked him for his co-operation. His solicitor would be informed of any further developments but in all likelihood they would be moving to press charges.

'What about me dad?' he said.

'I can't discuss that,' said Janet.

'He'll be back inside, that's right, isn't it?' Gloria Tandy said. 'And none of this need have happened but for you. He'll be inside and so will you, won't he?' she said to Janet.

Janet didn't answer. Her silence said it all.

Gill was giving a speech to the press and media. She had rehearsed it until near word perfect so she could look at the cameras for most of the time.

'This afternoon Manchester Metropolitan

Police charged a fourteen-year-old boy, who cannot be named for legal reasons, with the murders of Victor Tosin and Lydia Oluwaseyi. I would like to thank the community of Manorclough for their help and to thank my officers for their dedication and persistence' *but not their pig-headed reckless fuckwittery* 'in pursuing this case. The recent murders of Richard Kavanagh and Victor Tosin and Lydia Oluwaseyi we believe to be hate crimes and if those charged are convicted they can expect to face longer sentences as a result. We all have the right to live safely in our community. Attacking another person for no other reason than a dislike of that person's ethnicity, sexuality, subculture or lifestyle is an appalling crime and will be investigated with the utmost rigour and determination – as will any murder in our town. Our thoughts are with the relatives and friends of the victims. Thank you.'

Back inside the police station, the incident room was deserted. Plenty more to be done but nothing that couldn't wait until morning. A wave of exhaustion made Gill dizzy. A good night's sleep, that was what she needed, something decent to eat, an hour of telly, a chat with Sammy. Some routine. The team would be in the pub. She'd show her face, important to be there celebrating their success, to be part of it.

32

Just Rachel and Janet left now. The lads had stayed for a drink then gone to a pub down the road to watch the match. Mitch had gone home after showing his face. He had a young family and his work meant he missed out on a lot of the domestic stuff. He made up for it whenever he could.

'He wasn't thick, was he?' Janet said. 'Connor. Not like Noel and Neil Perry. He can't have thought he'd get away with it.'

'Search me,' Rachel said. You could drive yourself mad trying to work out why people did the stupid stuff they did.

'That hatred, living with it day in day out. It's easier to fix on that, to blame other people, outsiders, isn't it?' Janet said.

'What for?'

'For everything that you hate about your miserable little life. But it's like a split, isn't it?' Janet said. 'He's matey enough with Victor and Lydia, hangs around there. Probably likes the attention, he's only fourteen, they're dealing. Victor trusts him enough to hand him the gun, then it's like someone's flipped a switch. Bang bang. What did he think would happen? His dad pats him on the head and trains him up in the family business. No comeback, no repercussions. Did he think we wouldn't catch him?'

Rachel thought of Dom – it was the same, doing idiotic stuff, no thought of the consequences. Decisions that ended with you banged up with the other lowlifes and hard men, the nutters and the knob-heads. Going slowly demented staring at the walls of a cell twenty-three hours a day.

'He made a decision, a bad one. He pays the price. We all have to live with what we've done.' Rachel drained her glass.

'You should go,' Janet said. 'Sean'll forget what you look like.'

'He'll be watching the game. No rush. Anyway, shouldn't you be at home with Elise and everything?'

'I should. I will. Soon.'

The door flew open and there stood Godzilla, a raptor waiting to pounce.

'Oh, fuck,' Rachel murmured, 'now what've we done?'

She came over to them, stopped by the table. 'The others gone?'

'Yes,' Janet said.

'You're still here?' She fixed her beady eyes on Rachel. 'Could have sworn I sent you home. So, you'll have another?'

'Maybe I should get going...' Rachel reached for her bag, felt the tug of pain in her arm.

'You'll not have me drinking alone?' Her Maj said brightly.

'Course not,' Janet said, 'mine's a white.'

'Red, ta,' said Rachel, giving in.

Godzilla nodded. 'Chief super's calmed down,' she said. 'Violent crime stats are through the roof, our place in the league tables may be shot to buggery but our clear-up rate is, as of today, bloody amazing.'

Rachel waited for the sting in the tail; it didn't come. Instead the boss said, 'You all right mixing red wine with whatever the hospital's pumped you full of?'

'Constitution of an ox,' Janet said.

'What is an ox anyway?' said Rachel.

'Half horse, half donkey?' Janet said, like she wasn't sure.

'That's an ass,' the boss said, 'which is more like it. Not known for their forward planning and risk assessment.'

Bingo.

'An ox,' Her Maj went on, 'is cattle, a castrated adult male. Peanuts?'

They both shook their heads and she made for the bar.

Rachel turned to look at Janet, whose eyes were twinkling.

'Cheeky bitch,' Rachel said. Janet laughed and that set Rachel off. It hurt to laugh.

'Do you think we're forgiven?' Janet said.

'You, maybe. Me? Never.'

'Oh, go on, look at how she stood up for

you when all that stuff with Dominic went down. She knows you're a good copper, could be great. Just need some fine tuning...'

'I'd kick you if I wasn't in such bloody agony,' Rachel said.

Godzilla came back in no time, tray in hand. Deposited the drinks and sat herself down. Raised her glass. Rachel and Janet did the same.

'To us,' she said.

'To us,' they echoed.

'And sod the lot of them.'

'Sod the lot of them.'

The cab took Rachel back past the hulk of the warehouse, spotlit as the process of demolition began. She saw a shadow in a doorway at the shops. Someone up to no good? Someone with no place to sleep? She wondered what Shirelle would do after her stint inside, bound to be sent down as far as Rachel could see. Would she go back to the old life or turn her life around? Rachel knew the rehabilitation rates for prisoners were pitiful.

Information had reached them that Stanley Keane was in Spain, could take months to get him back to answer charges even if they could track him down. Some other person would move up the hierarchy of Williams's business. What would Shirelle think when she realized it was Connor who'd killed Victor and Lydia? Killed them because of the colour of their skin, to earn a few Brownie points with his father. A scrawny kid on a stunt bike who could have made something of his life, with the right support. Now the pinnacle of his life, the defining moment, a double murder.

Rachel tensed as the taxi swung left, not wanting to jar her arm.

Janet had waited outside the pub with her for the car. Godzilla had gone.

'She's a bit hot and cold,' Rachel said.

Janet looked then said, 'She's got a lot on.'

'Such as?'

Janet had given half a laugh but not said anything else. Just looked at Rachel, her big eyes smiling, then pulled a soppy face. 'If you'd–'

'Don't,' Rachel said.

'It's just–'

'Don't. I know.'

'It's going to be all right,' Janet said after a moment.

And Rachel didn't really know what she meant. Stuff at work or what had happened with Elise or whatever mystery trauma was going on with Her Majesty or if she was on about Dom and Rachel's mother.

Rachel said yes anyway. 'Yes, course it is.' Even though inside she didn't know. She really didn't know. Because anything might happen. Anything did happen. Day after day.

Year after year. A lot of it messy and shitty and wasteful and sad. But that was life. You got on with it.

What the fuck else could you do?

Acknowledgements

Thanks again to Sarah Adams, Bill Scott-Kerr and Rachel Rayner at Transworld for inviting me to write the Scott & Bailey novels. Thanks to Sally Wainwright and Diane Taylor whose wonderful characters continue to be a joy to work with, and to Suranne Jones, Lesley Sharp and Amelia Bullmore who bring them to life in such memorable ways. Thanks also to Keith Dillon for generous help and advice about police work – any mistakes are mine. Some are deliberate! And many thanks to my agent Sara Menguc for her unstinting hard work and encouragement.

The publishers hope that this book has given you enjoyable reading. Large Print Books are especially designed to be as easy to see and hold as possible. If you wish a complete list of our books please ask at your local library or write directly to:

Magna Large Print Books
Magna House, Long Preston,
Skipton, North Yorkshire.
BD23 4ND

This Large Print Book, for people
who cannot read normal print,
is published under the auspices of

THE ULVERSCROFT FOUNDATION

... we hope you have enjoyed this book.
Please think for a moment about those
who have worse eyesight than you ...
and are unable to even read or enjoy
Large Print without great difficulty.

You can help them by sending a
donation, large or small, to:

**The Ulverscroft Foundation,
1, The Green, Bradgate Road,
Anstey, Leicestershire, LE7 7FU,
England.**
or request a copy of our brochure for
more details.

The Foundation will use all donations
to assist those people who are visually
impaired and need special attention
with medical research, diagnosis
and treatment.

Thank you very much for your help.